David Elham live

He ◀━━━ does too much thinking and not enough doing.

Best wishes

D~ E

DIARY OF A PARALLEL MAN
BY MAHERSHALALHASHBAZ

DAVID ELHAM

HIRST
publishing

Diary of a Parallel Man by Mahershalalhashbaz
David Elham

First Published in the UK in January 2011 by Hirst Publishing

Hirst Publishing, Suite 285 Andover House, George Yard, Andover, Hants, SP10 1PB

ISBN 978-1-907959-09-7
Copyright © David Elham 2011

Cover Design by Carl Horne

Printed and bound by Good News Digital Books

Paper stock used is natural, recyclable and made from wood grown in sustainable forests. The manufacturing processes conform to environmental regulations.

www.hirstpublishing.com

This book is dedicated to
Alan, Richard and Theresa

Section One

ENTRY 1

This time it almost worked. I know the elders said I should stop it at once, but I can't help myself. I am so close to a breakthrough. Had I not witnessed the hints of a world beyond ours, had I not glimpsed particles of a somewhere and a sometime assembling before my very eyes for the briefest of moments, I would have given up long ago. But the images repeat in my mind over and over. I simply must see it again.

I've got most of the plants I used last time and a few new ones. The collective energy of these newly engineered specimens should be enough to repeat the process. The two chimps I used are adequate.

The tree dwelling where I'm conducting the experiment is deep within the forest. No one suspects a thing. The elders don't know anything about it. Naomi - who knows me better than anyone, better than I know myself – has said nothing.

There have been no hints, no half-suggestions or awkward enquiries or worried stares. It caused her so much distress last time, what with the elders' meeting and everything; there had been nothing like that for centuries, apparently. I'm glad she hasn't realised; she's so happy now. Her mind is at rest and I want it to stay that way.

No, the only ones who know what I'm up to at the dwelling are me and the Father – and no one has heard a peep out of the Father for months. If he really disapproves as much as the elders say he does, there would have been a summons by now. Makes me wonder how much the last summons was down to *them*.

My family is eager to sow the seeds of this year's crops, and I did my bit today, but all I think about is the experiment and how I will make it happen again.

ENTRY 2

'Tell us about Adam and Eve again, Daddy,' Boaz and Daisy insisted. I tucked them into their beds. Don't they ever get tired of it? I wouldn't mind, but Nathan, Cheran and Lily before them always wanted me to tell them that story, and Johanan and Sarai before them. I think their children, grandchildren, and great grandchildren all demanded to hear it too. The funny thing is I don't remember ever being so enthused by it in my own childhood.

I turned down the lamp to a flicker, pulled up a stool, and recited the account of human creation for the umpteenth time:

The Father creates the world and gives it an atmosphere, oceans, land, and plant life. Then he makes the fish and the birds and the animals, and finally man. The man is given responsibility over the other creatures and his beautiful world. The Father then gives him a partner, a wife, made from one of the man's own ribs. In a simple ceremony the Father marries them together and tells them to have children and extend their paradise garden until it covers the whole planet.

The bit my children seem to like the most is 'The Test'. Before procreation begins, the Father tests the obedience of the man and woman by allowing them to eat from all the trees of their park-like home except one: the Father's own tree.

Meanwhile, in the heavenly realm, one of the Father's spirit creations fosters a desire for the worship the Father receives from the man and his wife. And so the rebel plots to undermine the sovereignty of the Father.

In order to catch the woman's attention (she being the youngest and least experienced of creation) he speaks through the mouth of a serpent and tries to persuade her that the Father is withholding good things from the married couple, implying that they would be better off without him.

The woman finds the proposition appealing for a brief moment but then tells the serpent that he is evil for suggesting that the creation would be better off living independently from the creator.

When the man catches up with her, the woman tells him what the serpent said, and the man is appalled. Both express their love for the Father and the Father rewards them with everlasting life. Then they are permitted to bear their children and the human family begins.

I got the chance to ask Adam about this a couple of cycles ago when Naomi and I were on vacation down the Hiddekel river. 'Was it exactly like that, as it has been handed down to us?'

'Yes,' Adam said. I could see the wisdom of the millennia in his eyes (he being the oldest human on Earth) and found it an unnerving yet strangely wholesome experience. 'The Father wanted a demonstration of our loyalty before he granted us endless life. When he saw the selfishness developing in one of his spirit sons, he permitted the condition to develop until it resulted in his challenging the Father's sovereignty.'

I was amazed at how cheerful he was about it. 'Didn't it ever bother you?' I said. 'I mean that the Father would allow you to be tested like that?'

'Not really,' Adam said. 'It was merely a question of who we loved most, the Father or ourselves.'

I found this utterly astonishing. Naomi, on the other hand, simply accepted it as fact and repeated what Eve had told her, namely that anyone in their circumstances would have reacted the same way.

So Adam and Eve were faithful and the Adversary's slanderous claims were proven to be the lies that they were. All spirits and all humans down through the ages now know for a certainty that the Father is God and his way is the best way.

And the moral of the story? If it wasn't for our first parents being loyal to the Father, we would now all be in a corrupt and dying state – that's assuming the Father wouldn't have simply destroyed Adam and Eve (and we, their potential offspring) straight away and start again, much as he did the rebellious angel in the story.

And the *real* moral of the story? Obey or die.

ENTRY 3

The children are sound asleep now. It's a warm spring evening and Naomi is preparing some juice for us both. I love her so much, and my children too. I suppose that the creation story is really a way of making us see how grateful we should be.

Without the Father, none of us would exist. Without the Father's power, the world would die, the sun would boil away, the Earth would cease to orbit, photosynthesis would not occur in plant life and oxygen would not be produced. The galaxies would wind down and collapse, the universes would die. We need him. Period. And without the Father's wise guidance, it would be utter chaos amongst the brothers and sisters of humanity.

That is the moral of the story. It's a good one. I'm glad my children love it.

10

Naomi and the children are visiting Cassia's great, great, grandmother's aunt Esther tomorrow afternoon. I'll have plenty of time to get to the tree dwelling and do the experiment. I can't wait!

ENTRY 4

It was incredible. I still can't believe what I saw. The younger chimps made all the difference. They and the engineered plants connected to the forest finally accomplished what I'd been hoping for; the globules of reality bounced together to form a complete picture. I could see grassy hills, water in the distance, blue skies with a few fluffy clouds, and people – people walking along stone paths.

It was a real place. I don't know if it was somewhere near here, or somewhere elsewhere in the world, or if it was else-*when*. I'm fascinated by the idea of being able to summon up the past and step into it like stepping into a photograph or a holo-recording. There is another possibility, though. It might actually be here and now, in this very spot, at this very time, but on another dimension plane.

I tried to put these notions to the elders a while back, but they just said I should wait on the Father to guide us. He will direct us there if it's in his purpose. In the meantime I should put my fanciful ideas on hold. But I had to ask, what did the Father give us these talents for if not to use them?

If I can just keep the reality window open long enough, I might be able to step through it. Imagine if I could do that!

ENTRY 5

Oh no. I'm in trouble, big trouble. The elders know I've been working on my experiment again. They say the Father has told them. Obviously someone has been spying on me and they've told the elders.

Naomi is disturbed by it; she's very weepy and can't look me in the eye. She has managed to keep it from the children, grandchildren and the other generations. I feel terrible. She looks as though I have betrayed her in some way. I really do feel wretched.

ENTRY 6

It was a strange thing to enter not just the Holy Reception but the Holy Hall itself. Two elders, Caleb and Ludim, stood outside making sure no one entered while I was in session.

The hall was spacious, decorated with pleasant colours. The lights were dimmed. I sat down on the rose chair that dominates the room and waited. And then it came – a voice, deep, resonant and strangely reassuring. It filled the room, yet not audibly; it wasn't something picked up by the ears, but was something in one's head.

The Father.

'Mahershalalhashbaz.'

I bolted upright in the rose chair. Of course, I've heard the voice countless times over the last nine hundred years, but usually in assembly with many others outdoors. This was different. This was just me, alone in a room, with the Father, the creator of Heaven and Earth. I couldn't speak.

'Mahershalalhashbaz, I have been watching you.'

I could barely speak. 'Father.'

'What were you doing in the forest yesterday?'

'I –.'

'Were you conducting experiments again?'

Once more, I froze, a hundred different emotions warring away inside. The main one was boiling rage. I resented the line of questioning.

This was the Father, creator of all things, the Universal Parent, all knowing, all seeing. He knows when a sparrow falls from its nest; he knows and names every star in the night sky seen and unseen by human eyes; he counts the very hairs on our heads; he is aware of elemental forces and the delicate balance that needs to be maintained to keep life a reality.

He knows all of this, and if he chose to stop knowing it, everything would stop. It would blink out of existence as though it had never been.

'Father,' I said slowly. 'You know what I have been doing. You see and know all things. You search the mind and heart. Nothing is hidden from you.' I desperately wanted to add, 'So why are you asking me?' but thought better of it. I cringed at the realisation that he would have known what I was going to think before I thought it.

'You are peering into things that you are not ready to know, child,' the Father said.

'But if I have guessed right,' I said, more confident now, 'if I have generated a reality field, if I have broken into another realm of existence, why can't I follow it through?'

'I am your Father.'

He made his statement as though it answered everything. I knew I was expected to accept his word as law.

But I couldn't.

'Father,' I said. I don't know where the courage came from, but there it was. I challenged him, I actually challenged him. 'I do not mean to be disrespectful. It's just that I cannot see why I should be held back if I have made progress.'

'You know nothing.'

'Please tell me, Father, what is it that I have been tapping into?' I was desperate for an answer, a hint, some clue of what that place was. 'Is it somewhere else on the Earth, or is it another world up among the stars?'

Nothing.

'Or have I found a means of crossing into another time? I have a theory about this, which of course you will know. I think I might be seeing the past or the future.'

Still nothing.

'Or is it another plane of existence altogether?' I pondered on this last thought. It was the most mind-blowing concept of all; another world going on around us, here in this area, in this time, but somehow not.

The Father spoke, his voice firm but still kindly: 'Mahershalalhashbaz, there is much frustration and anger in you. You must master it, and if you do, there will be exultation.' His tone changed slightly, and I shivered. 'But if you fail to master it, I will not rescue you from the consequences of your actions.'

'Yes, Father,' I said, my voice trembling again.

'I am your Father,' the Father said. 'Nothing I ask of you will be to your detriment. Everything I command is borne of my love for you and your brothers and sisters in the world. Follow my words and your path will become like that of a river, like the peace of the sea. But truly I tell you, on the day you step through that dimensional gateway, you will surely die.'

And with that I was dismissed.

Of course, he knows this very instant that I am writing this. Nothing escapes his attention.

14

ENTRY 7

I am greatly troubled by my audience with the Father. My emotions are a tangled mess. By calling the phenomenon a 'dimensional gateway' he has basically given me the answer. I now know what it is I've been glimpsing – a world of this time and this Earth, but parallel. We know nothing of them and possibly they know nothing of us, but the Father is Father over both realms. I cannot stop thinking about it. I am consumed.

MARCH 15

I can't believe I've actually done it. I am sitting writing this, my hands trembling. I am trying to take in the new environment. It is different and yet the same. My head is a mess. I'm trying to come to terms with the reality of what has happened, and the simple truth that I am now sat elsewhere and elsewhen.

I feel nauseous.

It began when Naomi took the children to see Esther. Daisy was being difficult. Children always are at that age, I suppose. So in the end I said she could stay home with me and help repair the skylight over Boaz's hay bed.

And so Naomi and the children waved. 'Goodbye, Daddy. Goodbye, Daisy. See you later.' And we waved back. 'See you at meal time.'

Once they had gone, we got to work on the skylight. Together we took off the old one and then I began sawing the fresh wood to size and making the dovetails. Daisy held the new screws and watched with fascination.

Everything was fine until she asked, 'Daddy, you know how you're making this, and the Father of all things made us and the world?'

'Yes.'

Then the killer question – and I knew it was coming. 'Well, who made the Father?'

I stopped sawing. 'No one made the Father. He has always been. He has no beginning and no end. He is eternal.'

'I kind of know all that,' Daisy said. At that moment I was filled with pride. She was a thinker like her dad. 'I just don't understand it. I mean, if he has always been, his memories must stretch back and back in time. Before he made the world, he made the rest of the physical universe, and before he made this universe, he made the spiritual one with all his spirit sons in it. And before he made his spiritual family, he was alone, just him and no one else forever, forever into the past.'

I smiled. I remembered asking the same questions when I was her age. 'Do you think he was lonely all that time by himself?'

'No,' Daisy said. 'The Father is complete in all things, lacking nothing. He doesn't need to have company to be happy.'

'So, what's the problem?' I asked.

'Well, how could he have just sat there for millions of years on his own just sort of thinking?'

I smiled. 'So what's the alternative? If the Father isn't eternal, if he was actually made, who made him?'

Daisy just stared at me.

'And if somebody made the Father, who made that person, and who made *him*? Do you see the problem?'

Her brow furrowed as she thought it through logically, like her dad. 'You mean that if the Father was created by somebody, and that somebody was created, and the somebody before him was created, we end up with the same conundrum? It still stretches endlessly into the past without beginning.'

'Exactly,' I said. 'All we can understand is what we have experienced. To us there is always a beginning. Seeds are planted, they germinate; they grow into plants. Foetuses are conceived, they are born as babies; they grow up into adults. It's all we know. The Father's existence is beyond that knowledge, beyond our experience, so we grapple with it and fail to truly comprehend it.'

I resumed my sawing, only to be interrupted again. 'Is that why you went to the temple, to ask the Father?'

I stopped sawing, taken aback. 'Who told you I had an audience with the Father?'

'Everyone knows you went into the Most Holy. Mummy said it was to ask the Father some questions. Did you ask him about how he has no beginning?'

I frowned. 'Why would I ask him that?'

'Because that's what I've always wanted to ask him,' she said.

I smiled. 'No. That's not why I went to see the Father.'

'Are you in trouble over something?'

I felt a shiver run right through me as the words tripped from my young daughter's lips, so innocent, so without guile. 'The Father was displeased with something I was trying to do,' I said. 'But I've stopped it now, so I'm all right. Everything's going to be all right.'

I had lost heart with my sawing now. I just sat back and stared into nothingness, bewildered. Daisy touched my arm. 'It's all right, Daddy. There's nothing wrong with asking questions, is there? That's what you always say, there's nothing wrong with asking questions.'

I smiled, not looking at her. 'No.'

'So, what were you doing?'

'Trying to satisfy my curiosity. Trying to get ahead of myself, ahead of the Father's guiding hand. I found something, found it by accident.'

'What did you find?'

'Another world. A world parallel to ours, on this planet, right here, going on around us.'

Daisy frowned, trying to comprehend. A chip off the old block for sure. 'Like the spirit world: there but invisible?'

'No,' I said. 'Not like the spirit world. This was a physical place just like our Earth, with people and animals and trees just like ours. Here but not here, like a reflection of a mountain in the lake, but not upside down. Clear, real, solid, and yet not.'

'I don't understand.'

I laughed. 'Neither do I! But I saw it. It was as real as we are now – a reality conjured up by the combined telepathic energy of the most highly advanced plant life and the minds of two of our best bred chimpanzees. With more power I'm sure I would be able to step across.'

'More power?'

'Greater mental energy, a stronger mind.'

She touched me again. 'Something stronger than a chimpanzee? You mean like a person?'

'Yes,' I said. 'I suppose so.'

And then it came to me in a flash, and I loathe myself now for even thinking it. I told Daisy to put on her shoes and pack a bag. We would be there and back before Naomi returned with the children. I took Daisy to the forest.

Everything was as I'd left it. I had assumed the Father would have told the elders to destroy the arrangement of plants, but no, they were all still there, even the chairs for the chimps and the glass solar panels. Before long, I had the special plants connected to the forest network and the two young chimps in place. Finally I sat Daisy in the centre.

'It won't hurt, will it, Daddy?' Daisy asked.

I couldn't look at her. 'No.'

She sat patiently as I strapped her on to her chair and fitted the leaf headdress. 'Now don't try to take this off, you understand? Not until I give you word. Promise me.'

'I promise, Daddy.'

'Good girl,' I said. 'Now I'm going to adjust the panels and then switch on. The chimps might get a bit noisy, but you must sit still and wait. Promise?'

'I promise,' she said.

I hate myself when I think of her innocence.

And so I began the process. I adjusted the glass panels and the build-up of heat was immediate. Excited, I rushed up the ladder into the tree dwelling and activated the sequence.

Straight away there was a hum of power. The leaves of the trees curled and moved. The smaller animals shuddered. Then I heard the chimps screeching and howling, and above them Daisy, her voice trembling. 'Daddy, Daddy, where are you? I'm scared!'

I ran down the ladder and into the clearing where she could see me. 'I'm here, sweetheart. Don't worry.'

The chimps struggled to get free, but could not. I cared little as droplets of reality began to form in the clearing. I punched the air with the thrill of the moment. 'It's working!' I screamed. 'It's *working!*'

This time, the globules of elsewhere were bigger. I could see grass and a pathway connecting, forming a larger, more complete picture. More of the floating images gelled into one, coming together like pieces of a giant jigsaw. 'Look, Daisy, look - distant mountains and a blue sky like ours.'

Above the din of power and the hullabaloo of the chimpanzees, I heard my daughter weeping. 'It's hurting me. It's hurting my head. Turn it off.'

I gazed at the water-like bubble floating in front of me. Someone in the image was walking up the path in the distance, with an animal, perhaps a dog on a line. 'In a minute,' I said, not quite turning around.

'My head is hurting. I feel sick. Daddy, I'm scared.'

I turned reluctantly. My reluctance gave way to horror as I registered what Daisy was trying to do. 'No! Daisy! Don't take it off, not until the power is down!'

But it was too late; the leaf helmet was off her head and she was undoing the straps. I turned back to the image. It was fragmenting, bursting, breaking up. 'No!'

Without any hesitation I grabbed my paper book and a writing implement, threw them into my satchel and slung the bag over my shoulder. Then I sprinted for the unstable image, and hurled myself up into the air and into the evaporating projection.

I landed hard on the gravel path, winded, and looked up to see the floating bubble breaking apart, my frenzied daughter running and crying. And she was gone. The smaller bubbles burst into nothingness. I sat, stunned, taking in the enormity of what I'd done.

The man with the dog approached. His clothes were similar to mine, a series of woven fibres, only more of them. They had a home-made look to them and were well worn. He doffed his cap. 'Owl reet.' His voice was cracked and tired, his words strange and yet oddly familiar. Then I caught full sight of his face.

He was hideous, like a grotesque caricature of a human being. His flesh was lined and worn. He looked as aged as the dog he was walking. He frightened me at first and I had to apologise for staring. It took some time for what I had seen to sink in; an aged man, his skin like that of a withered piece of fruit.

The atmosphere of this place is more alien than I had anticipated. It's much cooler for a start. Then there's the smell. The air has a peculiar mix of gases. Some I can recognise, like the fragrances of the flowers, but others are oddly sickening. I have to fight to resist vomiting, but that might also be due to the shock.

The knowledge of what I have done.

MARCH 15 (b)

I have just been sick again. The dizziness is overwhelming. I have to lie back on the grass and close my eyes.

A few moments ago, three young persons walked by. I heard them laughing and jeering, and then realised it was me they were making merry about.

'Look at him,' one of them cackled. 'He's pissed.'

The words are completely different to anything I have ever heard. In my travels around the world, to the great mountains in the South and the region of Eden in the East, I have encountered many variations of speech, but none like this. It is *completely* different. And yet, I am able to understand. It is like listening to the gibberish of a dumb animal and somehow being able to decipher it. I can only assume that the Father is enabling me to understand. Perhaps he has altered the speech centre in my brain to allow me to communicate? He is certainly capable of such a thing.

The only word I do not comprehend is 'pissed'. There must not be an equivalent in my vocabulary.

MARCH 15 (c)

I'm feeling a bit better now, though still disorientated.

I have decided to explore some of this other world. I'm aware of what I have done, and the state I left Daisy in. No doubt the Father will ensure her safety. But I am growing ever curious about this place.

The stone path crosses a wilderness and rises up into the hills. I know I said mountains before, but now I am here I see that they are not as immense. They are still appealing, though. There are a few people scattered about, going up the path. I think I should go the opposite way. I should go down, and see where the people have come from.

MARCH 15 (d)

The descent is steep. A valley opens up below. It is truly a picturesque scene, reminiscent of many places surrounding my home. I can see a dwelling in the distance and a man working the Earth with some bizarre apparatus. At first I thought it might be a creature of this land, until I descended further and came to realise it is some contraption with wheels. There is a line of blue smoke coming from its top and I can hear a sound as it moves. I am intrigued all the more. I have never seen such a thing.

A man and a woman have just passed me. They give the appearance of man and wife. Again they look aged, but not as old as the first man I saw. These look the way an animal appears when it is just beginning to deteriorate. Their hair has colour interspersed with occasional strands of grey and white. The skin is lined only a little. But they do not seem at all bothered by it. In fact they smiled and uttered a greeting as they passed me by. I smiled back and repeated the greeting.

I was astonished when the word came out. For, not only is the speech of the natives being converted, but my own words are different too. Instinctively I had responded to the greeting by saying my own usual greeting. I *thought* the word, but actually said their word, 'Hello'.

Very strange.

The Father has not spoken to me at all since I came into this realm. If these people do not have the genetic advancement that mine have developed under the Father's guidance, I am going to need his wisdom and help in getting back.

He knows my thoughts. I do not need to physically ask him.

MARCH 15 (e)

I got to the bottom of the hillside, and when I looked back I was amazed at how beautiful the scenery was. The hills now looked more like mountains, albeit modest ones. I rested for a while and took some water from the river. It tasted awful. It's not like the water we have at home. I don't know why.

I crossed the river by walking across a stone slab, and then I came to a line of dwellings. They were simple, pleasant houses. The road they followed was made of a smooth hard substance. We could do with roads like this at home. The carriages would be more comfortable to ride, for sure. Individuals passed, smiled and said hello, and I said hello back.

One of them had a paper tube pinched in his lips. The end of it burned slowly, and every so often he sucked on it, inhaled the smoke, and then blew it back out. It was an almost subconscious process. I am completely baffled by it.

The contraption I saw in the distance I now realise is made of some kind of metal alloy. Of course, I have seen the blacksmith working his metal in the village at home, but to produce a device of metal so huge is mind-boggling. I'm still trying to take it in. I am guessing that the smoke coming from the pipe at the top is something to do with the way the contraption is fuelled, but I cannot begin to comprehend it.

Two smaller contraptions passed me as I walked down the road. It would appear that the hard surface of the road has been especially made to accommodate the machines.

I am now seated on a bench at the end of the road. It faces an arrangement of buildings not unlike a village. There are signs on the walls surrounding the village, but I cannot read them. I am feeling sick again. There are far too many people in this place.

The people, like those at home, vary in nature and caste. Some have a pale colour to the skin, as though repelling the rays of the sun, while others have a light tan like mine, and still others are dark-skinned like those from the Far Land. But there is something else about them – something different.

The children appear like regular children and so do their parents, but those of the previous generation – the grandparents – seem altered somehow.

Their hair colour is faded in places and some of them actually have patches of hair missing. The skin on these ones is sagging around the eyes and the chin, like old worn leather. I now realise that the man walking the dog, whom I encountered up the hill, was in a more advanced state of this condition, and the married couple less so. I do wonder how far the phenomenon develops before it ceases.

MARCH 15 (f)

A woman sat next to me on the bench a moment ago. Her hair was like a grey cloud and she wore lenses in front of her eyes. I took in her odd assortment of clothes. She appeared to be wearing two woollen cardigans, one on top of the other. She said, 'Oh it's a lovely afternoon, isn't it?'

I realised she was addressing me, and so I replied, 'Yes it is.' Then I asked, 'Are there times when it isn't lovely?'

She looked at me quizzically and I saw that her eyes sagged ever so slightly. She was in the very early stages of the grotesque metamorphosis. 'We've been lucky so far with the weather. The sun has been out with virtually not a cloud in sight for the whole of the last fortnight.' She paused and then added, 'I hope you don't mind me asking, but are you foreign?'

I wasn't sure how to answer. What did she mean by foreign? Foreign in what sense? It was obvious I didn't come from the Far Land; I looked no different than the young parents here. Cautiously I said, 'What do you mean?'

'Oh, I'm sorry if I offended you.' She smiled. 'It's just that your accent is not one I recognise. I thought you might be on holiday abroad.'

I frowned. 'Hol-i-day.'

'Yes,' she said. 'Holiday. Or maybe you call it a vacation?'

'Vacation,' I repeated, and then suddenly (I don't know how) I knew what she meant. 'A vacation: a rest from work and my everyday assignments. Yes, I'm on vacation.'

'From abroad?'

'Yes, abroad.'

She smiled and I felt better, temporarily secure. 'Where are you from then, love?'

Love? 'My name is not Love,' I said. 'I am Mahershalalhashbaz. I am from Elohah Village in North Hemisphere.'

Her smile broadened. 'Ingland is in the Northern Hemisphere, darling.'

'Mahershalalhashbaz,' I corrected. 'So I am in the same geographic location, but on another plane. Ingland.' Her smile became a half smile, almost a frown. I looked at the people seated on the lawn and milling about the various shop windows. 'Do many people come to Ingland Village for vacation?'

The woman's hearty laughter startled me. 'This is Grasmere,' she gestured. 'Ingland is the country, part of the British Isles. Surely you must know?'

'I struggle with your language,' I said.

'Even so,' the woman replied. She got up. 'Well, I need to be getting back to my cottage. Tee won't make itself.'

25

'Tee?'

'My evening meal.'

'Thank you for speaking with me,' I said, grateful for any clues about where and when I am. 'What is your name?'

'Margaret,' she said.

'Margret.'

'Mar-gar-et,' she corrected.

'Mar-gar-et,' I replied. 'I confess I have never heard this name before.'

Margaret laughed again, and I saw her beauty – a beauty from before the time the sagging of her skin got underway. 'Well, I've never heard of Mayer… What is it?'

'Mahershalalhashbaz.'

'Yes.' She laughed again. 'Oh dear. It really was lovely meeting you. Enjoy the rest of the day.'

She set off in the direction of a row of houses set back from what looked like a large inn. There were many metal carriages parked outside it. I decided to stroll around this Grasmere Village and soak in the experience.

Looking in the windows of the shops, I saw that the layout was very similar to the market stalls we had at Elohah Village, only all of these were a under a roof. There wasn't a single outdoor stall to be seen. There was a shop of books, and I longed to be able to read their Grasmere words so that I might learn something of Ingland British Isles.

Another stall building had thin books and maps on a rack and bags that one carried on the shoulders. Men and women examined the items, picking up hats and sticks and sturdy boots. A man with sagging skin and patches of hair took a map to the counter and exchanged a piece of thin brown paper for small metal tokens. Some kind of bartering system, I guessed.

The road narrowed into a lane. On the left was a nicely designed three-storey house with gardens and metal carriages parked on a gravel surface. Another inn? To the right was an older building, dark and musty-looking with windows made up of coloured glass. It was more of a hall than a home. Perhaps a meeting place for their elders?

The road opened out onto a junction. A carriage trundled by. The driver was one of the grotesque man-creatures. His passenger, I presumed, was his life partner, although she too looked hideously deformed. The vehicle moved on and I took a lungful of the smoke emitting from the back. I coughed and spluttered, and even when I had recovered, I could still taste the emission in the back of my throat. What are they fuelling those things with?

I took the road to the left and fell upon another inn, and then another old building with coloured windows. This time it was surrounded by a spacious grass area with strange slab-like stones dotted about in sequence, each inscribed with a short paragraph or two. A group of visitors to the village were being guided by a man with a book of notes. I decided to join them and listen.

'Saint Oswald's was built in the thirteenth century on this site, which was, like many others, originally established by the Pagans and then adopted later by the Kristian church.' I had no idea what 'Pagans' and 'Kristian' meant, but 'church' I sensed was similar to 'temple' – a place to worship the Father.

The thought struck me hard. I was almost literally staggered by it. *The Father.* When would he speak to me? When would he direct me back to my home plane? I decided not to trouble myself about it. The Father would lead me home when it was his will to do so.

I followed the group into the temple. It was dimly lit inside and musty. Narrow benches filled the main area and a raised platform stood at one end where, I imagine, the presiding elder would give out instruction from the Father. I saw no inner sanctum where one could have private counsel, but I did see something else, and it nearly took my breath away, it was so disquieting.

Flicking through one of the books, I saw an image of a thin undernourished man, arms outstretched on what looked like a beam of wood, with pins or nails through the palms of his hands. His legs hung vertically down a second central beam, and his feet appeared to be fastened to the wood similarly. He was literally nailed to the wood!

I could not help but ask, 'Sir, what does this image of wood purport to be? It is hideous.'

The guide looked at me with uncertainty. 'I'm sorry,' he said, and then it was my turn to be uncertain. What was he sorry about? He approached. 'Have you never seen the kriste impaled before?'

I had to tell him the words meant nothing to me. 'What is this kriste?'

'You don't know who this is?'

I conceded that I did not. I told him I had come from abroad on vacation, but he seemed even more perplexed. 'You don't know who it is?'

I shook my head.

'You have never heard of Jeezuz Kriste, the Son of God?'

I shook my head again. I couldn't tell if he was angry or merely astonished. His tone implied that I should know something of this Jeezuz Kriste picture. Then I realised I recognised the words from the latter part of the figure's title. Son of God?

I frowned. 'Do you mean Son of the Father?'

The man looked relieved. 'God the Father, yes. Jeezuz is his Son. The Word made flesh.'

I stared at the picture. I felt in awe of it, but frightened of it at the same time. 'The Word made flesh?' I said. 'You made an image of the Word in human form?'

'Well, not me personally,' the guide said.

'It's blasphemy,' I said, barely able to contain my shock. 'To make an image of a spirit person.' I inhaled deeply through my nostrils, trying to regain some composure. 'Why is he nailed to the cross shape?'

The guide frowned again. 'It's the crucifixion. You know that's how he died, don't you?'

I almost choked on the words. 'He –' I could not bring myself to say it, it was so inconceivable. 'How can a spirit person die?'

The guide touched my shoulder, as if to comfort me. 'He was the Word made flesh, remember. That's how they were able to kill him. He let them do it so that we might have our sins forgiven and gain everlasting life.'

'This talk is deeply disturbing,' I said, resting on his arm. 'Please stop.'

'I'm sorry to have upset you,' the guide said. 'Forgive me, but I need to continue with the tour.' He steadied me and then called his group of students to join him outside. They did so.

I leaned on the wall, shaking, and then chanced another look at the image of the pathetic figure nailed by his hands and feet to the wooden cross.

The Word made flesh? Would the Father send his Son to walk amongst us? Who were these people who killed him? And what did the guide mean about gaining everlasting life? I closed my eyes, composed myself, and ran out of the church into the open air.

The sky was a little darker now. Evening was drawing in. I looked up into the blue. 'Father, I want to go home. These are an offensive people.'

The Father did not answer.

The guide and his group were standing by one of the hard inscribed slabs. I went across to hear his speech. 'His mother Anne died of pneumonia in 1778, and Wordsworth himself passed away seventy-two years later in 1850 from pleurisy.'

Were this Wordsworth and his mother killed too? I looked at the rows upon rows of slabs in the field. Did all of

29

these represent killed people? I decided to leave the guide and his group and explore more of the village.

I crossed a small bridge over the quaint river separating the church grounds from a small eating establishment. People drinking from small cups sat on a platform hemmed in by railings and overlooking the river. One woman sucked on a burning paper stick and blew the smoke up into the air. A pointless and potentially harmful practice, I thought. These were indeed a strange people.

Approaching the main counter of the food shop, I stared at the cakes and drinks on display. A young woman approached. 'Can I help you, sir?'

I smiled, hunger pangs getting the better of me. 'I have not eaten anything since I left home. That cake looks very appetising.'

'It's two pounds a slice, sir. Would you like some?'

'Pounds?' I said. And then I realised. 'Ah, your tokens of exchange. Sadly I do not have any pounds.' I paused, staring at the big brown cake nearest to me. 'May I not have some cake and give you the pounds later?'

The young woman smiled. 'I'm afraid not, sir.'

I bid her farewell and made my way back to the bench where I had spoken to the saggy-skinned woman called Margaret, and this is where I am now. I have tried requesting an audience with the Father again, but he hasn't answered.

I am now thinking about Boaz, Daisy and my dear wife Naomi. They will be settling down to their meal. Daisy will be upset, and Naomi will be angry at me. I do not mind facing her bitter words when I get back. It's a small price to pay to escape this bewildering Ingland British Isles where they killed Jeezuz Kriste the Son made Flesh, and Wordsworth and his mother. They are not like us. I hope the Father opens a gateway back home soon. I am beginning to feel lonely for proper company.

*

MARCH 15 (g)

I am seated at the dining table of Margaret. Her home is small and appealing, if a little dusty and cluttered. She has gone to bed. It is dark now and I write this entry aided by a light powered by a harnessed natural energy called electricity. Apparently it is similar to lightning, only tamed.

I am sleeping on a couch that Margaret has made into a bed. She invited me back when she saw me still sitting on the bench. I explained that I didn't have anywhere to go, and that I had no pounds to pay for a room at one of the inns. She gave me a nice meal and a drink of a herbal mixture similar to the one I like at home. I think she called it 'tee'. This is not to be confused with the evening meal. She said I should go into the city and find a hostel. She is going to give me some pounds tomorrow so that I may do this.

I hope the Father rescues me soon. I am deeply sorry for ignoring his commands and offending him. But he already knows this, because he reads hearts and minds.

Section Two

MARCH 16

I am sitting in a waiting room at what Margaret called the railway station. I came here on a bus, a metal carriage with two floors, one on top of the other!

The pounds are a strange currency. Each one represents one hundred units of a lesser value called pence. The gold coloured pieces of metal represent one pound, the larger ones with the silver centre represent two pounds, and the thin brown paper represents ten pounds. Margaret gave me two of these; twenty pounds in total.

The bus driver was annoyed when I gave him one ten pound note and asked him to take me to Windermere railway station. But he did it nonetheless and gave me the exchange of a smaller piece of paper, a turquoise one representing five pounds, and a few metal pounds making up the difference. It is a ridiculous system, but I dare not say so.

The bus took me out of Grasmere, along a meandering tree lined road, and there were many pleasant sights along the way, including a huge lake and a much bigger town called Ambleside. It was sprawling with people and I was glad to get away from it, it making me queasy inside. I have never seen so many people in one place.

I arrived at the railway station five minutes ago and offered pound tokens for a ticket granting me permission to travel to the city. The man at the counter said the nearest proper city is a place called Manchester, so I asked to go there. He took nearly all my pounds in exchange for the ticket. It does not seem right that it would cost so much, but I did not challenge him.

Minutes are a measurement of time. The people in Ingland British Isles split the timing of the day into twenty-four segments called hours. These are made up of sixty minutes each, and each minute is sixty seconds. A second is an instant of time. It lasts as long as it does to say one word. For example, if you were to say 'second' out loud, that would be how long a second of time is, it's that infinitesimal. I don't know why they want to count time down to such a tiny fraction, and I lacked the courage to ask Margaret before I left.

The railway is exactly what I thought it would be; two rails of metal stretching off as far as the eye can see. They are embedded in large blocks of wood that rest on a carpet of white stones. The carriages, like the buses, are self powered and are pulled by an engine at the front. It goes without saying that the fuel emissions smell awful and I have to suppress the instinct to be sick.

MARCH 16 (b)

I am sat at a table on the train. The movement was a little unsettling at first, but now I am enjoying it greatly. A man and a woman are sitting further up. The woman is attractive and reading a book. The man has his eyes closed and there are two thin threads plugged into his ears. A peculiar faint rhythm is coming from the threads. I am assuming he can hear it better than I can. He seems to be enjoying it, whatever the case.

The scenery outside the train is like nothing I have ever witnessed. There are great patches of farmland, but every so often I see huge sections of buildings, like big ugly overgrown villages. I cannot imagine living in such places.

Why would they want to live like that, all crammed together? I suppose Ambleside looks like this from the vantage point of the train travellers.

We actually went into one of the oversized villages and the train stopped at a platform. Two young boys got into my carriage, and then the train continued on its journey, pulling away from the big village and back into the fields.

The boys talk to one another loudly and rest their feet on the seats facing them. One of them has a small device in his hand which produces a tiny flame whenever he presses a button. He is clicking it on and off constantly and the flame goes in and out.

This action is beginning to irritate me.

The way the boys speak is not like the language of the people in Grasmere Village or like that of Margaret. Most of their words are recognisable, but they keep interrupting the flow of their sentences with a word that sounds like 'fukkin'. I don't know what the word means or why they keep interrupting their sentences to say it. One of their conversations went something like this:

'Hey, Makker.'
'Wot?'
'What time is it?'
'Ow the bleedinnell should I know?'
'All right, I was just askin, you dick.'
'Oos a dick?'
'You are.'
'Oh fukkoff.'
'Dick.'

I can only conclude that they must be on vacation from abroad like me.

*

35

MARCH 16 (c)

We have been through a number of big villages now, and the buildings are getting more and more intrusive each time. I heard one of the passengers refer to the last place as 'Bulltun'. I couldn't wait for the train to get away quickly enough. All those buildings and all those people. Truly overwhelming.

MARCH 16 (d)

Manchester is awful. I couldn't believe it as we approached. It is a massively condensed island of buildings. There are trees and little bits of greenery, but it is mostly roads and houses and old tall buildings.

I nearly vomited when we got near the centre of the place, the buildings being so dangerously high. Newer, even taller structures rise above them. Floors on top of floors. I counted one tower that had at least twenty floors. Why would they choose to live like this, on top of one another, when they could so easily spread out?

In the distance there is a giant metal wheel with boxes positioned around its rim. Do people live in the boxes? I think what they are doing here is grossly contrary to nature.

The train has stopped. I am about to follow the others into Manchester. I feel terrible.

MARCH 16 (e)

I am sitting in an eating establishment. I am trying to regain my composure after the vomiting fit I had when I first emerged from the station onto the street. The buses, the solo carriages, the huge vehicles carrying all manner of goods, the buildings dizzyingly high, the people, so many people, in front of me, behind me, at either side of me, talking and laughing and ignoring.

And the smell, *that awful smell* of concentrated fuel emissions.

I staggered backwards and hit the wall of the station, it itself dirty and neglected, covered in bright writing.

My stomach heaved and pushed; my mouth and nostrils bursting with a sudden flowing torrent, a river of acidic fluid. Passers by groaned their disapproval and stepped around me.

I slid along the unkempt wall to the even filthier floor, small globules of sick dripping from my chin.

I broke down and sobbed like an infant, overawed and anxious, crying myself silent and with an aching gut.

'Father!' I managed to shout. 'Please take me back! I'm sorry! Really I am.' I began to sob again, and then the sob became a wail. '*I'm sorry*! I'm sorry I disregarded your command! Father! *Father*!!'

Nothing.

Nothing but the crowd walking by, mumbling and pointing and sniggering. Stepping over me. They *stepped over me*, as one steps over a toy left strewn in the garden.

Following what seemed like quite a few minutes, a young man stopped. His hair was cut extremely short, his skin rough and unshaven, strange elaborate blue designs on his arms. He puffed on a lit paper tube. I recoiled as he bent down towards me, his face scowling and hideous. I was certain he intended to strike me, since the whole place provoked a stifled frustrated rage.

'You OK mate?' The man extended a hand. 'You OK?'

I glared at him, unsure of his intentions. His breath stank of the smoke he savoured so much. He seemed to realise I did not fully understand him.

'Let me help you up.'

37

'Yes,' I said, suddenly appreciative and grateful. 'Yes, please.' My legs were very shaky, but I was able to stand. 'Thank you,' I kept saying. 'Thank you. You are most gracious.'

He took my hand, as I would do with one of my children. I began to weep again at the memory of them. I missed my children like never before. The man led me down the street. I cowered every time a vehicle came near the pathway. I only really started to relax when he took me through a door and into one of the eating establishments.

'Oi!' the man shouted to the people busying themselves behind the counter. 'Get this gent a cuppa tee. And some o that carrot cake.' He turned to me, again parental. 'Do you like carrot cake?'

'I don't know,' I said. I didn't care, I was hungry.

'Give him some carrot cake.' He paused, and then added, 'and some wipes.' He turned to me. 'Sit down mate.'

I sat down.

A young woman came over with a cup of the tee drink and a plate of carrot cake, and a damp cloth for my chin.

'Thank you.'

The tee tasted horrible, nothing like the tee the woman Margaret gave me when I stayed at her cottage in Grasmere Village. It was mostly water, milk and sugar, with a bit of the tee taste lingering at the back of my throat. But I didn't care. I was just glad to get away from the people and the noise and the awful smell, and not see the buildings quite so much.

The man gave the young woman some pounds, nodded a farewell to me, and left.

I have been sat here for two hours now and the people behind the counter are wishing I would leave, I can tell. But I cannot bring myself to go back outside. I'm frightened.

*

MARCH 16 (f)

'We're closing now,' one of them said. He was big, overfed it seemed to me. His hair was wiry and going grey. It goes without saying his skin sagged around the eyes and jaw. 'You will have to leave.'

I was horrified. 'I cannot go,' I said. 'I am from abroad, I have nowhere to go.'

'Not my problem, mate. Now, come on.'

I pressed further. 'I have no pounds. I cannot go to an inn.'

'Not my problem.'

'Where can I go?'

He moved hastily towards me and I instinctively reached for the door. 'Not my problem. Now get lost.' As I exited I thought I heard him say something like, 'Bloody immigrants.' It can't have been that, though, for why would an immigrant be bloody?

Manchester is different at night. There are fewer solo carriages and no big carriers at all. Buildings are a lot less intimidating because, with exception of the ones immediately facing me, which are frightening enough, I cannot really see them. The lights are actually quite pretty.

There are plenty of people, smartly dressed and going about their business. The inns are well attended and I look longingly at the guests through the big windows until they start scowling at me.

Other people wander aimlessly up and down the street. Their attire suggests that they have a low supply of pounds. I am finding these people appealing. They seem to be like me in some ways.

I am sat in a doorway now, observing and writing, trying to keep myself warm and sane.

MARCH 16 (g)

The carriages are not coming by that often now. The lights on the road change from green to yellow to red and back again but there is nothing on the road for them to govern. I don't know how far into the night I am, but it is very cold. The climate bears no similarity to the lukewarm winter nights back home. No one seems to find it out of the ordinary, so I can only assume that it must be normal.

Every so often a person will come out of the inn across the road and get in a black carriage. Others arrive. Further down the street there is a young woman walking up and down a stretch of pathway. She is wearing very tight black clothes. Her bare legs are covered part way by knee length boots. The tops of her breasts are showing. I am dazzled by her lack of chastity. She seems not to feel the cold.

A carriage has stopped. She is leaning into the window. Perhaps the driver is lost? She is nodding and looking up and down the road. She has got into the carriage. Maybe the driver had agreed to meet up with her. Yes, that must be it.

MARCH 16 (h)

It is freezing cold. I can hardly make my writing stick work. Never have I trembled so much. Thoughts of Naomi and the children keep me focussed. I have stopped begging the Father to help me. I am going to curl up into this corner as far as I can and try to sleep.

*

MARCH 17

I dreamt I was back home, back in the fields helping to gather the harvest. It was a bright summer's day; Naomi and all generations of our children were there, they and their little ones too. Caleb the elder came to see if we were still available to come for supper. It was all so warm and beautiful and perfect.

And then I awoke.

The reality is hard to contemplate. It isn't quite light yet, but already the vehicles are moving, making their noises and sounding their horns. I can taste their emissions in the back of my throat. I want to vomit, but I suppress it.

A vehicle has pulled up just beyond the inn. The young woman dressed in black has just got out. This is strange because the vehicle and its driver are not the ones she joined last night. Maybe she visited a few people and this is one of the others bringing her back? But why here? Why bring her back here, to leave her standing on the pathway as before? The vehicle has gone now.

She is just standing there, hands in pockets, looking up the road. Now she's looking at her wrist. There's something tied to it, it seems. Now she's reaching inside her coat. She's pulled out a small box. She's slid something out and she's putting it in her mouth. I think it's one of those paper tubes. Now she's touching the end of it with something. A flame? Yes, it's one of those tubes. She sucks on it, inhales the smoke, and then blows it out. I remain baffled by the procedure.

A vehicle with blue and yellow colours and lights on the top is approaching. It creeps along as though cautious. The woman has seen it. She's walking at a pace in the opposite direction. Now she's running.

MARCH 17 (b)

I had to move from the doorway when the proprietor arrived. It is morning now, the sun has risen and the city is bustling with activity. I have been watching the way people stop the vehicles and cross the road. Some of the lights that change from green to yellow to red and back again can be controlled by a small console. The people press a button, the lights change to red, this signals to vehicles to stop at a line, and the people cross the road to the pathway on the other side. I put my theory to the test, and am pleased to say I was right. I crossed the road and determined to get to the outskirts of the city.

I am currently sitting on a bench in a very small area of grass near a place called Bleedin Deens Gate. I know it's called this because I overheard a man with long hair and with round lenses suspended over his eyes say it into a small communications transmitter he was holding to his ear. He didn't sound pleased to be on Bleedin Deens Gate. I smiled to myself. Yes I smiled. It is so nice to know that some of the natives here hate the place as much as I do.

Finding the outskirts of the city is proving to be a pointless exercise. It's nothing like Elohah Village. If I had not seen the towns and cities from the train, I would conclude that these places go on infinitely.

I am feeling a little rancid. My shirt is sticking to my back; my arms are itching with sweat. I desperately want to take off my boots, but I dare not. Even the grass here has hidden dangers. And I smell. I need a wash.

But worst of all, I am hungry.

I keep thinking of ways to get food, but they all depend on getting some pounds first. It seems nothing in this world can be achieved without them; be it food, clothing, shelter, even something as fundamental as a wash – without pounds I am lost.

The orgology of this world is primitive. It seems they have abandoned the natural route entirely in favour of man-made advances, if advances is the right word. The scale of the mining operation to produce the amount of metal needed to build their vehicles and towers must be monumental. I mean, if the whole world is supplied to the same level as this city of Manchester, they must have gutted the planet to have accomplished it.

The buildings seem to be made of an artificial kind of stone, again man-made. Their clothes are a mixture of natural fibres such as cotton and bizarre hybrid materials that I can only guess the composition of.

They pump the air with poison from their vehicles (I think they might be powered by burning some natural ore or residue), and for some even that isn't enough. They have their own personal supply of poison sticks, which they happily puff on.

How could they possibly contemplate the orgology that brought me here? Plants to these people serve as food and decoration, nothing more.

The Father seems to have left them to it. Either that or they have abandoned him. It's hard to tell. In all my travels and in all my years I have never before encountered a place such as this. I hate it.

And I'm hungry, so hungry.

I sit here, and every so often I weep with the desperation. The people pass me by as though it were normal and a common occurrence. Only one stopped. A young woman, average in height, hair coloured artificially blonde, smart trousers and shoes, a nice fibre coat and a shoulder bag. She stopped on the other side of the road and just watched me. I offered a weak smile as a child does a parent when it knows it's being silly. She cast her eyes to the floor and walked on.

*

MARCH 17 (c)

I have spent most of the day wandering about, looking longingly at the eating establishments and inns. I have never felt so empty physically.

I took refuge in another doorway until a man in blue clothes moved me on. He was like the people driving the blue and yellow vehicle before. He was a person of authority.

The light is fading now. I have found a couple of others, a man and a girl, who look as devoid of purpose as I feel. The man hasn't shaved for many days, his skin is raw and weather-beaten, and he wears a big woolly coat. The girl has long matted brown hair tied back in a tail. Her clothes are all of one design, green with brown and black shapes, like the colouring of the forest. She's carrying a red patterned blanket about her shoulders.

The pair huddle in the doorway of an establishment closed for the night. He sucks smoke from a stick he made himself from paper and a crushed brown herb, and then passes it to the girl. She inhales and passes it back. Then she passes it to me and I decline as politely as I can.

'Not seen you ere before,' she says.

'I arrived in the city the day before yesterday.'

'Where you from?'

'Abroad.'

The man chuckles. 'Ah, I thought you were a foreigner. Your accent gives it away.'

'What is that accent anyway?' the girl asks. 'Is it finish or sommat?'

I shrugged. 'Finish,' I say. 'What is finish?'

The man turns. 'From Finland,' he says.

'No,' I say. 'I am not from Finland.'

The man is called Jack and the girl's name is Kelly.

44

MARCH 17 (d)

It is night time. The vehicles – or the traffic, as Jack and Kelly call them – they are getting fewer again. Kelly has two bars of a sweet food made from a cacao plant. She has saved them for the night to help stave off the hunger pains. She and Jack have decided to snap off the individual 'fingers' and share them with me. I couldn't stop thanking them.

'All right, all right. Kriste,' Kelly said. It was strange hearing the name of the man who was nailed to the tree in this way. I realise from the way she said it that she wasn't really referring to him at all. She wasn't even thinking of him. None of them are. His name is just a word used to express embarrassment and exasperation.

I had caught snatches of this kind of talk during the day. There was a man stood in the market place holding up a collection of thin paper books, and he was shouting, 'The big issue! Help the homeless!' So I approached and said, 'I am homeless. That is, I have no home. I had to sleep in a doorway in the street last night.' He completely ignored me. When I tried to engage him again, he said, 'Jeezuz, mister. It's took me ages to get this gig. I have sympathy, I really do. I mean I've been where you're at. But if I don't sell enough of these –.'

I left him. I watched from across the big lawn, and sure enough, the odd person would give him some pounds in exchange for one of his books. I envied him his industriousness. But when he said Jeezuz, I knew he did not think that was my name. Nor was he trying to engage The Word in conversation. It was his way of expressing mild anger.

Strange mannerism.

In the end I decided to ask Jack and Kelly about the Father outright. I wasn't really expecting anything profound from them. I mean, in all the time I've been here, and in the few conversations I have managed to instigate, no one has openly talked about the Father or the family of spirits in the higher dimension.

'What?' Kelly said. 'You mean your dad?'

Immediately I was lost.

'You want us to find your bleedin dad?'

That word again. Clearly 'bleedin' is a corrosion of 'bleeding' and is employed in the same way 'Jeezuz', 'Kriste', 'bloody' and 'get lost' are. This is not Bleedin Deens Gate, after all. It's just Deens Gate. I am dealing with a very primitive culture; that much I have established. The youngest children back home have better communication skills than these adults who imagine themselves mature.

'I'm talking about *the* Father,' I said patiently. 'You know, the great spirit who created the universe and the life in it.'

'Eh?' Kelly said.

Jack rolled his eyes in what seemed like mockery. It is hard to read their faces at times. 'He means God the Father.' He said it as though it were the punch line to a joke. 'You're not gonna start preechin to us, are you, son? Cos if you are, you can kiss goodbye to the soup kitchen in the morning.'

I raised my eyebrows, and my hopes. 'Soup kitchen?'

'Yeah,' Jack said, his voice hard and insistent. 'That's why you're hangin round us, innit? Be honest. You want us to take you to the soup kitchen run by the Sally Army.'

I thought of the broth that Mary makes, brown and salty with a good roll of buttered bread to mop up with afterwards. I caught myself slavering and wiped my chin. 'You will lead me to the soup kitchen in the morning?'

'Only if you cut the Jeezuz crap.'

46

Strangely I know the word crap. It must be a proper word, since my brain translates it as excrement. Jeezuz excrement? I can only assume Jack meant he did not hold Jeezuz in high esteem. The very thought wounded me. I mean, the Word, the Son of God in human form, as they believe, likened to excrement. I nearly vomited again.

I kept telling myself he might not mean that, but the more I thought about this perverse world, the more it seemed likely. It is little wonder the Father has abandoned them, if indeed he has.

'Can I ask you one thing about the Jeezuz crap?' I said. He shot me a look, but I sensed I would be safe just to offer one question only. 'Can you tell me where I can learn about the Father and Jeezuz? Do you have any elders who I could go to?'

Kelly answered. 'You mean priests and shit like that?'

Again – the unsettling equation of holiness and excrement.

I felt my voice trembling. 'Er, yes. Priests,' I said. 'And things like that.'

She considered for a second. Then she turned to Jack. 'Isn't there some big church on ere?'

'Yeah,' Jack said. He pointed. 'Further along. There's a library too. It has books about God and that. I think there's a bit of ancient bible in there too. The book of John or sommat.'

Kelly elbowed him. 'Ow do you know all that, you old git?' she jeered. 'You used to be choir boy?'

He let out a raucous laugh. 'No, you daft cow. I had to supervise a special meeting they ad there when I was a copper. A load o big wigs turned up and I heard this professor chap saying there was a fragment of John's gospel. It dates back nearly two thousand years, near to the time of Jeezuz. They reckon it compares with modern bibles really well.'

'Bloodiell!' Kelly said. 'Sure you're not a bit of a bible basher yourself?'

'Fukkoff!' Jack snarled with a grin. Yes, he snarled *with* a grin.

Then, as if we had never discussed the subject of the Father and his son Jeezuz, Kelly began shouting and waving to someone across the road, and I saw it was the young woman from last night, the one dressed in tight black clothes. She skipped across the road to join us.

'Hiya,' she said, and then looked me up and down. 'Who's this?'

I smiled and introduced myself. 'My name is Mahershalalhashbaz.'

'Takes all sorts,' she said. 'What's with the farmer jiles outfit?'

The others laughed and I realised she was indicating my clothes. I decided it would be polite, and easier, to just laugh along with them. Though I didn't feel like laughing much.

They giggled even more when I flinched at her touch. She ran her fingers lightly over the tops of my arms. I was not prepared for that at all. The only woman who had ever done that back home was Naomi. Oh how I missed her now. 'You're the best lookin farmer I've ever seen, though,' the girl continued. 'Do you work out?'

'Do I work out what?'

Before she could reply, Kelly cut in. 'He's fit, in-e, Shaz?'

'He certainly is,' Shaz said. Her eyes dazzled. 'He's perfect.' She touched my face. 'Boy, I'd do you for free if I could afford to lose an hour. I've not had a good lookin bloke for months!'

More laughter as the trio discerned (quickly) that I had no idea what she was talking about.

'What's in the funny bag?'

I glanced down at my satchel. 'Just an account I am writing of my experiences,' I told her. 'It helps keep me focussed.'

Jack looked about cautiously and then asked, 'Got any weed on you?'

'Nah,' Shaz said. 'Not seen Jimmy all week, and I've used what he left me.'

Jack grimaced. 'Oh, I could really do with some and all. I've been feeling the cold really bad these last few nights.'

'Me too,' Kelly said.

'Sorry,' Shaz said. 'Fresh out.'

I had meant to ask about the coldness at night. Back home it never gets as cold as this. The water canopy here must be faulty. Or maybe they've ruined it like so many other things. But since everyone here accepts the temperature as normal, I thought better of asking them about the canopy.

'Got any booze, then?' Kelly asked.

'No,' Shaz said. 'But I'll see if I can pick some up for you after my first client. Will you still be here, or will you be going under the arches?'

'We should still be here, shouldn't we, Jack?' Kelly turned to her friend.

'Yeah,' he replied, unsmiling. 'We'll be here for another hour or so.'

'I'll try and get you some then. But it'll be the cheap stuff, *White Lightning* or sommat like that.' She broke off as a vehicle pulled up on the other side of the road. The driver sounded a horn. 'It's Ron,' she said. 'First one of the night.'

Kelly studied the man. 'An oldie?'

'He's all right,' Shaz said. 'He's easy. Just wants what his missus won't do, that's all. Every man's secret desire.' Shaz signalled to Ron and he gave a slight movement of the hand to indicate his reply. 'Ay, Farmer Giles?'

I have no idea what she was talking about.

'No, Ron's one of my best. He's easy to please, always gentle, pays up every time, and he's safe.'

Kelly raised an eyebrow. 'Safe?'

'Always wants it with protection, so there's no worries.' She skipped across the road. 'See you in an hour or so.'

Jack cleared his throat. 'Don't forget the booze!'

'I won't!' Shaz called over her shoulder. She got into the vehicle. Within seconds the driver had engaged the engine and driven off. The more I thought about it, the more it occurred to me that the man was not the same person she had met last night. And what did she mean by client? What was she selling? Again I thought better of asking Jack and Kelly.

Kelly shivered. 'I couldn't do what she does. I hope I never have to.'

'Don't start taking, then,' Jack said.

'She's taking?'

'Of course.' Jack's voice was stark and unfeeling. 'You don't think she goes with these losers because she loves it, do you? It's why they all do it. They need money and lots of it.'

'Not necessarily,' Kelly replied. 'My flatmate used to do it part-time, whenever she needed the cash. *And* she did it in my bed, the bitch.'

Female dog?

'I'm telling you,' Jack said, 'that Shazia is injecting. That's why she's on the game every single night.'

'Not heroin.'

'Yep.'

'God, I hope I never end up like that.'

'Don't start on the stuff then,' Jack said. 'No matter how cold and depressed you get.'

Kelly fell silent for quite a few seconds. Then she reached into her pocket. 'Right, shall we get started on the Kit Kat? I think we've held it off long enough.'

The three of us huddled round and took a stick each. We savoured every bite and chewed it slowly. It was short-lived, but it was good.

*

50

MARCH 17 (e)

I'm sat on my own. Writing this is the only thing keeping my mind off the hunger. Shazia did come back an hour or so later. She was pleased to report that her client was as easy and clean as ever and that she had stopped by at 'The Offy' to get some *White Lightning*. I took a mouthful and then spat it out. It was horrible.

'Hey!' Kelly and Jack shouted in unison. 'If you don't want it, leave it for us.'

'It's horrible,' I said. 'I thought it was going to be from the grape of the vine.'

Shazia laughed hard. 'The grape of the vine?'

'He means wine,' Jack confirmed.

'I know what he means,' Shazia said. 'You really are a child, aren't you? An innocent.' She studied me. I followed her eyes as she once again looked me up and down, hovering momentarily over my biceps and crotch.

If I was reading her facial expressions correctly, and I'm not sure that I was, but if I *was*, it seems she was imagining herself to be my wife and having sacred union with me. My face might have registered the disgust I was feeling toward her. She was like an unreasoning animal of the field.

'Do you think you will get some weed tonight?' I was grateful for Kelly's interjection.

'I've told you,' Shaz said, suddenly annoyed. 'That all hangs on whether or not I see Jimmy.'

Kelly coughed. 'Won't you need to see him for yourself?'

'Well, yeah. If I don't bump into him by tomorrow night, I'm screwed. I'll have to look elsewhere.'

'But when you see him, you'll get us some weed?'

'Look Kelly,' Shaz said. 'I'm not made of bleeding money, you know. I've got to see to myself first. But if I can, I'll get you some weed. Now leave off.'

Suddenly there was a man stood nearby. His head was shaven, but he was younger than the man who helped me when I first arrived in the city. He looked nervous, apprehensive, and kept glancing about as he approached.

"Scuse me, love,' he said, trying not to look at Jack, Kelly and me. In fact, he could barely look at Shazia. 'You a hooker?'

Shazia smiled and her whole countenance changed to that of a kindly mother. I was staggered by the transformation. 'Yes,' she said, leaning forward slightly so – at least it seemed to me – he could get a look at her breasts. I followed his gaze and felt my own member swell with desire.

Desire gave way to guilt and self-loathing. This world is cursed. I grappled to remain in control and not burst out crying again.

'How much for the works?' the man stammered.

'With or without protection?'

The man shot each one of us a nervous look. Then he stared Shaz right in the eye. 'Without,' he said.

Immediately I felt anxious for Shaz. I had no comprehension of what he was asking of her, but I knew from her earlier remark that 'without protection' meant that it, whatever *it* is, would be more dangerous for her. She paused, not anxious at all, and considered. 'Two hundred,' she said.

The man was appalled. 'Two hundred!'

'One-fifty with protection, two hundred without.' She said simply, 'I'm not prepared to negotiate.'

'Oh, come on,' the man protested.

'No.' Shazia was adamant, and I found myself championing her cause.

'You know to have it without is more dangerous for her,' I said. Jack and Kelly glared at me, horrified. Shazia shot me a reproving look and I recoiled immediately. She did not want me involved in her bartering, that much was obvious.

'It's more dangerous for me and all,' the man said. 'I don't know ow many fellas she's been wiv tonight, or what she might av picked up from em.'

Shazia reacted, her motherly countenance evaporating. 'Oh get stuffed!' she said with a snarl and headed off down the street.

The man scrambled after her. 'All right, two hundred!' She carried on walking. He shouted louder. 'Two-fifty, then!'

Shazia stopped dead. 'Where?'

'I don't have anywhere,' the man said lamely.

'I need to be able to clean my teeth and freshen up.' Shaz's voice had authority in it. She knew she had power over him now.

'My place then,' he said. 'They're on holiday with her mother. But I don't want any noise. I don't want the neighbours to hear.'

'I can do quiet,' Shazia said. 'Lead the way.'

Kelly watched them walking down the road. 'I couldn't do it,' she said quietly. 'I'm sorry, but there's no way I could do it. I mean, what about AIDS and all that crap?'

'Told you,' Jack said. He reached into his big woollen pocket and pulled out a tin. 'Heroin.'

Jack prised open the tin and took out a hand rolled paper tube. He put it between his lips, lit the other end with a steel rod that produced a flame at the click of a button (like the one the boys on the train had), and sucked smoke into his mouth.

As I had seen many others do since I arrived here, he held the smoke in his mouth and then inhaled it deeply into his lungs. Then, after he had blown the smoke out, he handed the paper roll to Kelly. She did the same and then offered it to me.

'Want some?' Kelly asked. 'Keep you warm.'

I just stared at the roll. I could not see how it could keep me warm. 'What about the pollutants?' I said. 'They'll rot my tongue and throat, not to mention my lungs.'

Kelly groaned. 'God, I'm sick of you, with your bloody bible talk.' She tugged at Jack's sleeve. 'Come on Jack, let's go see what's going on down the gay village.' Jack did not need asking twice.

I called after them. 'What about the soup kitchens and the arches?'

'Find em yourself!' Kelly shouted without looking round.

I was instantly panicked, my breathing faltering. 'But what about food? What will I do? How will I keep warm?' I began sobbing, I couldn't help myself. 'How will I keep warm in this harsh climate?'

It was Jack who answered, again without turning. 'Get back to your own bloody country if you want it warmer!'

My own country? I thought of those warm winter evenings sat at the back of the cabin, Naomi lying back in my arms, gazing at the lanterns in the distance and the stars up above. There are no stars here because it's almost permanently cloudy, and when it isn't cloudy, the unnatural light from the street lamps drowns them out.

I dropped to the pavement and cried myself breathless. 'What will I do?' I kept saying. 'What will I do?'

I felt something land on my shoulders: Kelly's blanket. I wiped my eyes and she looked down at my pathetic form.

'Here, take this,' she said. 'You've not been homeless long, have you?' I shook my head. 'And you've never been homeless before.' This last sentence sounded more like a statement than a question. 'I can tell,' she said. 'Listen, go to the church in the morning. Tell the priests or whatever they are. They should help you. And go to the library. You need to learn some Inglish if you are going to get by.'

A glimmer of hope. They have libraries here as we do back home. I took the blanket about my shoulders and crawled over to one of the doorways. 'Do they teach your language to children?' I asked. 'What I mean is, do they have elementary books for learning how to read your language?'

She studied me thoughtfully, not with scorn. 'You're weird,' she said. 'You're bright, intelligent, too intelligent to be on the streets. You're like a teacher or sommat.' She frowned. 'But you're also like a child. You're like Shaz said, an innocent. You really don't know, do you?' I shook my head and dried my tears.

Kelly crouched down and smiled. 'There are books for children in the library, you know, to teach them to read and that. Get a look at them. I think you'll pick it up in time.' She stood up. 'Just don't hang around the kids too much, OK? I know you. They'll bang you up for being a perv.'

Again I could not understand. My brain had no word for perv. 'Someone who eyes up little kids,' she non-explained. 'A child molester.'

She put a lot of emphasis on the words, but I still couldn't comprehend. A child molester? A person who molests children? In what way? It made no sense.

But I promised not to speak to the youngsters and only talk to the adults, as Kelly advised. Satisfied with that, she skipped off to join Jack at the gay village. Wherever that is.

I am exhausted. And cold. The blanket helps a little but the taste of sour wine lingers in my throat. I am distracted by my thoughts; thoughts of speaking with an elder and learning to read Inglish.

This could be the start of me learning how to generate a dimension gate and get back home. Back to Elohah Village, back to Naomi, the children, their children, their children's children's children, and the other families, my mother and father and my brothers and sisters. Back to the warmth of the sun, the lushness of the grass and trees and the splendour of the mountains.

Hopefully, I will get a couple of hours' sleep to dream.

*

MARCH 18

I slept for about an hour on the bench facing the small square of grass. Like yesterday morning, I was moved from my doorway by a uniformed elder. I am now back on the bench and sitting up watching and writing, trying to take my mind off my hunger. I weep and dry my eyes. Again the people busy themselves on the way to their destinations, and again they act as if I don't exist.

The only person who stopped to look at me was the young woman who stopped to look at me yesterday morning. She turned the corner on the other side of the road and stood there watching me. But this time she crossed the road and spoke. Yes, she actually spoke to me.

'Don't cry,' she said, the way my mother used to do when I was a small boy. Her voice was soothing and I could not help but look up into her clear, yearning blue eyes. She was pretty, but different from Kelly and even from Shazia. She was kindly with no edge to her voice at all.

'Forgive me, miss,' I said. 'I have not eaten a proper meal for three days and my hunger pangs are extreme.'

'Haven't you eaten at all?' she asked. Her voice was faintly husky, like that of my aunt Rukhsana. She is very pretty too.

'I have had some soup and tee, and I had a piece of Kit Kat last night.'

'You're not an illegal immigrant, are you?'

'I am sorry,' I said. 'I do not understand these words. I think you mean I am from abroad, yes?'

'Er, yes.'

I told her I am from Elohah Village, and like those before her, she had not heard of it. She asked how I had travelled to Ingland. Inglish? So their language is *Inglish*. I found the woman easier to translate.

'I'm not sure I can explain it to you in a way you would understand,' I said.

She shrugged. 'Did you come by plane or on a ship?'

'Neither,' I said. 'You see, I have not come a great distance of space at all. I was in an area near Grasmere Village. Have you heard of that?'

She knew it. I explained my experiments in harnessing the energies of life, be they plant, animal or human, and that I'd opened up a dimensional gateway to this realm. I'd walked through it and it closed behind me, and now I am trapped here.

The young woman's eyebrows rose in a way that indicated she did not accept my story. 'OK,' she said.

I looked at the floor tearfully. 'I have not eaten for three days.'

She took a deep breath and sighed. 'Well I'm not giving you money.' There was determination in her voice. 'You'll just spend it on booze or fags.' I shook my head slowly, but she smiled. 'I'll tell you what I will do, though.'

'What?' I said. 'What will you do?'

'I'll get you a Mac Donalds.'

I was none the wiser. 'What is a Mac Donalds?'

She laughed heartily. 'Forgive me. You don't know what a Mac Donalds is? You must be from another planet, never mind another dimension.'

I smiled. She was still not accepting of my account, I could see that, but at least she was talking to me in a kind way. She told me to stay on the bench. Then she walked over to a brightly coloured inn and exchanged some pounds for a package and a cup. She hurried back over and handed them to me. 'Here you are,' she said. 'Breakfast and a hot drink of tee.'

I filled up again. I kept on thanking her.

'It's the least I can do,' she said. 'Listen, I've got to go now. I've got to get to the Job Centre.' She chastised herself. 'Jeezuz. I'm sorry, I forgot. Forgive me. At least I have a chance of *getting* a job.'

I sunk my teeth into the breakfast. It tasted good. 'I am going to the church to talk with the elder,' I said. 'Then I am going to the library to learn to read Inglish.'

She pulled her shoulder bag tight and a breeze ruffled her artificially coloured hair. 'You can't read English at all?'

'No,' I said. 'But I am told it will be easy to learn in time. Kelly said I should go there. Do you know her?'

'Er, no. No I don't.'

'She's not the one who is a hooker,' I said.

'I'm pleased to hear it.' She paused. 'Well, good luck with the library.'

I asked her what her name is. 'Kirsty,' she said. 'What's yours?' I told her my name. 'Now why doesn't that surprise me?' she asked, and then she laughed, and I realised she was not asking me a question. It was a statement of fact, implying that my having a strange name is not at all surprising.

She wished me well and went on her way.

Kirsty is a nice woman. I hope she comes this way every morning. Now I am resolved to find the church.

Section Three

MARCH 18 (b)

I walked right past the church, it blending in effortlessly with the surrounding buildings. Not like the temple at home at all.

Thankfully, a young man and woman standing outside one of the buildings and drawing smoke from paper rolls were more than happy to point it out to me.

At closer inspection I saw that it was vaguely different, especially with respect to the shape of its windows and roof. Filled with both excitement and apprehension, I went in.

A man dressed in smart attire approached. His skin was in the early stages of sagging and his hair on the turn from brown to silver-grey. His approach was swift and I felt a little unnerved by his cheerfulness.

After three days of gloom, over crowded streets, heavily polluted air and a tangibly aggressive populace, I now found myself startled by the genuinely cheerful. Hand outstretched, he beamed and said, 'Hello there!'

I extended my hand in the same fashion (he seemed to be indicating that I should) and he shook it vigorously.

'Have you come to look at our library, or are you after something more specific?'

His acceptance of me was refreshing, my unshaven face, windswept hair and body odour apparently not causing him revulsion as it does the people in the streets (with exception of the other homeless ones, of course).

'Are you one of the elders of the city?' I enquired.

He smiled broadly. 'Ah, a foreign gentleman, yes?'

'From abroad, yes.'

'Just visiting?'

I ignored the comment and got straight to the point. 'I need to speak with an elder.'

He cocked his head momentarily. 'Well,' he said. 'It depends what kind of elder you mean. Do you mean a councillor or an em-pee, or do you perhaps mean a religious elder, a clergyman?'

I knew at once this was not going to be as easy as I had imagined. I have no understanding of the words 'em-pee', 'religious', or 'clergyman'. I paused to think. 'I need to know about the Father.'

'The Father?' the man repeated.

'I do not mean my own father,' I clarified. 'I am referring to *the* Father, the Father of the Word, whom you call Jeezuz Kriste, the father of the universe and of all life.'

He smiled the smile of recognition. 'Ah, you mean God.'

I could not help grinning, I was so relieved. I had forgotten they called him God here. 'Yes,' I said chuckling, delighted to have found someone at last who did not regard the Father with scorn or a hint of loathing. 'The Father, God.'

The man folded his arms. 'So, what do you want to know about him?'

That was easy enough. 'I want to know why he has stopped speaking to me.'

The smile slackened and the arms loosed. He cleared his throat and shuffled backwards ever so slightly. 'What do you mean?'

'Well, back home, I can talk with him openly, sometimes as I am working, but mostly in the inner sanctum of the temple. But –'

I broke off, staring at the floor, suddenly lost and hopeless.

The man prompted me after a moment's hesitation. 'But?'

'But since arriving here I haven't heard him at all. I keep imploring him but he does not answer. I've asked odd individuals since I got here and they don't seem to understand me. It's as if the Father staying silent is normal.'

Seeming to realise, the man smiled and nodded, slightly at first and then more emphatically. 'Yes, yes,' he said. 'We can all get those feelings from time to time, that God has abandoned us. It might surprise you to know that I sometimes feel like that too.'

At last!

'You do?'

'Oh yes. Even a man of the faith can become riddled with doubt.'

I was lost again. 'How do you mean, riddled with doubt?'

'Well,' he said, shrugging. 'Doubt that there's anybody up there at all.'

Repelled by the idea I said, 'No, no, no. I don't doubt he is there. How can he not be? I just don't understand why he doesn't speak.'

He nodded again. 'I had similar feelings when my dad died.'

I was shocked, and I think it showed. 'Your dad?' I had to clarify before I went any further with this, so as not to offend. 'When you say your dad, you mean your own father, yes?'

His smile was less certain now. 'Well, yes, of course.'

I didn't know what to say to him. I tried to imagine my own father dying. To know he had expired, ceased to be conscious, like one of the aged animals.

'And that's when you beseeched the Father?' I said.

'Well yes.'

'For him to restore the life of your dad. He is the giver of life. He would be able to restore it easily.'

The man frowned. 'I did not expect God to bring my father back to life,' he said, uncertain again. 'That would be

61

unrealistic. No, I asked that I be given the strength to cope, to endure the pain.'

Now it was my turn to frown. 'But not to bring him back?'

He gave a slight shake of the head. 'No.'

'What did he say to comfort you, then?'

'What do you mean?'

'You said you asked him to help you to endure. What did he tell you?'

He gave me a pathetic non-smile. 'Well he didn't actually speak. But then I didn't expect him to. But I thought there might have been *something*, you know, some indication, some feeling.'

I nodded. 'Well, I certainly understand that.'

His father *died*. How? It was incredulous to conceive: A human being ceasing to exist, after how many years? One hundred, two hundred, three hundred? And God staying silent when approached? I tried to conceal my astonishment, but I was unable.

'Does the Father never speak?' I pressed.

The man shook his head. 'He speaks through the spirit of creation and through the good of mankind, but when we are low, we sometimes fail to discern it.'

That was not what I meant. 'But you never hear his voice – literally?'

'What, like Abraham and Moses and people like that, you mean?'

The names mean nothing to me, but I gave a brief nod.

'Well, there are claims of such encounters,' he said, laughing, 'but no one takes those seriously. No, I can definitely say, in all the time I have been serving the church, no disembodied voices have ever communed with me.' He paused, and then added, 'Or with anybody that I know, for that matter.'

I found myself staring at him again, the shock gripping me. 'He does not speak.' My voice was fading into a croak. 'Ever.'

The man touched my shoulder. 'I'm afraid not.'

'It must be because you have ruined the creation,' I said, not quite to myself. Then I started to weep. The man comforted me and waited. 'I need to know,' I said as I sobbed. 'I need to know why the Father is silent. I need to learn your history, how you got into this pitiful state.' Then I remembered. 'I need to learn to read your Inglish language.'

The man beamed at me. 'The library does evening classes.' Then he reconsidered. 'But I'm not sure they would take a homeless person on.' He looked at me in earnestness. 'You are homeless, aren't you?'

I nodded.

'An immigrant, perhaps?'

'Perhaps,' I said, and dried my eyes. 'But I do not need the classes. A young woman called Kelly told me they have elementary books to teach children to read. All I need do is study one of them.'

'Well, I'm not sure it's that –.'

'I can do it,' I asserted. 'And when I have I will come back here and examine your library dedicated to the Father, especially the fragment of ancient scripture by John.'

'Well, that's written in Greek, actually,' the man said. 'And it's at the John Rylands library on Deens Gate, not the central library, but you're welcome to go and look at it.'

I headed for the door. 'Thank you.' Then I realised I had not sought his name. He told me his name is Grey-am. 'Thank you, Grey-am,' I said. 'Thank you for all your help.'

And that's when I came here to the central library. It is huge and has rows upon rows of books. All I need do now is find the ones for teaching children to read.

MARCH 18 (c)

I forgot about how hungry I was as soon as I caught sight of the youngsters in a segregated part of the building. They were sat together in a group, all wearing the same cut of clothes, with an adult presiding over them. The adult gave me a hard stare and I recalled what Kelly had said: keep away from the children.

A second adult, a woman with lenses suspended over her eyes (like Margaret in Grasmere Village) sat behind a counter. I told her I could not read the native language and asked her to point out the books for teaching children to read. Somewhat apprehensively she did so and I took one of the books from the shelf. With permission, I took it into the main part of the building and sat at a table.

I am sitting at the table now and want to laugh out loud. The language is so primitive and elementary. Again, comparisons with my own children are inevitable. The infants of my world would have this mastered in a day.

There are twenty-six letters in this Inglish alphabet, and different combinations form short words, some of which are remarkably similar in sound, but the variations are easy to remember.

'A' is for 'apple'; 'b' is for 'boat'; 'c' is for 'cat'; 'd' is for 'dog'. This process goes on, with pictures to illustrate full words, until the whole twenty-six letters are covered. 'Z' is for 'zoo', a sort of home for animals, it would seem.

I now know that Deens Gate is actually Deansgate. I recall the spelling on the name plate. Grasmere Village is probably right, but should it be one 's' or two, one 'r' or two? It is not easy to determine. Once I have seen the word written down I will know. I wonder…

I have just asked the woman at the desk if they have a book explaining what words mean. I blushed, feeling that the question was probably ridiculous, but she pointed me towards the 'reference' section where she said I would find a selection of 'dictionaries'. And sure enough, they have books explaining the application of diction!

Oh, and I was right, the language is actually *English*. It would help enormously if the populace would pronounce their words the way the dictionary implies they should.

There are many books in the library, including books about the different areas of the world. England Great Britain, if I am understanding correctly, is segregated from other areas. Each area is called a 'country' and is governed separately by its own elite of elders. The countries all have different languages too, English being just one of many, as is Greek, the language of the ancient writing in the John Rylands library. There is so much to learn here. I must come back.

I must ask the woman some more questions. I want to know if I can take the dictionary out of the building and if the woman will get me a Mac Donalds like Kirsty did this morning. I would also like to know why people say 'fukking' a lot.

MARCH 18 (d)

The woman at the library got very angry. I am still shivering with fright! It seems the youngsters learning to read do not know the meaning of expletives, and the use of them is forbidden in the presence of children, even though everyone says them all the time on the streets. How bizarre. Thankfully, before she started shouting, the woman told me that I will have to buy a dictionary from a place called Waterstone's if I want to take it away.

Presumably, Waterstone is the name of the proprietor. If it is, no one knows his whereabouts. I am sat at a table in Waterstone's now. The smell of food and hot drinks is affecting my very powers of reason. I keep wanting to take a biscuit without exchanging some pounds. I am so hungry.

MARCH 18 (e)

After browsing the many books I went over to the food counter and stared longingly at the cakes, biscuits and other delicacies on display. The young man guessed that I am homeless and, after I had hovered by the counter some minutes, signalled a uniformed man with a handheld communication device to escort me off the premises.

'I am tired and hungry,' I protested. 'Are you going to put me back on the street to freeze?'

As we reached the top of the stairs, a familiar voice called up. 'What are you doing here?'

'Looking longingly at cakes,' I said candidly.

Kirsty laughed. 'I'll buy you a cake,' she said, 'and a drink. How's that?'

I released my arm from the grip of the uniformed man, who was now somewhat confused, and thanked Kirsty profusely. She led me back to the food area, sat me down at a table, and ordered two 'chocolate fudge cakes with ice cream' and two 'coffees'. Then she sat opposite me at the table. I was so filled with gratitude I was moved to tell her that she is not like the other people I have met in this world.

'And you're not like any homeless person I've ever met,' Kirsty said. 'I mean, where exactly are you from?'

'I've already told you,' I said. 'I'm from a place situated in the same geographic area that you call Easedale Tarn in Grasmere, but on a different dimensional plane of reality.'

She sighed. 'Of course, I was forgetting.'

'I crossed over what I choose to call a gateway between the two realities and it closed behind me.'

She finished the account for me. 'And now you're stuck here, right? A man out of time.'

'Not out of time,' I said.

'But lost.'

I gave a half smile and she looked into my eyes. 'You know,' she said. 'I've heard all kinds of tales from people like you. I'm sorry if this sounds offensive.'

'It does not offend me,' I reassured her.

'Well, usually when they come out with the kind of thing you've just said, they are deranged in some way. Delusional. But you are quite obviously clued up.'

Clued up?

'Which means,' she said, 'you're either a very good liar or you really believe what you're telling me.' She laughed at her own circular logic. 'And if it's the latter, you must be delusional.'

The young man behind the counter, somewhat hesitantly, it has to be said, brought our cakes and coffees over on a tray. Kirsty gave him a warm smile. 'Thank you.' Then she picked up a sachet of sugar and tipped the contents into my coffee and stirred the drink with a spoon.

'What makes you different?' I asked.

She shrugged. 'Different? In what way?'

'You care about strangers,' I said. 'You care, when others simply walk by.'

She stirred her own coffee and did not look up. 'Not so long ago it was my job to care.'

'Job?'

'I was a clinical psychologist.' The phrase means nothing to me, but I let her continue uninterrupted. 'It took me eight years to qualify from leaving school, right through university and a shed load of debt, to get a placement and actually start to make a difference in people's lives. The money was good, I moved in with a boy I'd had a relationship with on and off, my parents were proud, and best of all I felt like I had some purpose to my life.' She sipped her coffee. 'And then I blew it.'

'Blew what?' She did not make sense.

'Everything,' she said.

'Everything?'

'Yep, everything.' She took her metal fork and cut into her cake. 'There was this lad. He had what we call a personality disorder. An unusual world view, a bit off the wall, but honest with it. He couldn't understand why the world is the way it is, why one half lives in luxury while the other half is starving, why the people of the various nations support the politicians' decisions over war and sanctions when deep down they don't agree with it.'

Was it one of their typical exaggerations or did she mean it literally? I could not help but speak. 'Half the world is starving?'

She ignored my question. 'I mean, we all think about that stuff, but we push it to the back of our minds, otherwise it'd drive us insane.' She pointed her fork at my cake. 'Come on. I thought you were hungry.'

'I am,' I said sheepishly. I dug into the cake and shovelled it into my mouth. The sponge-like substance was similar to the one the man with the blue line drawings on his arms had bought, but the taste was like that of the Kit Kat bar Kelly had shared with me. The sauce made all the difference; that and the ice cream. It was delicious. I sipped some coffee to wash it down. I winced as the hot liquid hit my cold teeth.

'Anyway,' Kirsty resumed. 'He couldn't push it to the back of his mind. It was part of his condition, his disorder, a kind of obsessive compulsive thing. He drove himself demented dwelling on all this heavy sh-.'

She stopped for a fraction of a second, looked at the people browsing the books and corrected herself, 'stuff. His dad got tired of hearing it. I mean, he did go on about it day in, day out, and in the end his dad threatened him.'

My face must have looked a picture. He *threatened* him?

'He told him if he didn't get his act together and get a job and pay his way, he would throw him out.' She sipped her coffee again and I did likewise. 'He was probably trying to shock him or something. But if you ask me, his dad's approach, how ever well intended, had contributed to the boy's state of mind. I mean, can you imagine the effect that would have had on his self-esteem?'

I cannot.

'So what happened?' I pressed.

Kirsty took another mouthful of cake and then dabbed her mouth with a paper towel. 'Well, he got worse, really depressed, you know, and was, like, spending whole days sleeping in bed.'

I found myself nodding. 'I can see why he would want to. When you're sleeping you are not aware of the world around you.'

'Exactly.' She sipped her coffee. 'Well, his father blew his top and told him to find somewhere else to live. Now we're talking about a recluse here, you know. He struggled with social skills at the best of times, and found the whole idea of approaching housing officials terrifying. So he bunged a load of clothes in a bin liner and tracked me down.'

'This was because he knew he could trust you,' I said. 'You were his friend.'

I thought about the man who helped me when I first arrived and how different he was to the majority of the people who had simply walked around me or stepped over me. Then I recalled the casual aggression that was a natural trait in Jack, Kelly and Shazia on the streets at night. I could see how the young man in Kirsty's account would be moved to find her. 'Were you surprised when he arrived at your home?'

'Kriste, you bet,' Kirsty said, her eyes widening at the thought. 'My boyfriend wasn't too pleased either. But I couldn't turf the lad out on to the street, so I let him stay over. The idea was to help him get a place of his own. But it wasn't as simple as that, and my boyfriend had issues with it.'

I was confused. 'He did not like you taking care of the boy?'

'He wasn't jealous, don't get me wrong,' she said. 'But he knew that those in the profession aren't supposed to befriend their patients. He was like me, he'd just got established and he didn't want to get the boot.'

The boot?

'So he moved out.' She finished the last of her coffee. 'Anyway, when the council finally found the lad a flat, he didn't want to go. I didn't blame him, it was a right dive. Drug dealers and all that. But because he wasn't deemed mentally ill, he didn't qualify for any of the programmes we could've offered. So he refused to go.'

I was entirely absorbed in her story now. 'So, what did you do?'

'Well I had no choice but to call the Law.'

'The Law?'

'Yeah, you know, the cops, the police.'

The police? The uniformed guards who patrol the streets, perhaps? I thought back to the vehicles they drove; blue and yellow, flashing lights and loud wailing sirens, and a word on the doors: *Police.*

'And then all hell broke loose,' Kirsty said. 'I had to tell them I was a psychologist and that I worked with the National Health, and the lad's father milked it for all he could, oh yeah. Said I'd taken advantage of his son. Ha!'

'So what happened?'

Kirsty ran the edge of her spoon around the rim of the cup and sighed deeply. 'Well the father took the lad back, my boyfriend packed me in and I was dismissed from my job.'

'That's awful,' I said.

She offered an excuse for a smile and for the first time I noticed how hard her eyes are. 'I'm not as bad as you, I know. I mean, I've still got a roof over my head, albeit a council one, and I'm on Job Seeker's, so I do have some money coming in, enough to tide me over until I get another job. But I've blown the psychology big time. Eight years down the drain because I couldn't keep a professional head.'

I took her hand and gave it a gentle squeeze. 'It's what makes you different,' I said. 'It's a good thing. A rare thing, in my very limited experience.'

Her eyes softened. 'Who are you?'

'Mahershalalhashbaz', I said.

She laughed, and suddenly was pretty again. 'Is that really your name?'

I laughed too. 'Yes!'

'Well, I'm going to call you Baz for short.'

'Baz,' I repeated, not quite sure what to think of it.

She withdrew her hand. 'Ee, I don't know why I told you all that. I'm sorry.'

'You have no reason to be sorry.'

'Sometimes it's easier to talk to a stranger.'

I agreed that it is.

Kirsty got up and exhaled noisily. 'I'm dying for sig.' I just looked at her. I couldn't be bothered asking her what a sig is. 'They're cracking down on smoking so much now. I reckon there'll be a complete ban before long.'

Then I realised: a sig is one of those paper rolls with herbal mixture inside. So she does it too? How disheartening.

She turned to leave. 'Oh,' she interrupted herself. 'Did you go to the library?'

'Yes,' I said with a smile. 'I learned to read your language from the books they use to teach children. It's very simple, but invaluable. I can learn all I need to know about this place now.'

She arched an eyebrow. 'About *this place*?'

I nodded.

'Something tells me, Baz, that you don't mean Waterstone's!'

I laughed. 'No!'

'You mean this world, right?'

'This dimensional plane,' I said.

She gave a snort, but smiled with it. 'Now why doesn't that surprise me?' Before I could answer, she was trotting down the stairs. 'Gotta go, Baz. I'm gasping.'

Gasping? She was as strange as the rest of them, but friendly.

I am savouring my cake and coffee. It is very tasty. The guard and the young man keep looking at me. They don't want me here, that much is obvious. It's back to wandering the streets then.

MARCH 18 (f)

The night is drawing in. I walked as far as I could and looked at many things. Being able to read English has made all the difference. I now understand the signs and notices in windows and on street corners. I found the Job Centre that Kirsty goes to each morning, I saw a place with pictures of dwellings of various sizes and shapes which one could buy with a lot of pounds – or what did Kirsty call it? – money. I am now sat on a bench in the area with the large lawn with the fountains, which I now know is named Piccadilly. I am tired and the hunger pangs are returning.

Other homeless people approach from time to time, but it doesn't take long before they are asking me for booze, dope and sigs. They all tell similar stories.

Some had good jobs like the one Kirsty described and made a series of foolish decisions culminating in the elders refusing to give them shelter and an allowance of money (Job Seeker's?), while others befriended rebellious types during their youth, began smoking sigs, progressed to dope and then substances which when taken alter one's perception of the world.

Apparently these induce feelings of euphoria, which makes them all the more appealing, but when the effect wears off the user feels dreadful ('like crap', they say, which is ridiculous because excrement is inanimate and has no feelings. I can only assume that this phrase is yet another metaphoric expression. Excrement, if not disposed of, can poison the body, and so it is unwelcome, like substance abuse).

These 'drugs' are addictive and demand that the user continues to take them. Doing so requires money, but because the users no longer have a job, or never had one, they resort to taking other people's money (I think they call it steeling, though how steel relates, I don't know).

This is fascinating. In all the time I have been here, it has never truly occurred to me that I might simply take the food that belongs to others.

Understandably, the system put in place by this world's elders is not sympathetic to these people, and so they are denied jobs, a place to live and a means of buying food. They live on the streets and beg the populace to give them money. They even beg one another, which is why I try to keep a distance from them.

They hate their world and they hate the system. They blame it for making false promises and for not giving them a chance (even though some of them were at one time enjoying to the full everything it has to offer).

None of them hate being here as much as I do. None of them have lost what I've lost.

I haven't seen Kelly and Jack this evening. Maybe they went to the gay village again. I don't know if it really is a gay village or if the phrase is just another metaphor.

I did see Shazia again, though. She was upset because one of her clients 'got violent' and hit her so hard in the face that one of her eyes has a black bruise all around it. I shudder, not just with the cold, but at how normal it seems to her. She appears to be more concerned about not being able to earn as much money with a black eye.

I have not yet discerned exactly what it is Shazia sells to her clients. It might be the dope Kelly was asking about last night.

When it gets quiet enough, I'll find a doorway in one of the back streets and see if I can get to sleep a bit earlier. With a clear mind I will be able to read more books in the library and see if there's any way I can grow the necessary plants to build a circuit and disrupt the dimension field enough to crawl back to my own world. It only needs a small opening to wriggle through. I just hope their orgology is advanced enough.

I did think of beseeching the Father again and then thought better of it. I don't believe I'm any more likely to receive a reply than these people here. Maybe it's his way of teaching me the folly of pursuing ideas independent to his guidance and purpose. Even so I do feel it is unkind.

I wish I hadn't written that last line or even thought it. He knows my every thought. I find it morbidly fascinating how easy it is to forget that the Father is there. The people here carry on with their everyday lives as though he doesn't exist. The illusion is a potent one. Thankfully, he also knows that I regret my presumptuousness.

This is getting silly. I need to sleep.

MARCH 19

Hungry again. I'm sat on the bench in front of the small patch of grass. It's feeling like home to me. I slept as best I

74

could in the back street. It was quieter and darker, but it also attracted intoxicated homeless people who insisted on talking to themselves or to one another until the early hours. I could understand how a human being might be driven to strike another, and felt wretched for thinking it.

Father, forgive me, please.

Then there was the moaning. That woke me up. A man pressed a woman up against a wall in the darkest part of the street. They moaned and sighed as one does in holy union. When I focussed I could see that their leg and thigh coverings were unfastened. They *were* having holy union!

I was both repulsed and aroused, as I had been the previous night when Shazia deliberately provoked sensual feelings in the man with the short hair. They treat sexual intercourse here the way dogs do at home. Maybe that is why the city is so overrun with people.

Finally I returned to my bench and slept for a couple of hours. Now I'm sat here watching people travel in their vehicles as they make their way to their jobs to earn money. The library will be open soon. I am hoping that the woman will let me in to look at the books about orgology.

Kirsty will be here soon. I keep asking the Father to influence her so that she will bring me a McDonald's again. But I know it's futile.

MARCH 19 (b)

Well, not only did Kirsty arrive on time, but she brought me some sandwiches and a steel cylinder of coffee with a screw-on top that becomes a cup when one removes it.

'This is much better than McDonald's,' I beamed appreciatively.

'I hope so!' Kirsty said. 'I made them myself. And you've got a full flask of coffee there, so if you're sparing with it, you should be able to make it last you a couple of hours.' She reached into her bag and pulled out a small pouch. Inside it there was money. She handed me a couple of pounds. 'Here. Buy yourself some food later. You should be able –.'

'To make it last,' I concluded for her. 'Thank you.' She hesitated. I tried to prolong the conversation. 'Are you going to the Job Centre?'

'Yeah. Gotta keep looking. I think I'm gonna have to settle for a crap factory job, though.'

Crap is excrement. It is synonymous with poor quality.

'No one in the mental health profession is going to take me on now. I've been trying for low profile roles, but as soon as they check me out, they don't want to know.'

'So a crap factory job is your only option?' I asked, not really knowing what I was talking about.

She grabbed the strap of her shoulder bag. 'Yeah. I'll have to do some mind-numbing monotonous job for piss poor wages.'

Piss is urine.

'Still, it's whatever pays the rent.'

I warmed my hands on the hot flask. 'Could I get one of these crap factory jobs too, do you think?'

She gritted her teeth and at first I thought she was angry. Then I realised - she was trying not to discourage me.

'Oh, I don't know, Baz,' she said. 'I mean, you have no address, you have no history. If you're an illegal immigrant, they won't want to take you on. And then there's the way you look. You're dirty, you smell of sweat. Your breath stinks. You'd never get past an interview.' Then she reproved herself. 'Jeezuz, I'm sorry.'

'You have no need to be sorry,' I told her. 'You brought me sandwiches and coffee.' She gave me a helpless smile and I felt warmer, not because of the coffee, but because of her smile – my only friend in this awful wilderness. 'If you do find someone I could work for, though,' I offered

76

meekly, 'please tell them I will work for piss poor wages too.'

Her pitiful smile became a broad one and she laughed heartily. 'You're one on your own, Baz. That's for sure.'

'Like the lad you helped?'

She considered, a little apprehensively I think. 'Yes. Like the lad I helped.' Then without saying another word, she continued on her way to the Job Centre.

I finished my sandwiches and drank one cup of coffee before putting the flask and the blanket in my satchel. My plan for the day is to learn as much as I can about the plant life here and discover what provisions there are to construct a circuit. I am determined to get back home before the day is over.

MARCH 19 (c)

I am sick at heart. I persuaded the woman in the library to let me in on the basis that I would stay away from the children and not say the metaphors aloud. I asked her for the books on orgology and she said she didn't know what I meant. After some clarification she pointed me to the gardening section, and from there I learned enough to know that this society only uses plants for food and for deriving certain drug compounds.

When I expressed my disappointment, the woman recommended I try the science section. Science is the word they give to the process of investigating the natural world. The workings of the Earth's physical resources and mechanisms, the biology of various life forms, the chemical make-up of the elements and so forth. But nowhere did I find a book on orgology.

Instead they have a concept called 'technology', which is the very antithesis of orgology. It makes depressing reading.

As far as I can discern, in the last two hundred years or so they have been harnessing the Earth's resources to such an outrageous degree that, if they don't stop soon, they will have gutted the planet of all its precious minerals and stones. They are like locusts.

For example, the huge structures of metal, the vehicles and the other things in the city have been mass produced. Great groups of people work together to make as many items as possible to be sold around the world for money. Those who instigate the selling are given a lot more money than those who do the actual work. I now have a greater appreciation of what Kirsty means by 'piss poor wages'.

The electricity that powers the night lights and automatic machinery does not come from natural sources like lightning, but is generated by burning excessive amounts of natural ore (called coal) and other substances, and in some cases, by splitting atoms and utilising the energy within.

Of course, the latter method is incredibly dangerous. The danger seems not to bother the populace at all. It bothers me a great deal, and I just hope there isn't an atom splitting factory near to Manchester. I also can't help worrying about Kirsty. I truly hope she doesn't get a job in such a place.

The amount of filth that has been pumped into the atmosphere over the last two hundred years must be tremendous. What effect it is having on natural equilibrium, such as the seasons and weather cycle, I can only guess.

If the tribes of the Earth are all like this one, the long term effects will be catastrophic. These people seem determined to poison themselves into death, whether it be by burning oils mined from deep down under the sea or by inhaling the smoke from mass produced cigarettes (the proper name for the paper rolls, so I've discovered).

Again I find myself in agreement with the Father over his decision not to have any dealings with this people. They have ruined everything he has created. I just wish he would have some dealings with me!

It has become woefully clear that this society never engaged in orgological studies. They do not have the means to get me back home, though they may have the raw materials.

'I think *Science Digest* or *Nature* magazine might be more up your street,' the woman advised when I told her of my disappointment, but I have no idea what she means.

MARCH 19 (d)

I'm sitting in a doorway trying to keep out of the rain. It's going dark earlier than normal because of the clouds. It's also much colder.

I am so hungry.

MARCH 19 (e)

The rain is coming down hard. I have never seen anything like it before. The gentle dew that waters the land back home is not like this. But I can't say I'm surprised. Even the rainfall is off-balance here.

The whole of the ground is soaked, with water running off the pavements and into specially made grooves that run between the pavements and the roads. I hadn't noticed them before. For all of their immaturity in splitting atoms and pumping colossal amounts of filth into the atmosphere, this society can also be ingenious. The system of grooves and grids is quite compelling and makes good for passing the time.

Shazia has joined me in my doorway. I have learned a bit more about her. She was brought up by a strict family, has an older sister who went to study biology in a university and had all the support she needed to succeed. The sister is now living in a place called Australia, which I think might be an underground city ('Down Under'? Nothing surprises me about this place any more).

When Shazia reached her teen years she became jealous of her sister and her parents' favouritism. She 'got in with the wrong crowd' and began committing crimes against the Governmental system. She had sexual intercourse outside of wedlock and had 'an abortion' without telling her parents.

I did not dare ask her what she means by this, as her countenance implied something deeply disturbing. She said she doesn't feel bad about it, but her eyes, her voice and the very fact she chose to tell me suggests that she does feel bad.

Following the abortion, she went 'really off the rails' (even worse?) and began taking drugs. At first she enjoyed the 'buzz' of 'getting high' and then she became 'dependent' on them. Presumably the intake of these chemicals interacts with one's natural body chemistry and destabilises it, the body then making demands on the conscious mind to keep up the intake.

Shazia said that as she adjusted to it she needed more to 'get the effect' (an artificial feeling of euphoria?). She went from 'soft' drugs to 'the hard stuff', which is more expensive. She took money from her parents at first, and then began taking items she could sell, all just to be able to buy the drugs and 'just feel normal'.

In the end, her parents evicted her from their home. Determined not to become homeless, and equally determined to maintain her doses of 'the hard stuff', she 'went on the game'. I think this is the line of work she is involved in now (a Hooker?).

She has a number of regular clients and she does them favours. If I am understanding correctly, some of these favours include stimulating fantasies in a sexual way, things their wives would not feel comfortable doing. (What could they *be*?!). These favours pay well enough to keep her in her new lifestyle. She works through the night and sleeps in the day.

I find her curiously appealing, though I wish she would cover up her breasts and legs. I keep staring at them while I'm talking to her. This makes me feel as though I am behaving treacherously toward my dearest Naomi, which, of course, I am not.

MARCH 20

I am shivering with cold and hunger. This world is like a bad dream. I hate it, I truly do. It has dawned on me that these people are not simply going to the same places every day, but they are doing the same things every day. What a tedious way to live. Do they have no sense of passion or curiosity? Why do they not get bored with it? I have only been stuck here a few days and I utterly loathe it. I cannot imagine living this life for a year, or many years.

There is one positive aspect to the predictability, though: Kirsty.

MARCH 20 (b)

True enough, right on time, Kirsty walked around that corner, with her bag hanging from her shoulder and a larger bulkier bag in her hand. I hoped the second bag contained food and a flask. And it did. She smiled as soon as she caught sight of me and walked toward my bench.

'God, you look freezing,' she said. She was not addressing me as God. That was just a figure of speech like the others.

'I am,' I confirmed, passing her my empty flask. 'The rain last night –.'

'Oh, Kriste, yeah. I heard it belting on the windows last night. It must have been awful for you.' She poured me some coffee from the fresh flask.

'It was,' I said and nursed the warm cup in my numb fingers. 'The whole weather system seems to be malfunctioning. I mean, the water canopy in my world prevents such harsh temperatures from ever developing. What have you people done to it? It must be drastic, whatever it is, to affect the equilibrium like this.'

Kirsty stared at me. 'The water canopy? What's that?'

It was incredulous. I looked into her eyes and saw nothing but bafflement. She really did not know what I meant by the water canopy.

'There is a blanket of water just above the atmosphere,' I explained. 'When the sun's rays hit it, they are dispersed, creating a natural greenhouse environment.' I laughed, more to myself than to her. 'Or at least it would if it were working!'

Kirsty continued to stare. 'Baz,' she said. 'I have never heard of that before in my life.' She considered this. 'Though it is a fascinating concept. Did you think of it yourself?'

Now it was my turn to stare. 'I didn't think of it, Kirsty. It's real.'

She snorted. 'Er, I don't think it is.'

'It isn't?'

'Nope.'

I was stunned (I still *am* stunned. No water canopy?!) 'But if there is no water canopy,' I said, 'the two poles would freeze and the equator would be far too hot. It would be crazy. Not to mention uninhabitable.'

Kirsty did not react. I cleared my throat. 'You're going to tell me that is in fact how it is, aren't you?'

She tightened her grip on her shoulder bag, as if readying herself. 'Baz,' she said finally.

'Yes?'

'I have made an appointment for you.'

I frowned. 'An appointment?'

'At Glendenning House, to see an ex-colleague of mine, a Doctor Neil Collier. He's cleared it with my old boss, Stephan Prescott. Prescott thinks you're an outside referral, which you are in a way.'

'I don't understand,' I told her.

She sat next to me on the edge of the wet bench and took my hand in hers. It was warm and gentle, motherly almost.

'Don't take this the wrong way, Baz. But I want him to assess you. If I can convince him that you need his care, we might be able to get you into the system. Once you're in the system, they would get you off the street, might even find you a job.' She broke off, hesitant.

'There's just one thing,' she said. 'If you mention any of this stuff about other dimensions or coming from a different time or a parallel world, he's likely to think you're just putting it on, and he'll dismiss you.'

'Define "putting it on",' I said in all seriousness.

'He will think you have invented the story simply to court his favour,' she said. 'He will think you are pretending to be mentally ill just to get in his good books.'

Mentally ill? What a bizarre concept.

I felt awkward. It was clear that Kirsty herself thought my account of my origins was little more than fanciful dreaming, the product of desperation. But how else could I explain myself? Avoid the truth and tell an alternative fanciful dream, an un-truth? (another bizarre concept, but one which sits well with this ridiculous world).

'Neil will see you at five, right at the end of his surgery.'

'Will you be there too?'

She bit her lip. 'If I can get in without anyone seeing me. I'm kind of off-limits these days.'

'Very well,' I told her. 'I will go to talk to this man, if it will help get me off the streets and into a proper dwelling place. And a job, even a job that pays piss poor wages, will help me acquire the things I need to open up a way back to my own world.'

Kirsty laughed heartily again. I was bemused. 'What is funny?'

'It's just the way you say "piss poor wages"'' she said. 'It sounds funny when you say it.'

I conceded that it probably does, and laughed too.

MARCH 20 (c)

I am in the library again. Kirsty showed me the location of Glendenning House where her friend Neil works. I will be meeting her there at five.

I've been reading books about the weather cycle. It actually works pretty much the same way as the one at home, only, due to the disruption brought about by this wayward society, it sometimes operates in a very erratic way, even destroying towns and killing hundreds of people. Again, there is no hint of the Father recreating these individuals.

A terrifying notion – dying and staying dead. No more permanent than plant life.

I have also found a book of drawings of the Earth. They show the land as if the artist were looking down from the sky. I also found a three-dimensional model of the Earth depicting the same designs.

The green areas represent land and the blue areas represent water. It is incredible: the land mass as I know it back home has been broken up and moved about, as if some great force has hit the world and disfigured it. By closely studying the shapes of the various portions of land, one can see that it was once all joined up as one big mass like at home. I cannot mentally grasp the amount of water that covers this planet. There is a *lot* more water here than at home. Indeed, even the authors of the book acknowledge that *two thirds* of the Earth's surface is water!

From what I have been able to discern, there are many cities like Manchester on the Earth and some of them are much, much larger. Conversely, there are other areas that are completely uninhabited. It seems this version of humanity is excruciatingly simple minded and cannot organise itself into smaller villages now that it has developed technology. Little pastoral communities cannot mass produce metal and plastic and cigarettes, and so they have abandoned the pastoral way of life.

I am beginning to understand what Kirsty means by mentally ill. It is a malfunction of the mind. By this definition, the whole populace should be attending Glendenning House.

I am trying to read, and eat sandwiches, without the woman at the desk seeing me. Eating in here is forbidden for some reason.

MARCH 20 (d)

The meeting with Neil was awful. I was left feeling completely worthless and empty. Rogue animals are accorded greater dignity in this world.

Kirsty met me outside the building and spoke into one of those tiny plastic boxes with even tinier buttons on it. She would speak, go silent momentarily, and then resume her conversation.

I mentioned this in an earlier entry. The boxes are two-way transmitters, communication devices. Presumably the vocal patterns are converted into electrical ones and transmitted over the airwaves. They are much more crude than mental projection, but just as effective.

'Just ten minutes, Neil,' she was saying, 'that's all. Just an initial assessment.' Silence. 'Yes, he's here now.' Silence. 'Well I would prefer to, obviously. Is Prescott still there?' Silence. 'Then I want to be present when you interview him.' Silence. Then euphoria. 'Great! Thanks Neil, I really appreciate this, I really do.'

Kirsty turned to me excitedly. 'Come on. We're going in.'

Neil was a tall slight man with thin brown hair. His complexion was ruddy and his eyes raw and tired. He was very healthy looking, though. His skin was clean, his clothes smart: black trousers and shoes, a white shirt and a pointed strip of blue material hanging dead centre from his neck. He smiled at Kirsty and then shot me a look, one of apprehension I think.

He extended his hand. 'Hello.'

I shook it. 'Hello.' As an afterthought I added, 'Thank you for agreeing to see me.'

'Don't thank me,' he said bluntly. 'Thank Kirsty here.'

He led us down a brightly lit corridor and into a sparsely decorated room. The walls were white; a white board with black handwriting on it dominated one of them.

A wooden table occupied the middle of the room, with two chairs on either side. Neil took a chair and indicated that I take the one opposite him. He opened a book of blank faintly lined white paper, a writing tool in his hand poised and ready to go. Kirsty chose to remain standing.

I savoured the light and warmth the room provided and ignored the stench of my body as it mingled with the artificial fragrances.

'First things first,' Neil said. 'Your name is Baz.' He wrote it at the top of his book.

86

'That is the name Kirsty gave me,' I said with a smile.

He looked at me. 'What is it short for? Barry?'

'No,' I said. My reply was instinctive. Kirsty seemed uncertain, but I was confused as to how I should interpret her body language. 'It's short for Mahershalalhashbaz.'

'Is that your Kristian name or your surname?'

Baffled already.

He seemed to realise. 'Your first name or your last name?'

I shrugged. 'My only name.'

'Well you'll forgive me if I ask you to spell it.'

I interpreted this question/statement as an indication that I should spell out the letters of my name. Thankfully I was right, and relished going through it in the English alphabet.

'How are you feeling at the moment, Baz?'

I shrugged again. 'Glad to be in here rather than out there, grateful for the warmth and the light.'

He wrote something on his book. 'And how do you view yourself at the moment?'

That was easy. 'Lost,' I said.

Neil frowned. 'In what sense?'

'In every sense,' I said. 'I am lost geographically, lost socially.'

'How about mentally?'

'No,' I replied, and immediately sensed Kirsty burrowing holes in the floor with her eyes. 'I am mentally sound. But your world –' I corrected myself. 'The world. The world is mentally deficient.'

He began writing again. 'In what way?'

'You are determined to destroy yourselves. Your history, from the little I've seen of it, is full of strife and hardship, most of which you have brought upon yourselves. Since the arrival of what you call the Industrial Revolution, you have pumped toxic fumes into the atmosphere, stifled the ground with artificial rock, ruined the weather cycle, and abandoned all that is natural in favour of selfish convenience.'

Neil stopped scribbling. 'Interesting.' Kirsty stared at him, her eyes pleading with hope. He ignored her and continued to look straight at me. 'You do not include yourself.'

I frowned. 'What do you mean?'

'You said *you* are determined to destroy the world, not *we* are determined.' He scribbled a sentence. 'You do not regard yourself as contributing to man's guilt.'

'Well I'm not guilty,' I said simply.

'But everyone else is?'

'Yes.'

He arched an eyebrow and took a deep breath. 'So you don't regard yourself as having a mental illness of any kind?'

'No.' I considered. 'But I do think of myself as *emotionally* ill.'

He smiled, as if to himself. 'Go on.'

'I have felt wretched ever since I got here.'

'Ah.' He waved his writing implement at me. 'Since you arrived here. Do you mean here as in Manchester or here as in Britain?'

'Both.'

'And from where have you come?'

I gave a nervous cough. This question was one of the crucial ones, I understood that. 'From a place near Grasmere village.'

'In the Lake District?'

'Yes.'

'Whereabouts did you live?'

'Near Easedale Tarn.'

'But *where*?'

'On a farm.'

'Where was the farm?'

'In Elohah village.'

This time both eyebrows went up. 'Elohah?' I was not sure what the question meant. There was a look of recognition in his face. I nodded. He smiled. 'Elohah as in Elo-*him*?'

'I suppose so, yes.'

Kirsty frowned at him. 'What is it, Neil?'

Again, Neil ignored her and looked directly at me. 'Tell me, Baz. Do you have religious feelings?'

Religious – religion – their word for trust in God.

'I look to the Father for guidance,' I said, with almost a sense of shame.

Neil smiled at the frowning Kirsty. 'Elohah and Elohim are ancient He-broo for God. One is singular, the other plural.' He grinned at me. 'Isn't that right, Baz?'

I shrugged. 'I suppose so. Yes.'

Ancient He-broo? Is that their name for my language? Did they once speak it here?

'And what does God say to you when you look to him for guidance?'

I glanced to Kirsty for inspiration, but she dared not give the impression she was aiding me at all. I returned to the expectant Neil, who remained cold and neutral, like the passers by who stepped over me on the pavement on my first day. I said:

'Nothing.'

'Nothing?'

'Nothing,' I repeated. 'Nothing since I came here.'

His eyes darted at the remark and I failed to understand the significance. 'What about before you came here?'

'I do not understand.' I was stalling.

'It's a simple question, Baz,' he retorted. 'What was your relationship with God before you came here?'

I could do nothing but shrug again. 'I talked to him whenever I needed to. During my work, when I had an idea I wanted to test with him. When I went to seek counsel from the elders, or when I went into the inner room at the Temple Hall.

'And you stopped talking to God when you arrived here?'

'No,' I corrected. '*He* stopped talking when I came here.'

Kirsty held her chin and glared at the floor. I had made a big mistake. No one I had met in this world ever expected the Father to converse with them, why would it be different in this house of mental illness?

Neil wrote one long word on his book. Then he put his writing tool down, clasped his hands, and stared at me intently. 'Schizophrenia? Unlikely. Exaggerated view of self? Definitely. Lacking in social skills? Very probably. Confused by and angry at the world? Aren't we all? Delusional beliefs? Well, beliefs are beliefs. Borderline Asperger's? Could be.'

Kirsty gave a vague uncertain smile. I smiled back. I had no idea what Neil was communicating to either me or my friend.

'The trouble is, Baz,' he continued. 'I can't help you at all unless you tell me who you really are.'

But Kirsty said I mustn't.

I kept my face as blank and clueless as I could, which wasn't difficult. 'What do you mean?'

'As much as you hate the system,' he said, 'you are going to have to subject yourself to it before you can avail yourself of its benefits.' He bent back the fingers of his left hand one by one. 'Your real name, your last address, your National Insurance number if you know it; some way of identifying you.'

Kirsty instinctively took a step closer to the desk. 'You know very well the homeless often cannot supply these things, Neil. Be realistic.'

'I am being realistic, Kirsty. The system will want to know who he is.' He pointed a finger at me. 'Who are you? Where are you from?'

His tone alarmed me. 'I have told you,' I spluttered. 'I am Mahershalalhashbaz.'

'Your accent is foreign,' the man barked. 'Are you an illegal immigrant?'

Kirsty's eyes bulged. 'Neil! Don't insult him!'

Neil ignored her.

I began to panic. I had never been attacked in such a way before. He pressed closer. 'Are you an illegal immigrant?'

'Why does everyone keep asking me that?' I cried.

'Are you?'

'No!' I yelled. I was in a rage now. 'I come from Elohah Village in the Northern Hemisphere. It is a place that runs parallel in both space and time to the area you call Easedale Tarn in Grasmere, only it's much more beautiful and lush. I found a way of pushing open a door between my dimensional reality and yours, and in my foolishness stepped through it. Now I am trapped here; trapped with no family, no friends, no one who understands. Yours is a miserably primitive society. You are aggressive and animalistic – it is little wonder the Father has abandoned you.' I was sobbing in real earnest now. 'Me,' I spluttered. 'He's abandoned me.'

Images of home flooded into mind: the trees, the meadows, the rivers; my dear wife, my daughters and sons, all wondering where I am; my cabin and my bed; the stars at night.

Kirsty nursed her face in her hands and stared at me through spread fingers. Neil just looked, mouth agape, completely astonished by my outburst.

'I am sorry,' he said slowly. 'You are clearly in great distress. But I cannot help you if you will not help yourself. I am accountable for every name I put forward for our programme. You have emotional problems, it is clear, but you are mentally sound. You are intelligent. At the end of the day, if the authorities even begin to suspect that I am sheltering an immigrant, I will be in big trouble.'

He walked toward the door and opened it. 'It's not a risk I can afford to take. I'm not prepared to jeopardise my job.'

Tears filled Kirsty's eyes as they met his. 'No one's asking you to, Neil. You can see what he's like.'

Neil mumbled through gritted teeth. 'He's a tramp, Kirsty. He's no different than any of the other poor sods out there. They all talk about the system and hypocrisy and God. It is part of what makes them what they are. The world has broken them. If he won't give me something to work with I cannot help him out of his slumber.'

I got to my feet and shuffled to the door. 'Thank you,' I said, wiping the snot from my nose with the edge of my sleeve.

As I made for the exit I heard Kirsty behind me hiss, 'For God's sake, Neil, he's like a child.'

'No he isn't,' Neil replied, his voice even and unconcerned. 'He's a desperate man who will say anything to relieve that desperation. Anything but the truth. The truth will ship him back to whatever poor state of affairs he has fled from.'

I heard Kirsty walk out the room. Her footsteps were determined, angry, but I did not look back. Neil half followed her. 'This is the last time, Kirsty,' I heard him say. 'Don't bring anyone else to see me unless they have an address and a national insurance number.'

I have spent most of this evening recounting this conversation. There is something good and honest and selfless about that girl. She's like me, she doesn't belong here.

I'm so hungry. Neil didn't even offer me a cup of tea. The more I think about it the more I feel certain he had decided the outcome before our interview had begun. Clearly I am not the first person Kirsty has taken to see Neil. But I will be the last.

It's raining again, but not as bad as last night. I'm sat under the arch at Piccadilly, the only place I can write without wetting my paper. It's difficult avoiding the other 'tramps', but I'm doing my best to. Their conversation is wearisome. Most are intoxicated with that awful wine they call *White Lightning*, and that other stuff, *Meths*.

There's Kirsty!

My heart is beating faster now I have seen my only friend in this dreadful place. She's appeared from a corner on the opposite side of the square. Maybe she's just eaten in one of the establishments. I feel bad about running off from the mental house. I could not face her.

She's standing in front of one of the money dispensers now. She's inserting her card. She's waiting.

But there is something else, something stirring around her: four young men, three circling behind her, the fourth standing a few paces back, looking left and right, watching keenly. But for what? The man nearest her is talking to her. She's looking over her shoulder, shaking her head.

The men are closing in on her. What are they doing?

I am going to go across.

MARCH 20 (e)

'Ere that, Waz?' the man closest to her jeered. 'She's on the dole, it's all she's got.' The four men laughed. 'Well you look all right to me, darling.'

They were threatening her, intimidating her. I felt sick to the pit of my stomach, but chose to remain concealed in the shadows. Kirsty had not seen me and the men certainly hadn't.

Kirsty slowly and carefully removed her card from the wall and slipped it into her pocket. 'Please,' she said. 'Leave me alone. I'm just a girl on my own.'

'Aw,' the ringleader sneered. 'She's a girl on her own.' Again they laughed. Then, as if reacting, they began to close in further.

Her back hit the wall. 'No, don't. Please.' Her eyes darted about, frantic. She shouted. 'Help! Somebody please!'

The ringleader launched at her and cupped her mouth. 'Shut it, bitch!' The other two stood very close to her. The fourth remained in position, giving sharp looks to the left, the right, and behind. 'Get on with it,' he commanded.

Just as when the people stepped over me in the street, so the majority continued as though nothing was happening. One or two looked on pitifully, but seemed too scared to go to her aid. Then the ringleader produced a small knife and held the blade against the smooth young skin of her neck. He grabbed her by her hair, gritted his teeth and mouthed the words, 'Give me the card.'

Instinct got the better of me. I stepped out of the shadows and onto the wet pavement, lights and colours reflecting and glistening. The second man looked at me and called to the one named Waz. 'We've got company.'

I advanced upon them. 'Leave her alone!'

I was furious.

Waz made a grab for me. 'Going to have a go, big boy?' But I took his arm and twisted it up his back. He screamed. I formed a fist and punched his back hard, like I was punching a block of wood into place in the barn at home. The man gasped and fell into the curb.

The ringleader scowled at the third man. 'Jav, get him.'

As Jav turned, I hurled myself at him. My weight knocked the breath out of him. In his fright he became like jelly and I slung him across my shoulders and tossed him into the road. A vehicle screeched to a halt and sounded its horn. I advanced on the ringleader. 'Let her go, you despicable man!'

94

He turned and pointed his knife at me. 'You don't scare me. I don't care whether you're built like a brick shitter or not.' He stabbed at me, but my reflexes were much quicker.

I took his fist in mine and squeezed it as hard as I could. The tips of his fingers went white as they pressed into the handle of the knife. His eyes watered in agony and he let out a silent cry. I took the knife from him and threw it across the road. Ringleader dropped to his knees, nursing his lifeless hand.

The remaining man just stared at his friends in a fright and then ran. The others scrambled after him as best they could. I could not help but laugh, as one does at an animal when it performs an amusing act.

They were an insult to the human race, endowed with self-awareness, the ability to think and create, but they chose to threaten a defenceless young woman. A good, kind-hearted woman. The nicest, loveliest person I had met in this bereft horrible place.

She stood there, shivering with fright. I approached and put a comforting arm about her shoulders. 'Do not worry. It is over. They have run off like cowardly cows.'

'Kriste,' she croaked, her teeth chattering. 'I feel terrible. I can't move.'

'It's all right, I am here now.'

She reached into her bag and pulled out an oblong red and white card box. I saw the word 'Marlboro' on it. Then, as she slid open the box, I groaned. She ignored my objection and I felt bad for sounding my disapproval.

The cigarette was different to the ones smoked by Jack and Kelly. It was smooth and had a synthetic material at one end. I marvelled at it, a mass produced poison for general consumption. She put it between her lips and brought out a plastic lighter device. Her nerves were so bad, her hand shook. I took the device from her, clicked the button, and touched the end of her cigarette with the little flame.

Eyes closed, Kirsty sucked on her cigarette. The end burned orange. She removed the tube of paper and crushed leaves from her lips, breathed the smoke deep into her lungs, held it briefly, and then blew it back out. And I realised. It was an act of self comfort. She repeated the process again with her eyes closed, after which she held the cigarette as was the custom, pinched between her first and middle finger.

She looked at me with a near smile and then linked my arm. 'Baz.'

'Yes?'

'Will you take me home?'

'Yes.'

We walked arm in arm, she leading me across to an area where a number of black vehicles were parked. Called taxis, she leaned into the window of one of them and spoke to the driver. He started up the engine and we climbed inside.

The movement of the taxi is curiously enjoyable as it works its way through the streets. I have to keep reminding myself that it is not an intelligent machine and that it is being manipulated by the driver, such is his skill at driving it.

We are waiting at the red light now, and I am writing this. Kirsty half watches me, half drinks in her smoke (the driver didn't want her to smoke in his taxi, but gave her concession because of her bad experience at the money dispenser), and half stares out of her window.

MARCH 20 (f)

The taxi is on the move again. I am finding it difficult to write. I will wait until we get to Kirsty's home.

I have just seen Shazia standing at a corner.

Section Four

MARCH 20 (g)

Kirsty is having her bath. I feel immense gratitude as I reflect on her goodness.

The taxi brought us to the foot of a tower of bricks and windows. Kirsty's window is the eighth one up. I felt dizzy as I looked at it. She led me into the building, past the stairs, to a metal door that parted in the middle at the touch of a button. A steel upright oblong room lay beyond. We stepped in.

Kirsty touched another button and the whole room shuddered and vibrated. I found the sensation most unsettling, but appreciated that we were being hauled up through a shaft to the eighth floor.

Sure enough, when the doors parted and we emerged, I walked over to a window and found a bird's eye view of the city. Lit windows and bright illuminations make the city appear a lot prettier than it really is. The giant wheel stood majestic in the distance.

As we walked to the end of the corridor, Kirsty pointed to a door. 'Bob lives there,' she said. 'A divorcee. He's all right.' Then she pointed to the adjacent door. 'Rich and Glynis live there. They are Church of Yahweh, so be careful. They're nice people, don't get me wrong, but they can turn any conversation you have with them into a conversation about the Bible and the end of the world. So watch it.'

'I've heard about that Bible,' I said. 'Everyone I have spoken to seems to think I'm its advocate.'

She paused, her key slotted into the door at the far end. 'You're not, are you, Baz?'

'I've never read it,' I said. 'But I would like to. It sounds fascinating.'

She turned the key. 'It is one of the greatest pieces of fiction the human race has ever produced.' She pushed open the door, stopped suddenly, and faced me. 'You're not going to turn out to be a weirdo, are you, Baz?'

'Weird-o?' I repeated slowly.

She peered deep into my eyes. 'Can you really be the innocent you seem?' She touched my arm. 'You stopped those bastards when no one else would even stop to look.' She recoiled. 'No,' she said, to herself more than to me. Then she took my hand. 'Come in, Baz.'

I went in.

Once the artificial lighting was on, I could see that the apartment consisted of one main room, a smaller room for cooking, and two other rooms. And once the curtains were drawn across the windows, I found it surprisingly easy to forget that we are as high above the ground as we are.

She took off her coat and scarf and hung them near the door. I'm ashamed to say it but I noted how the shape of her body became more apparent, not perfect by any means, but not terribly overfed either.

She wore a white shirt affair, and a silver cross of the shape Jeezuz was nailed to, hung from her neck on a fine chain.

Planting her bag on the table dominating a corner of the room, she unloaded some of its contents: a hairbrush, a small steel canister decorated with pink flowers, her red and white box of cigarettes and her lighter. I could not take my eyes off them, they fascinated me so.

Kirsty pointed at the small cooking room. 'The brewing up gear is in there. Tea and coffee in the cupboards. I don't have any sugar, but there are sweeteners in there if you can find them. Make yourself a drink. I'll have coffee, white.'

Before I could reply, she thrust open the door next to it and turned on the light. Inside there was a white room with a sink, a long white tub and a basket of towels.

'Listen, I know you're desperate to get out of those stinking clothes,' she said, kicking off her shoes, 'but I feel so dirty since those more-ons attacked me. I've got to take a bath.' She leaned across the tub, moved something in its base and turned a tap on the right hand side. Hot water shot itself from the silver piping. Liquid from a pink bottle caused bubbles to multiply like a swarm of bees emerging from their nest.

I smiled, not really caring about stinking and itching, just appreciative of her kindness and to be in a warm sheltered environment with someone who did not loathe me or think me very strange. 'That is fine,' I told her. 'Go and wash away the filth of their violation.'

'It's a combi boiler,' she said, walking into the third room. I could see her bed and a big cupboard in the darkness beyond the door.

She re-emerged holding a light coat that I could see was of a similar material to the towels, and shut the door behind her.

'You won't have to get in my water. Just run a fresh one when I'm done.' She went into the bathroom and took the door by its handle. 'See you in a bit.'

I heard her slide a latch across the door once it was closed.

What a fearful and paranoid culture.

I made for the cooking area and examined the small boiling pot, the cups and the contents of the cupboards, and then thought better of it.

I am now in the main room. A cabinet lines one wall, and pictures of different persons are positioned at various intervals and angles. Most are very colourful and catch the likenesses of the persons remarkably well.

The one that stands out to me, however, is as clear and detailed as the others, but is composed entirely of grey. The picture is of a man with an infant girl sat about his shoulders. He stands strong and confident, holding the girl secure; a happy moment.

Next to the cabinet is a square plastic box with a glass screen. I have seen these in the windows of some of the buildings of Deansgate. They display moving pictures which have been captured by some sort of recording device.

From what I have been able to discern, some recordings are played back from a separate machine, some are converted into electronic signals and broadcast through the air to special receivers, and some are received images of things that are actually going on right now elsewhere in the world.

A regular session involves a man and woman sat behind a desk reporting affairs of the world, and they speak to people on a screen of their own to learn more of the detail.

I dare not touch Kirsty's plastic box.

A second much smaller box occupies the opposite corner. It sits on a small table and a chair is stationed before it. I have seen these in the windows of the city too, but they are not for broadcasting recorded material or images of world incident. These are machines operated by working people. They sit looking at the screen and summon written information at the touch of a button.

I dare not touch this device either.

I am more interested in Kirsty's bookcase. I have noticed her copy of the *Reader's Digest Great World Atlas* like the one in the library and her volumes of *The New Encyclopaedia Britannica*. I long to engross myself in them, but the sound of Kirsty submerging herself in water is distracting. Anyway, there is something much more fascinating to investigate.

I am looking at it now. The cigarette box is red and white and made of a stiff kind of paper. On the lid there is a word written in black:

100

Marlboro.

The lid also has the number twenty on it, which I presume denotes how many cigarettes are in the box. The bottom half of the box has a white square with two words, again written in black:

Smoking Kills.

I am utterly astonished.

Smoking Kills. So they know *the danger, and they do it anyway.*

I have opened the box and I have slid one out. The paper is very fine and the herb is crushed and packed tight inside. At one end - the end that is put in the mouth - there is a compact white material like cork, wrapped in orange paper speckled with yellow. I am guessing that the cork filters the smoke so as to make it more palatable to the tongue and easier to inhale.

I have the lighter in my other hand. The flame is ignited at the touch of a tiny button.

'Everything all right in there?'

Kirsty's voice.

My hand is shaking. I am about to venture into the unknown, maybe the forbidden.

'Yes,' I manage to reply.

'It's a bit quiet in there.'

'I am fine.'

'Put the telly on, if you like.'

'Telly?'

'The television.'

Ah, tele-vision. The plastic box with the glass screen. 'I don't know how,' I call, knowing she would have to leave her bath to demonstrate it to me.

'Oh,' she says. 'Well, don't worry, I won't be long now.'

'It is fine,' I call.

MARCH 20 (g)

I took a deep breath to slow my heart and tried to steady my hand. The cigarette felt strange in my mouth, the cork filter touching the tip of my tongue.

My hand trembled a little as I clicked the lighter and brought the flame to the exposed herb. As it touched and a thin line of smoke rose up in the air, I sucked on the cigarette as I had seen others do to make the end burn with life.

Then I took the cigarette from my lips and held the smoke in my mouth, allowing it to permeate, the strong woodland taste soaking itself into my tongue. It wasn't the pleasant sweet taste I was expecting. I blew it back out.

Looking at the line of smoke rising to the ceiling, I wondered what the appeal of this practice might be, because it certainly wasn't the taste. Then I recalled how they take it deep into the lungs. So I drew more smoke into my mouth, held it for a second, and then inhaled as though it were the sweet air of the valley. Only it wasn't. It took my breath away. I coughed and spluttered the smoke from my lungs.

Kirsty's voice. 'You all right, Baz?'

'Yes,' I said, choking. 'I am fine.'

'Hope you're not coming down with a cold after that night of rain.'

'I might be.'

What is a cold?

I decided to try again. I sucked, held the smoke, inhaled. It didn't seem so shocking this time. I could feel it, I could taste it, I was a little light-headed. But that was all.

How can they take comfort from this?

The cigarette had burned down by about a third now. I needed to get rid of it. I held it upright and made for the cooking room. The sink seemed like the best option. I saw that the taps were similar to the ones on the bath and that

102

the thing in the base served as a plug to hold in the water. The hole clearly led outside, and so I pushed the burning cigarette through the tiny bars, the hot end being killed by the dampness before it dropped through into oblivion.

I felt relieved once it had gone, grimacing at the vile aftertaste it left in my throat.

I am sat at the table now, writing this. I have closed the cigarette box and I just hope Kirsty does not notice that I took one of them. It has been a strange day, but it has ended well.

MARCH 20 (h)

'What is that you're doing?' Kirsty asked when she came out of the bathroom, her pink robe tied about her with a single cord belt. 'It looks like hieroglyphics or sommat.'

I smiled; her clean face was more appealing to me now it was rid of the paint. 'It's an account of my experiment and my life since arriving here,' I told her. 'I don't know why I keep adding to it. It's not as if I cannot remember any of it. Maybe I will pass it round my community when I get back. That's what we usually do with books.'

'Well, I like to keep a diary. I like going over it months later.' She paused. 'But why write it like that? Is it some kind of shorthand?'

'It's my way of speaking,' I said, and then I recalled their word for the difference. 'My language.'

Her eyes bulged at the thought of it. 'That's your language? I thought Finnish was more like English.'

I laughed. 'Why does everyone think I am Finnish? This writing is not Finnish.'

'Then what is it?'

'Your serious friend at Glendenning House called it Ancient He-broo.'

Kirsty chuckled. 'Male tea bag.'

'What?'

'That's what you call a male tea bag. He-broo.' She took in my confused expression. 'I know, crap joke. Forget it, it was a crap joke.' Then she frowned and put her hand on her hip. 'Hang on,' she said. 'He-broo? Isn't that, like, the language of the Joos?'

'I do not know,' I confessed. 'I do not know what the Joos are.'

'So you write in He-broo, the language of the Joos, but you don't know what the Joos are?'

'Yes,' I said. 'All I know is it is my language, the language I write in. Where I come from everybody speaks and writes this Ancient He-broo language, or perhaps something like it. There are variations in accent and dialect, but it is the same set of characters and letters.'

She frowned. 'Where you come from?' Then she grinned and scrunched up her nose. 'Oh yes,' she said, and I detected mockery in her voice. 'I was forgetting. You're from the other dimension.'

'Yes.'

'OK. Answer me this. How come, upon arriving in this dimension, you could speak good English?' Before I could answer, she cut in, waving a reproving finger. 'And don't give me any of that "my ship translates for me" bollocks.'

Again she was losing me.

'I wondered that myself when I first arrived,' I told her. 'The speech matrix of my brain must have been altered. I heard your strange words, recognised them as alien, and yet understood them. And whenever I tried to speak my own words, they came out as the English equivalents.'

She arched an eyebrow.

'My only problem is there are some words which do not correspond with anything in my Ancient He-broo language. And there are others which do translate perfectly well but do not make any sense in context.'

'Such as?'

'Well, "my ship translates for me bollocks" is a good example. My understanding is that bollocks are testicles, yet the phrase is used to denote incredulity and displeasure.'

She laughed. And I smiled, unsure of how to interpret the laughter. 'You must be a star trek fan.'

A star trek fan? What could that be? A fan that treks the stars?

'Sliders at least.'

I was none the wiser.

Kirsty shrugged and made for the cooking room. 'Oh, Baz,' she moaned. 'You haven't done anything in this kitchen. You haven't even put the cups out.'

I stood at the door, itching and smelling and tasting the smoke in my throat. 'May I get in the bath now?'

She turned, startled. 'Kriste, yeah. I'm sorry, Baz, yeah. I'll get you some clean clothes. You can wear Neil's robe. I doubt he'll ever be coming back for it. I think he left some tracksuit bottoms too, which you might just get into. I don't have a shirt that will fit you, though, so we'll have to improvise.'

Kirsty touched my arm. Her feminine odour caressed my senses and I felt guilty again. 'Hey,' she said excitedly. 'This shirt you're wearing is handmade, it's high quality.'

I nodded, quite weary now. 'It all is. We do not wear the uniform garments of your culture. We are much more individualistic in our dressing.'

'It's all handmade? Even your boots?'

'Yes.'

'Then I won't throw your clothes out. I'll wash them. And tomorrow we'll go round the charity shops and kit you out.'

Tomorrow? I had not even thought of tomorrow.

'You get cleaned up, I'll make us some supper, and we'll watch Blackadder. They're showing it on Bee-bee-see Two tonight at nine.'

Kirsty filled up the bath for me. I undressed in the bathroom, delighting in the peeling off of my rancid socks and underwear, and then sank my sweaty stinking body into the warm water, savouring every moment.

I giggled to myself as my muscles relaxed, my hair and beard thanking me for immersing them. I used the block of animal fat to make up some lather and scrubbed my body. The water turned grey, but I cared not.

Later Kirsty handed me the leggings through the partially open door and I put them on. Then she sat me down on the seat of the small sink-like bowl opposite the bath, filled the actual sink with clean warm water, bathed my beard in lather, and shaved me with a blade.

'I must say you are a fine specimen, Baz.'

I thanked her for the compliment.

'And don't take that as a come-on.'

I frowned. 'A come-on what?'

'You haven't been on the streets for long, have you? Tramps and vagrants don't have muscles like this generally.'

'Where I come from all the men are well defined,' I said.

'I wouldn't mind going there some day.'

'I do not think you would be permitted to enter.'

She stopped shaving. 'Why not?'

'I do not mean to offend you,' I said. 'But you are far removed from the standard of the Father. You all are. You have ruined yourselves and your world. I cannot imagine the Father allowing you to potentially ruin my world too.'

'Thanks a lot,' she said. 'You do realise I'm the one with the razor here.'

I did realise it. But I did not comprehend the meaning of her statement. She resumed shaving me until the task was complete.

I tied the robe about my waist and followed her into the main room. She made coffee for us both, lit a cigarette, sat with her legs coiled up on her chair and picked up an oblong plastic box. At the press of a button, the television came to life.

'I don't suppose you've ever seen Blackadder in your perfect dimension?'

I conceded that I had not.

'You'll like it,' she said. 'It takes the mick out of English history. It'll make you laugh.'

Blackadder is a sort of theatre production. There are different settings and scenes and the acting is presented before an audience located, I presume, behind the machines used to record/relay the pictures and sound.

All of the elders in the story are depicted as having the mentality of primitive children, while the central character, Edmund Blackadder, makes unpleasant remarks, mostly out of earshot of the primitive elders, but sometimes to their faces. Every time he does so, the unseen audience laugh raucously – and so does Kirsty, in-between inhaling her smoke and sipping her coffee.

I did not laugh at all, and even now I find I am puzzling over the way someone so without guile and spite as Kirsty could find this grossly disrespectful man amusing.

The story itself involves a man who is so like a homeless person he wants his daughter to earn money by allowing men to have holy union with her for wages. (Kirsty actually knew the dialogue of the play. 'Yes Kate,' she said in synchronisation with the old man, 'I want you to become a prostitute,' before laughing along with the audience.)

When I asked Kirsty to define a prostitute, she said. 'I thought your mate on the street was one.'

'My mate on the street?'

'The hooker. What's her name?'

'You mean Shazia?'

'Yeah.'

I shook my head. 'Shazia the hooker is not a prostitute.'

Kirsty laughed and then apologised for laughing. 'Oh, I'm sorry, Baz,' she said. 'A hooker *is* a prostitute. That's what it means.'

And then I saw that it is true. Shazia stood on the cold streets wearing clothes designed to arouse sexual feelings in men; her clients, men who want her to do the things their wives would not. I still do not know what these things might be, and I felt like crying. I didn't, though.

Anyway, in the story the girl disguises herself as a boy and goes to work for Blackadder, who, although believing she is a boy called Bob, falls in love with her. Much amusement is gained by the way Blackadder says 'Bob'. (Again Kirsty knew the dialogue: 'I want to marry you, Bob.')

When the silly song started at the end, Kirsty stubbed out her cigarette in a glass dish and mumbled, 'I guess the humour doesn't translate.'

At ten o'clock Kirsty made the long couch into a bed with blankets and a pillow and showed me how to turn off the lamp.

I write this, my heart full of love for Kirsty, who has saved me from this awful world.

MARCH 21

Kirsty let me sleep for as long as she could before it became a necessity for her to begin her daily routine. I woke to the sound of her movement in the kitchen.

Her routine today, though, is going to be a little different. Her visit to the Job Centre has been rescheduled for the afternoon. This morning we are to tour the city's charity shops in search of new clothes for me. Thankfully, my own clothes have dried sufficiently for me not to have to venture outside in the attire Kirsty gave me last night.

I have eaten the corn flakes with milk and they were very tasty. I'm now waiting for the bacon and eggs, which is the staple breakfast in England. I'm not really happy about eating meat from dead animals. Bacon is a dead pig, but Kirsty says it's a common food and that I'll like it. I know I can trust her, though I still can't help feeling sorry for the pig.

MARCH 21 (b)

My clothes smell lovely. I smell lovely too. Kirsty sprayed a fragrance into my armpits and slapped a stinging fluid on my cheeks and chin after she had shaved me. Kirsty smells of a similar fragrance until she has a cigarette. Then, as she passes me by, there is a grotesque hybrid of flowers and stale smoke.

Unbelievably, she began smoking cigarettes when she was eleven years old, starting with just one a day during her time at school (a centre for education where youngsters are parted from their parents and taught by specially trained instructors on a variety of subjects) to ten a day when her brain chemistry became dependent on the nicotine ingredient.

This is something I have not considered until now. They start this smoking when young, motivated by a desire to rebel against those who propagate the ethics of the world system and a need to feel adult.

Ironically, most of the adults who smoke do so only because they are addicted to the mix of chemicals, nicotine being the main one, while lethal substances like formaldehyde, arsenic and cyanide rot away the tongue, throat and lungs, poison the blood and interfere with the natural balance of chemicals in the brain.

Kirsty says I am obsessed. I think she isn't nearly obsessed enough.

MARCH 21 (c)

We are inside McDonalds. I am sat at a table and Kirsty is buying lunch, which will consist of shrivelled lettuce, a congealed slab of dead meat, a sliced tomato and a strong sauce. Kirsty likes to drink a flavoured black water called Coke. I'm sticking with tea, although it isn't as nice as the tea Kirsty makes, or indeed my own.

I am grateful for all that this young lady has done for me, but her insistence on visiting a great many shops became tiresome. I have a number of clothes now, but I am sure we could have bought similar items all from the same establishment.

MARCH 21 (d)

We've just got back from the Job Centre. What a depressing place it is. Not so much a place of despair, since the persons whose role it is to help us find jobs do work hard in our behalf, but there is a sense of helplessness.

Kirsty searched for a number of different jobs on the machine, printed out the ones she felt she had a chance with, and took them to the man called Gerald. He was a really pleasant man, always smiling and zealous in his arranging the interviews.

Kirsty has an interview tomorrow morning with the manager of a factory complex known as Stein's Beans ('Sounds dodgy,' she said), and an interview with an independent psychologist for the position of assistant. She's hoping to get the latter because she will be paid a higher wage and it might be a way of getting back into that line of work.

I noticed something quite strange while we were at the Job Centre. Not only do they measure time in increments of seconds, minutes and hours, but they also measure days.

I asked Kirsty about this and at first she just laughed. When she saw that I was serious she shook her head and whispered, 'How have you survived in this world? You are like an infant.' Then she corrected herself. 'I'm sorry. That was insulting.'

She explained that there are thirty to thirty-one days in a month. The current month is called March. Today is the twenty-first day of March. When I asked her what the 2006 bit was, she boggled again. 'Have you been a vagrant all your life? Did you never go to school?' I conceded that I never have. At home parents educate their children.

She explained that the modern 'calendar' is based on when Jeezuz Kriste was thought to have been born. We are over two thousand years away from that event. I asked her to tell me more about Jeezuz Kriste, but she completely ignored my question and started talking about her interviews.

We are having a 'Marks and Sparks Ready Meal' for dinner. Kirsty promises it will taste better than a McDonalds. She also wants to watch a play called *East Enders* on the television and a documentary about the New Romantics, whatever they are.

MARCH 21 (e)

Eastenders is extremely depressing.

*

111

MARCH 22

'You know how to work the telly, don't you?' Kirsty asked as she put on her gloves. 'You've got all these old books that you like to read as well.' These include the *Reader's Digest Great World Atlas*, the complete set of *Encyclopaedia Britannica* (twenty volumes, wall to wall, across two shelves), and the *New International Bible*, all of which were given to her by her dad. He, like the dad of the man in the church on Deansgate, has died. And as with that man, the Father has not reanimated him. Kirsty does not want to talk about it, which is understandable.

The television only interests me conceptually. The actual presentations are pitiful. My own children would be able to engage in more stimulating conversation.

For example, one presentation featured a woman conducting a discussion between a young man and a young lady before a large assembly of people. The theme of the discussion was 'Could you forgive a cheat?' and the young lady was accusing the man of having engaged in holy union with another woman, a practice that is bewilderingly common in this world.

Should she forgive him and try to repair the relationship or should she abandon him and choose another partner? Well they took thirty minutes to discuss that, with many interjections from the audience and parental observations from the presenter.

Pathetic.

Another presentation was made by a man and woman who kept giggling and making childlike jokes to one another in-between their interviews with a person who had written a book about how to lose excessive weight (stop eating too much food and burn off the excessive body fat with plenty of physical exertion, surely?); an actress who is in a television play about a woman who has holy union with

112

another woman instead of a man (Who thought up that premise?); a group of young people who have won a singing competition; and a strange man who claimed to be able to discern future events simply by studying the movement of the stars.

There was also a lady who provided solutions to problems brought to her by people around England via a telephone communicator. The problems consisted of ridiculous things like 'I'm having a midlife crisis.' I almost opted to telephone the presenters and tell them I have been in crisis ever since I arrived here, but thought better of it.

At lunch time there was The News. I find these programmes the hardest to decipher. Some of the things in them are so shocking I cannot believe that they are really happening in other parts of the world.

For example, they have built huge machines that roll along on tracks and project capsules containing explosive material. The purpose of these machines is to destroy villages and communities. It is an organised effort too. They deliberately set out to kill other human beings. I cannot understand why this world is so full of hatred and anger.

The images are so pervasive they dominate one's thinking: to end the life of another human being in full knowledge that they will not be reanimated by the Father. Why would anyone want to do such a thing?

This society is malfunctioning on a level I can but only attempt to conceive. I have the disturbing feeling that it is in fact much, much worse.

I found that after ten minutes of News, I could not bear to watch any more television. I went into the kitchen, made myself some sandwiches and a cup of tea, and then headed for what I had been saving for last: the books.

MARCH 22 (b)

The books absolutely intrigue me. One of them I initially believed to be a children's book, it being so full of fanciful ideas. Entitled *A Brief History of Time*, its author, Professor Stephen Hawking, attempts to explain how the universe came into existence. There is little mention of the Father.

Stephen Hawking appears to believe that the pattern of the universe just fell into place of its own accord. The absurdity of something so complex and well ordered coming about of its own accord without any guiding intelligence at work is striking – and yet the concept is remarkably appealing in a beguiling way. It stayed with me for a good two hours, especially since the author expounds his belief as though it is fact.

Another book, called *The Selfish Gene*, makes similar claims about the genetic code of life, what author Professor Richard Dawkins calls deoxyribonucleic acid, or DNA.

He puts forward the notion that all the ingredients from which a protein molecule is comprised were already here on the Earth, which, of course, they were. But he then says that through a sequence of random events, twenty 'left handed' amino acids were fused together to form the very first living cell. I laughed out loud at that one, it was so funny. Living matter from dead matter, a complex functioning DNA organism brought into existence arbitrarily?

Richard Dawkins believes that the cell somehow survived long enough to reproduce itself, and that all life on Earth – the plants, the fish, the reptiles, the birds, amphibians and mammals – descended from it. Again, this process is said to have occurred purely by chance; and again the appeal of the theory is beguiling.

And still another book on a similar theme: *Ape Man – The Story of Human Evolution* by Robin McKie. The front cover depicts a bizarre hybrid creature, a man with apelike

114

characteristics. The human race, says the book, is descended from apes. Pictures of malformed skulls, some of apes and some of humans, are presented as proof.

The theory has it that the metamorphosis took place gradually over millions of years. I am not sure how many skeletons they have unearthed, but the pictures in the book suggest a collection of skulls and bone fragments as the core evidence.

The fact that not a single one of these intermediary hybrids is walking the Earth today suggests to me that the fossils represent freak variations of ape and man, rather than a gradual transformation from one species into the other.

The author also appears not to see that the inferior model to the ape man, the ape itself, still exists in all its varieties. So men exist in their billions, apes and monkeys exist in large numbers around the Earth, but not a single ape man. And yet it is said the proof of their existence is conclusive and beyond doubt.

Well I laughed so hard, my head hurt.

In the end, I found myself drifting back to the *Encyclopaedia Britannica*. I read the entry about this concept – called 'evolution' in the two books – and it seems the notion of self-generating life has been popular for hundreds of years. The current version, though, has its beginnings with a man named Charles Darwin, who wrote a controversial book entitled *On the Origin of Species*.

It seems Darwin questioned the existence of a Heavenly Father when his young daughter Annie died of an illness. He was so overcome by grief that he sought an alternative explanation for the origins of life on Earth.

I tried to imagine how I would feel if Daisy died. Again the very question of such a thing happening is utterly preposterous, for a child to die like the animals die. I suddenly found myself appreciating Darwin's motives for searching out an alternative to the Father, even though I cannot at all embrace his theory.

It seems I am right in thinking no one in this world has ever had an audience with the Father. In a way, if this is true, I cannot blame them for rejecting him.

Sorry Father. I know you know I thought this. Please forgive me.

I also read the entry about the origin of television. The precursor to it was something called Radio, a process whereby the sound of one's voice can be converted into electronic signals and broadcast via invisible waves in the atmosphere ('sound waves' as they call them).

An organisation known as the British Broadcasting Corporation, BBC, started writing and producing broadcasts, including educational presentations, fictional plays, and music.

Then a man named John Logie Baird experimented with the principle of sending images through the air in a similar fashion. Thus tele (from a Greek word meaning 'far off') vision (from the Latin meaning 'to see' – apparently English is a hybrid of other complicated languages) was born.

The BBC monopolised the broadcasts, and at first television was thought to be 'radio with pictures'. Later it acquired a style all its own. As this technology has advanced, more organisations around the world have surfaced, rivalling the BBC in England and other groups around the globe.

This is utterly fascinating. There has never been the need for such an invention in my world. Plays are always performed live in front of an audience. We remember them perfectly and so do not require recordings.

All news is fine and is passed on by word of mouth. Hourly updates are totally unnecessary. All this said, I wonder if the invention of television might be of some use to my people if employed in a more wholesome way. Here it just seems to serve as a distraction and as a means of perpetuating the populace's already insatiable appetite for self-indulgence.

Kirsty and her generation appear to think that their world has always been like this. They do not question the origin of such things as electricity and motorised vehicles. They don't seem to know that this 'technology' (as opposed to orgology) is a very recent trend and that only one hundred years ago communities were much smaller and that one hundred years before that their ancestors were living in little villages.

This fashion of making complex machines and fuelling them with the Earth's natural resources happened suddenly and quickly escalated. The populace is entranced by it.

No one seems to have realised that such resources are finite and if they continue to gut the Earth at the current rate, it will not be long before their machines and inventions are obsolete. They will be plunged into darkness before many years have passed.

I find myself thinking about cigarettes again. These too are a very recent creation. A man named Sir Francis Drake was introduced to the tobacco plant on one of his voyages around the world. It is he who cultivated the idea of crushing the plant into fine strands and wrapping them in a tube shape, lighting one end and sucking the smoke up the other.

Later these crushed leaves inside a rolled leaf became known as 'cigars' and were manufactured and sold to those earning large amounts of money in favourable employment. In time smaller cigar products wrapped in paper, 'cigarettes', were also sold.

They became very popular when characters in recorded plays at the cinema (before the advent of BBC television) were seen to enjoy a cigarette. Thus smoking became synonymous with being a mature figure. In men it was deemed 'cool' (wise, deep thinking, popular) and in women it was regarded as 'sexy' (attractive to men). Apparently the populace's desire to be like these fictional characters was so strong that cigarettes sold the world over, flourishing the manufacturers with money.

For a time it was believed that smoking was good for the health and could even help cure malfunctions in the lungs. Astonishing.

More recently, this world's studies have revealed that cigarette smoke contains lethal compounds such as formaldehyde, arsenic and cyanide. Ha! They needed to conduct *studies* to prove it! I don't know whether I should laugh at the ignorance or weep over their foolishness.

They have put filters in modern cigarettes to lessen the damage to the tongue, throat and lungs, but that won't make much difference. And putting slogans on the boxes reading 'Smoking Kills' and 'Smoking Harms Your Unborn Baby' does not stop youngsters taking up the practice, nor do they provide an antidote to the addiction to nicotine.

I must say something about 'cinema' too. In a similar manner to television, actors in costume are assembled on a specially created set or in an outside location and are 'filmed', a process where many hundreds of still pictures are recorded at high speed. Then, in a sizeable venue, those pictures are projected at the same speed with a bright concentrated electric light shining through them on to a huge white screen.

These 'movies' became a popular form of entertainment in very recent history, after the advent of the radio, but before television. In a way, television is an amalgam of the two ideas. Again I would like to suggest something like this to the elders when I get back.

The Bible: The *Encyclopaedia Britannica* has plenty of information on this too. The word Bible comes from a Greek word (again!) meaning 'little books'. The Bible is a collection of sixty-six books, the first of which was written approximately 3,500 years ago, and the last of which was completed just under 2,000 years ago.

The first thirty-nine books were compiled by Hebrew people of 'ancient' times and the books were recorded in a corrupted form of my language. When Greek became the common tongue, copies were converted from Hebrew into Greek. After that the twenty-seven remaining books were written and compiled by a group of Hebrew people who either witnessed the activities of Jesus Christ (ah, *that's* how it is spelt!) or compiled reports based on the testimony of others.

About three hundred years after the original writings were completed, an agency called the Roman Catholic Church had copies of the whole collection made in Latin.

In a period of time known as the Dark Ages (not that long ago at all. Ha! The current generation think themselves so advanced) the Church forbade the translation from Latin into other languages to make sure that 'ordinary' people would not detect the contradictions in the agency's philosophy. But educated men who understood Latin and the original languages defied the Church and translated the Bible anyway. Incredibly some of these were burned to death at the order of the Church!

The Bible writers claim to have been inspired by the Father to record their experiences and because of this it is known as 'God's Word'. However in the last one hundred years or so, educators have questioned the validity of the claim and many regard the book to be nothing more than a collection of fanciful stories based loosely on real historical events.

It is approaching five o'clock. Kirsty will be back soon. I think I shall save the Bible until after our meal when she starts watching her dreary plays on the television.

119

MARCH 22 (c)

'God, it's cold out there,' Kirsty said as she half walked, half staggered through the door with two large bags in either hand. She dropped them, unwound her scarf, hung up her coat, and placed her shoulder bag on the table. 'I got you some more clothes on the way home. Good bargains, they were.'

Without even looking at the bag on the table, she opened it and took out her cigarettes and lighter. 'What have you been up to all day?'

Cigarette goes in mouth.

'I watched some television,' I said. 'And then I got bored of it and examined your books.'

Lighter flicks into life.

'Now why doesn't that surprise me?' she said. I knew she wasn't actually asking me why. Like 'God' isn't actually a reference to the Father and 'crap' doesn't mean she believes the poetic rhythmic recordings of Eminem are literally made from excrement. It is a figure of speech.

Flame touches cigarette and she sucks hard. The end burns ferociously. Inhales sharply.

'I'm dying for a brew.' Before I can reply, she is in the kitchen filling the kettle with water. 'Now I thought we'd do the chippy tonight,' she said. 'I'm knackered. I'm certainly not in the mood for cooking anything.'

Knackered means worn out, drained of energy, tired – I think.

'Does that mean we're going outside?'

She reappeared at the doorway. 'Jesus. I forgot you've been cooped up in here all day. Sorry. Yeah, we'll go together.'

Kirsty is like a baby sister or a niece. She has her funny ways, and although I am moved to reprimand her, I am also moved to love her. She is easy to love.

120

MARCH 22 (d)

Chippy consists of chips (finger sized slices of potato dropped into a boiling fat), fish ('battered' by boiling fat) peas, and gravy (a water based substance mixed with residual juice from dead animal meat and a man-made compound). It is actually very tasty, though it is also patently obvious (to use one of Kirsty's expressions) that this is how the populace here can overfeed. Really a diet of vegetables and fruit would be best, since they have been designed for consumption by the human body and do not do it any harm.

Kirsty had a steak pie. Imagine that! A pie made from a cow's steak! This went alongside her chips and was smothered in gravy, salt and vinegar. A truly vomit inducing concoction. At least I had peas.

Following our meal we had a 'sweet.' Astonishingly, this *is* literal. A sweet cake made from that lovely food called chocolate. She heated it up in the 'microwave' (I am slightly troubled by what that implies, actually. It sounds dangerous) and poured an equally warm thick milk based yellow substance all over it. I have to say it tasted great, though again I will need plenty of exercise if I am to avoid expanding out of shape.

I sit here writing this as Kirsty prepares to watch something called *Coronation Street*. It doesn't induce melancholia in the way that *Eastenders* does, she promises, but I am not convinced. She says it is set in this part of England and is full of eccentric characters.

I am watching Kirsty as she watches the television. I must draw her one evening if she will allow me. She is sitting with her legs coiled up, resting a cup of coffee on her thigh, a customary cigarette pinched between her first and second fingers. She's watching the sequence of vignettes in which people attempt to persuade the viewer that they really

121

need a particular type of car or floor cleaner. Some of these are like little plays with a beginning, middle and end. The music is upbeat and cheerful.

She sits silently absorbing them, transfixed by the pictures and sound. It is clear to me now how the television, radio and cinema are able to convince the populace that something like inhaling poisonous fumes can be enjoyable and to one's benefit. These short set pieces are deliberately coaxing the viewer, suggesting and implying – and it seems Kirsty's culture absorbs everything it is fed without question.

They are like children. She is an innocent. I am fighting back the tears.

Coronation Street has begun and Kirsty has sat up. The opening music is a brash whining affair, and the recording device is slowly hovering down over the roof-tops of houses. Kirsty is right; it is setting the scene for a story in this city of Manchester. The final image establishes the street itself and the play begins.

It is exactly what I thought it would be; a simple set of stories about different residents of the street. A husband and wife have an aggressive confrontation, a child sulks when she is denied permission to visit a friend (unbelievably infantile!), an oversized man opens his shop and sells some brown liquid to a man covered in a dark oil.

Then we witness workers in a factory. A man dressed in smart attire shouting and frowning at the women who sit at machines which weave cotton at an incredible speed. Older women tease a younger one, and a man with blond hair behaves like a girl.

'They know she's been slagging them off,' Kirsty suddenly says. I almost answer her, and then I realise she isn't really talking to me. Her eyes never leave the screen. She draws hard on her cigarette, savours the taste (how *can* she?!), blows the smoke up into the air and sips her coffee.

I think it's time I made a start on the Bible.

MARCH 22 (e)

'Don't start preaching at me,' Kirsty said with a reproving glare and wagging finger. I frowned. What could she mean? She had only noticed that I was reading the Bible when *Coronation Street* stopped briefly to run some more persuasive vignettes. 'I only keep that thing because my dad wanted me to.'

I did not answer her. No sooner than *Coronation Street* had resumed, her annoyance at my choice of reading abated. She was entranced again.

The first book in the collection is 'Genesis', and as the title suggests, it recounts the beginning of the Earth's formation by the Father, the sequence in which life forms were brought into existence, the creation of Adam and Eve. I am in wonderment. The account is exactly the same as the story we tell our children at home: the same beginning, the same Adam and Eve. The same test of obedience. The fruit representing the right to decide and define what is good and bad. I must show them this when I get back. Adam will be greatly amused by it.

The account has been broken down into chapters and numbered paragraphs, for I assume, easy reference. I am about to start Chapter Three. This is no doubt the bit my children love, where the spirit son of the Father uses a serpent to persuade Eve to eat the fruit in a foolish attempt to undermine the Father's sovereignty.

MARCH 22 (f)

I am still shaking. I cried myself to sleep when Kirsty gave up and went to her room. Now I am awake.

'Hey, what's the matter?' she had said, the way a mother does when her child has suffered a shock. 'What's wrong,

123

Baz?' When I told her, her complexion changed to one of bemusement and then to one of tempered rage. 'That bloody book!'

Her attempts at comforting me took the form of insisting that the Bible is just a lot of nonsense dreamed up by primitive men who were trying with limited knowledge to make sense of their world. But I just kept saying the same thing over and over, and in the end Kirsty lost what little patience she had and went to bed.

I am stunned.

This dreadful world now makes a terrible, twisted, sick, unnatural kind of sense.

Why did I not realise it?

They ate the fruit.

MARCH 23

I woke up at eleven o'clock when Kirsty started making brewing up noises in the kitchen. She emerged, still dressed in her bed clothes.

'Hi,' she said softly. 'Want some cereal?'

I nodded sheepishly.

'I'm going to get you a key cut after I've been on these two job interviews,' she said, returning to the kitchen. 'I remember what it was like when I first went on the dole, cooped up in here all day, depressed, with nothing but bloody *This Morning* for company.'

She was avoiding discussing last night. That was fine by me, as she would have just grown angry again if I had started talking about Adam and Eve.

It is true that they occupy my every thought. I am still greatly disturbed. But explaining the complexity of humankind's rebellion against the Father and the issues it has raised would be utterly pointless at this stage.

'I've got some DVDs you might like in the cupboard by the telly,' she said, putting on her coat. '*Stargate, Sliders.* Borrowed them off our Steve. They're all about parallel worlds and that. Right up your street.'

'My street?' I said.

'Yeah. And last year's *Doctor Who* box set. You'd probably like that too. You've heard of *Doctor Who*, haven't you?'

'No.'

'Oh, you'll *love* it!' she enthused. 'Time travel, other dimensions. All the stuff you're into.'

'Thank you.'

Kirsty went across to the smaller telly situated on the desk. 'I'll sign you into the computer, if you like,' she said, flicking the main switch. 'Give you your own password. If you like encyclopaedias, wait till you get on Google. Information at your finger tips. I'll just go throw some clothes on while it boots up.'

The computer screen lit up blue, followed by black screens of scrolling text, and then settled on an image of a young woman with long brown hair holding a long musical instrument about her shoulders on a strap. Little square symbols popped up along the left hand side, denoting, I presumed, the functions of the machine.

When Kirsty emerged from her room she was dressed in a long skirt, a modest blouse and moderately applied face paint. She was transformed, suddenly very pretty; even prettier when she smiled.

And then she slipped a cigarette in her mouth, lit it, and savoured the taste as it hit the back of her throat. Suddenly not so pretty.

Kirsty sat me at the desk and placed my hand on the plastic control she called a mouse (because it is white and has a long tail?). 'Have you ever used a computer, Baz?'

I shook my head. 'No.'

125

'Now why doesn't that surprise me?' She smiled and passed her cigarette from her right hand to her left, holding it at a distance so the smoke wouldn't go to my face. Then with her free hand she gently touched the top of my knuckles. 'Let me guide you,' she said.

I saw that the movement of the mouse corresponded with that of an arrow on the screen, and whenever the arrow connected with one of the icons it changed into a crude picture of a hand. We hovered over the one marked 'Internet Explorer' and she pressed my first finger down twice very swiftly.

The reaction was immediate. A symbol with fat ends and a narrow middle replaced the hand and the picture changed to a white screen with a narrow slot dead centre and the word 'Google' suspended above it in large appealing letters.

'Now, all you do is type in what you want to know about,' Kirsty advised, 'press "Enter", and a list of web sites all about your subject comes up. It really is the repository of all knowledge. I've even set up job interviews with it.' She stood up and checked the tiny clock strapped to her wrist. 'Which reminds me.'

I watched as she put on her coat and slung her bag across her shoulder, stopping only to stub out her cigarette and slide what was left of it back into the box from which it came. I indicated the computer: 'How do I turn this off when I've had enough?'

'Click on "Start" at the bottom left, then follow the instructions to close it down,' she said. 'Once it's back on the blank blue screen, press the main button on the oblong box there.'

'Thank you.'

She turned at the door. 'And don't spend the morning trawling through loads of porn, because I'll know. OK?'

I had no idea what she was talking about, and as she took in my expression, she seemed to know it instinctively. She smiled. Pretty again. Then she approached and touched

126

my face softly with the palm of her hand. It felt warm and full of love, like the touch of my mother. I thought of her working the land with father and baking cakes for my children and grandchildren.

'The man with a child in his eyes,' Kirsty said, her voice cracking. She cleared her throat. 'Is there anything you want me to bring back, a magazine or something?'

I thought of my family again. 'I would like something about plants.'

'Plants,' Kirsty repeated. 'What, like a gardening magazine?'

'Well, something to do with the science of plants,' I said.

She smiled. I love her smile. 'Like *Science Digest* or *Nature* magazine.'

'Yes, I suppose.'

'OK,' she said and returned to the exit door.

I called after her, 'I hope you do well in your interviews.'

'Cheers!'

She's gone now. I am following her instructions to turn off the computer. The Bible awaits.

MARCH 23 (b)

So now I know.

Adam and Eve were condemned to age and die like the animals. They were cast out of the Eden region into an uncultivated world. Their sons Cain and Abel were not as I know them back home, or at least Cain wasn't. He grew envious of Abel's favour with the Father and killed him! My very spirit turned within me when I read that bit. The human race multiplied, but each child inherited genetically the corrupted state of the original parents: born to die, in effect.

127

It was at this point I had to face the truth. Everyone who has ever been born in this version of humanity has grown up, reached a prime point, and then deteriorated until their bodies have given out and expired. Adam himself died at nine hundred and thirty years, just a little younger than me.

No age.

I wondered how far along the span of life Kirsty might be. To see her wear out, wrinkle up and expire, literally cease to exist – well, I cannot bear to contemplate it.

There is no direct mention of the Father's spirit sons or the one who had introduced rebellion in Eden until the seventh generation. By then things had got so bad a man named Enoch was spared persecution by his fellows for remaining loyal to the Father by having his life prematurely ended.

Shortly afterwards, spirit sons formed human bodies for themselves and had holy union with women, who in turn gave birth to hybrid humans called Nephilim. Under their influence, the human race turned rotten. All bar one family consisting of a man named Noah, his wife, their sons and their daughters-in-law.

The Father destroyed that world by collapsing the water canopy onto the Earth. I cannot help but reflect on the impact that must have had. It explains how the land mass was divided up, where areas like the Grand Canyon came from, and how the polar regions were formed (and also why they have found mammoths encased in ice with vegetation in their mouths and undigested in their intestines. It was an instant freeze).

I have noted that the lifespan of humans recorded in this Bible radically drops after the flood. Perhaps this is due to exposure from the undiluted sun? I cannot be certain. But they lived for a much shorter period of time, in some cases less than one hundred years. I wept a little as I realised how fragile they had become.

Only Noah and his family survived the wipeout, they and primary species of animals.

After only one generation, the people began to revolt against the Father again. Under the influence of a wretched man called Nimrod, they built the first ever city and established the system pattern that mankind currently slaves for. A huge tower was constructed (as an insult to the Father?). The Father got so angry he confused their language, forcing them to move out from the city and form other communities.

This explains the massive differences in language in this dimension.

It might also explain the complex variations of religious belief that appear to have spread through the world. The different language groups took their beliefs with them.

Only a few individuals at any given time remained loyal to the Father, despite their dying condition. One such man was Job (pronounced 'Jobe' I think). He was targeted by the Father's rival. Fascinatingly, it is only at this point, many books on from Genesis, that this spirit being is properly introduced to the reader and described as Satan (from the Hebrew word 'hasatan', no doubt: adversary, but in this case the definite article).

The Adversary highlighted Job's faithfulness to God and charged that his apparent loyalty was just a means of selfish gain. The Father then permitted Satan to test Job to the limit. I found this section very disturbing. Why would the Father do such a thing? I can only imagine that if he had destroyed Satan, others would have begun to wonder if the Adversary was right in his claims.

I would never have conceived such a thing could be possible in my own world. I mean, a child of Almighty God daring to challenge his sovereignty like that, succeeding in winning support, and forcing him to prove his worth. How can the creation have such control over the creator? Again I can only think that destroying the accuser would have given credence to the accusations.

The main focus, though, in the first thirty-nine books (dubbed 'The Old Testament'; surely 'The First Testament' would be better?) was the man Abraham and his descendents. He was promised that a 'seed' would come through his genetic line.

The promise was repeated to his son Isaac, and then again to his grandson Jacob. Jacob was renamed Israel, and after four hundred years had elapsed, his descendents had become a small nation. The remaining books of this testament tell the story of the Israelites, favoured by the Father as the line which would produce the seed.

The trouble was, the nation repeatedly tried the Father's patience. He sent men to show them the way he wanted them to live, and they had the men killed! Finally, he allowed their nation to be defeated by an aggressor called Babylon and they lost their national sovereignty.

It was while they were in this captive state that the Father gave a man named Daniel symbolic visions of future empires, showed him the spirit sons in the heavenly realm, and presented a mathematical calculation pertaining to 'Messiah the Leader'.

Most of the other books in the testament consider these themes in detail (too much detail in some cases. I'm baffled by much of it), the rebellion of Israel, the Babylonian captivity, the coming of Messiah (the seed?).

I thought of this world with its technology and advances in science, all in the last couple of hundred years: six millennia of simple pastoral living, and then suddenly, these developments.

Where is the Father now? Ever silent, seemingly inactive, to the point that Kirsty does not even acknowledge his existence. She thinks we created ourselves somehow.

My head hurt so much with this new realisation I shut the Bible and put it back on the shelf.

I stood at the window and watched the cars and the buses on the main road, everybody going about their business as they did each and every day; all continuing as though their dying state was the most natural thing in the world.

It is all so normal to them; and all so depressing to me.

I thought of that dreadful play series *East Enders*: a reflection of this community. I found myself getting tearful again and left the window.

I turned on the television and clicked on the different channels. On Five there was a play about law enforcement officers (similar to the police people I saw in Manchester). I think it was set in a different part of Britain, or maybe even a different part of the world. They spoke English, but it was a variation of the English I know.

For example, these people put a lot of emphasis on the letter 'r'. An overfed black man standing in a room full of desks and writing devices greeted a poor abused woman and her family members. 'Gech yer self a cup o caw-fee,' he said to one of them. 'There's a machine down the hawl.'

The buildings in the city were much taller than the ones in Manchester too, and the cars were longer. I soon got bored of this play and switched off the television.

I returned to the computer. The Google searcher thing is very impressive. I put in different words to see what would be displayed, 'Plants', 'Science', 'Father', 'Bible', and each one turned up pages and pages of information. It was all so overwhelming I didn't really read any of them.

Idleness had now taken me. What was that word which Kirsty said I must not put in? Prawn? No that wasn't it. Pawn? I tried that. It brought up a lot of stuff about bartering. Why would Kirsty be upset by that? I tried another spelling, Paun. Nothing. Nothing but a question at the top of the screen. 'Do you mean *Porn?*'

I tried that.

I clicked on one of the highlighted lines and the display appeared. My heart raced as the images manifested one after the other. Naked women, bare breasts, couples engaging in holy union, not to mention the most outrageous acts that can only be described as contrary to what is natural.

Immediately I went to the 'Start' button and followed the deactivation sequence as Kirsty had instructed.

She said she would know I had looked at it. How would she know?

I went back to the window and tried to interest myself in the comings and goings of the people, but all I could think about was those disturbing pictures: men, women, the things they were doing to one another. They seemed to be really enjoying it too, their obscene indulgences. How could they enjoy it? I returned to the bookshelf, pulled out the Bible, opened it anywhere and read. But it had no effect.

I could not help myself. I had become enslaved to my emotions in a way I had never conceived was possible. I sat back at the desk, turned on the computer, went to Internet Explorer, typed in 'Porn', clicked on the first line, and studied the pictures. As the arrow hovered over one of them it became a hand. Instinctively I clicked the mouse, and many more pictures filled the screen.

My lips were dry now, my eyes staring, my heart thumping hard in my chest. The images were disgusting. They were also extremely potent. I felt like Kirsty, having to obey the dictates of my loins as she does her nicotine. I sweated and swallowed and cleared my throat.

Then I jumped. A sound, a key inserting into the outer door. Panic. Click start. I can't make it move! I can't steady my hand!

Click start.

Click 'Turn off your computer.'

Click 'Turn off.'

Come on blue screen, *come on!!*

Press the switch.

132

The computer screen died, the surrounding box crackling like static on a woolly jumper.

The door opened. I stood up, red-faced and overcome with shame.

'You OK?' Kirsty grinned as she bustled in.

I coughed. 'Yes.'

'I got *Nature* magazine for you. And guess what?'

I did not answer. It took great discipline to remain composed. Kirsty advanced, smiling with joy. She took my hand and placed in its palm a jagged piece of metal. 'I got you a key cut.'

I burst into tears.

She touched my cheek as she had done earlier. 'Hey, what's the matter? You're not still upset about Adam and Eve eating the apple, are you?' She smiled, full of pity.

'No, it's not that,' I stammered, snot rolling into my mouth. I could taste it. 'It's much worse than that.'

'It is?'

'Yes,' I said, looking at the floor now. 'Kirsty, I'm sorry.'

'What is it? Just tell me. I won't be angry with you, I promise.'

'You will,' I said. I wiped my eyes and looked straight at her. Gaining some composure I said, 'I looked at porn on the computer.'

Kirsty stared at me. It was an intense stare, as though she had not fully comprehended the meaning of my words. I did not know what to expect. And then, without warning, it came. She broke into relentless laughter. 'Is that *it*?' she said. 'You looked at some porn?'

I began to stammer again, not sure how to interpret her reaction. 'Well you said you would know if I did, and –.'

She walked over to me and gave me a generous hug. 'Come here,' she said. 'You daft thing.'

'You're not angry, then?'

She smiled at me. She was very pretty. 'No,' she said. 'In fact I'm a bit relieved.'

I frowned. 'Relieved?'

'That you've finally done something *normal*, something so wonderfully ordinary at long last.'

I just stared, speechless.

Section Five

MARCH 23 (b)

Kirsty has gone to bed. She's had a tiring day. The interview process is a stressful one, apparently. One has to prove to one's prospective employer why one is best suited for the job. He or she then makes their choice based on the interviewee's appearance, performance and work history.

Kirsty believes this is not a very accurate method of assessment. A person not suited to the job could easily persuade the prospective employer that they are ideal, while those who are best suited for the job fail to get it because they do not communicate themselves well enough.

'It's all about how you look and sound,' she said, trickling gravy over her meal. She cooks well considering all the ingredients have been through a manufacturing process. They grow nothing for themselves here. It is all produced en masse like the clothes and the cars, and distributed to shops.

She pushed sausage (animal meat) and mashed potato onto her fork. 'I had a meeting with a careers advisor. God, that was depressing. No one is interested in the truth. No one cares why I was ousted from my job in psychology. No one is bothered that I took someone in because I cared about him and then he stabbed me in the back. All they're bothered about is me getting another job. Any job. And they're bent on teaching me how to bullshit my way into one.'

Excrement from a bull. A reference to lies. Another expression.

I could not eat. I was still thinking about the porn on the computer. It had disturbed my whole psyche.

'So I went to the private clinic,' Kirsty continued, 'and there were, like, two or three others; a couple of women in their thirties and a man. I was confident I stood a chance. I know my stuff; I have the upper hand on modern theory of the mind. But as soon as I got into the actual interview I could tell they weren't interested. They just went through the procedure, asked me about my qualifications and my experience.' She took a swig of tea. 'And then they asked the killer question. Why did I leave my last job?'

Kirsty got up from her chair and took our two plates into the kitchen. She hadn't noticed that I had left half of it. Her voice sailed in above the clanking of plates. 'I told her how Laurence had needed a stable environment and how I'd helped him.'

She briefly reappeared at the kitchen door. 'I've got chocolate fudge cake. Do you want it with custard or ice cream?'

I told her I would have whatever she was having. I couldn't concern myself over trivial decisions.

Clanking plates were replaced by the hum of the microwave.

'They weren't interested in any of that, of course. They just waited for me to stop talking and then said I'd been dismissed from the National Health Service because I had behaved in an unprofessional manner. They had it all in a file anyway. I mean, why ask if they already know? I tried to reason that I was actually doing my job, that I was caring for the young man's mental health, but they were having none of it, I could tell. It was a case of don't call us, we'll call you.' She returned to the main room and placed a bowl of hot chocolate fudge cake and ice cream in front of me, and took her own at her seat. 'I felt like crap when I came out.'

I remembered something. 'How did your other interview go?'

It was as though she had forgotten that she'd had another interview. 'Oh yeah.' She smiled and swallowed a spoonful of cake. 'That was sommat else, that.'

I dug into my cake as well. It was very tasty, though I winced a little when the ice cream met my teeth.

'Get this,' she said, half laughing. 'You know how the baked beans factory is called Stein's Baked Beans? At first I thought the bloke who owned the company was called Stein, but no, it seems the man I had the interview with, a Mr Hulton-Little, is the proprietor and he deliberately christened his business Stein's.' Now she *was* laughing. 'The labels even have a variation on that *Heinz* design. I was dying to laugh.'

She polished off the last of her chocolate fudge cake and took the bowl into the kitchen. 'And that's not all,' she said. 'As a sideline he sells broken biscuits that he's picked up cheap from some local factory, and dodgy DVD-R things imported from Finland.' She returned and lit herself a cigarette. 'I thought of you.'

I was surprised. 'Me? Why?'

'Well,' she said, vaguely apologetic and blowing smoke up to the ceiling. 'Finland.'

'I'm not from this Finland everybody keeps talking about.'

Kirsty laughed and picked up her television magazine. 'Let's see what's on the box tonight. *News*, *What Not to Wear*, *Dead Enders*.' That was her name for *East Enders*. It was supposed to be a joke. I smiled, for it was appropriate. 'Oh,' she said excitedly. 'They're repeating *Walking with Dinosaurs*. I love that. Don't suppose you've ever seen it?'

'Nope,' I said. That was one of Kirsty's words. It's a way of saying no but with a measure of humour.

'Oh, you'll love it,' she enthused. 'The animation is spot on.'

The News was as depressing as ever. The police had found the body of a ten-year-old girl in the canal and had

137

proof that she'd been 'raped.' I recalled from my reading of the Bible that this a gross form of abuse, whereby one person, usually a man, forces a woman into holy union (and in the part about Sodom and Gomorrah men forced other men into union!). In this instance it was a ten-year-old girl. Horrific is not strong enough a word to describe it.

I read up on the history of *Heinz* while *East Enders* was on. And then it was time for *Walking with Dinosaurs*.

Well, I laughed all the way through it. What Kirsty called dinosaurs were animated pictures of the much bigger reptiles and lizards that we use for clearing away dead forestry and for transporting heavy loads. But on this programme a lot of them were the wrong colour, had completely the wrong diet, and the world in which they lived was some kind of fictional period set millions of years before the Father breathed life into Adam. In one scene a creature is shown to extend a long flesh pipe from its body in order to lay an egg. I roared with laughter at that.

'This is the funniest thing I have ever seen,' I gasped, holding my tummy. 'It's much better than *Blackadder*.'

Kirsty just looked at me, half frowning, half glaring. 'This isn't a comedy, Baz,' she said.

I stopped laughing and joined her in frowning. 'It isn't?'

'No.'

'Well, what is it then? A programme for children?'

She drew on her cigarette and then stubbed it out on the ashtray. 'It's natural history. Science.'

I was dumbstruck. 'Science? This?'

'Yes.'

I suggested she might be mistaking it for science fiction, for it seemed to me that the story of these dinosaurs belonged in the realm of the sliders and the time travelling nameless doctor. But she insisted the narrative was based on fact.

I told her the programme makers should go and observe these creatures before they attempt to teach about them, and she countered that they would if they could. I did not understand her.

'Well, they're extinct, aren't they?' she said, as though it explained everything.

'Define "extinct".'

She raised her eyebrows as if to say, 'You're not serious?' That was one of her expressions. 'They all died out thousands of years ago.'

I could not comprehend it. Died out? How?

The end credits ran as the programme concluded. 'You don't see any dinosaurs walking about now, do you?' Once again I detected mockery in her tone.

It had not even occurred to me that I hadn't seen any of the great creatures since I arrived here. But now it was patently and obviously true. At last I asked, 'How did they die out?'

'A huge meteorite hit the Earth thousands of years ago,' she explained. 'That's what they reckon. Its impact was so devastating, the sun's light was blocked out, the plates of the Earth shifted, and volcanoes erupted; the whole climate changed. And the dinosaurs that didn't die when the meteorite hit the Earth later died of starvation. They were all wiped out.' She got up to go to the kitchen. 'Then when things settled down, life began to progress again, evolving into the species we have now. Fancy a brew?'

I indicated that I would. 'You know it's fascinating,' I said. 'All of what you have just described could have been caused by the flood.'

'What flood?' She filled the kettle and readied our cups.

'The flood the Father brought on Noah's contemporaries.'

There was a brief and awkward silence. I should have known better. Any reference to the Bible account provoked this non-reaction. Kirsty stood at the door of the kitchen and leaned against the post, arms folded. 'You don't believe that literally happened, Baz?'

139

'I do,' I said simply.

It seemed incredulous to her. 'How *can* you?' she said, tempering her incredulity. 'It's like Adam and Eve and the talking snake. It's an allegory. A terrific story, but that's all.'

'But it explains why you have no water canopy,' I offered. 'Why your seasons are so extreme and erratic.'

She screwed up her face in disbelief. 'You what?'

'It's why the mammoth was found with vegetation still in its mouth and intestines undigested.'

'That was because of the Ice Age,' she countered.

I pointed out that her imagined Ice Age was supposed to have taken many years to develop, whereas the Flood was immediate. It explained the mammoth frozen in an instant, its food still edible when thawed out, the tropical plants submerged in Iceland, and the uneven climate.

'But Noah's ark,' she said, chuckling, and returned to make the tea. 'Eight people and a load of animals floating about the Earth in a box for months while God wipes everybody out. Does that seem realistic to you?'

I took a breath before I answered. I knew I was expected to see the error in my reasoning. But I could not. 'It is realistic. The disobedient spirit sons had corrupted mankind to such a point that they had to be destroyed.'

She handed me my tea and curled up again on her chair. 'That's quite a sweeping statement, Baz.' She picked up the television magazine. 'Damn, I missed *Relocation, Relocation.* What else is on?'

I was irritated now. 'What's a sweeping statement?'

Kirsty looked up. 'Well, this God of yours. Destroying people. I thought he was an all loving, all wise heavenly father type.'

'He is.'

'So raining fire and sulphur on Sodom and Gomorrah and flooding the Earth is his way of demonstrating parental love, is it?'

I was angry now, but I kept my fury in check. 'Those people were utterly debased. If he had permitted them to live, they would have spread their corruption through the whole world until all creation was ruined.'

Kirsty reached for her cigarettes and slid one out.

'Does that include children and newborn babies?'

'What?'

Kirsty shrugged and clicked her lighter. 'Well, presumably there were little kids and babes-in-arms around in Noah's time, and in Sodom and Gomorrah?'

I scrunched my nose, trying to counter the point she was making, but could not think of anything. 'Well, yes.'

'So your all loving heavenly father wiped those out too?'

I was speechless.

'Sounds more like an abusive parent to me,' she concluded, touching the end of her cigarette with the erect flame. I watched her draw on her arsenic-and-cyanide tube, relishing the taste and the sensation. 'I suppose you're going to say I'm twisted and debased as well, eh?'

I shook my head, sheepish. 'No.'

For the remainder of the evening we barely spoke to one another. She indulged in her pointless television programmes and I read *Nature* magazine. It was a bit of a disappointment too, as the articles hardly touched on the kind of orgology I am expert in. I had been hoping that with a combination of their technological science and my knowledge of biological manipulation I might find a way of generating a link to my home world.

It was not going to be so easy.

I'm lying here on the couch and I cannot sleep. My mind is awash with law enforcement plays ('Getcha self a cuppa caw-fee, machine down the hawl'), shocking porn images, job interviews, bullshit, a science fiction animation about dinosaurs, arsenic and cyanide, and alternate history.

And I don't know what to make of any of it.

141

MARCH 24

Kirsty is excited because it's Friday. The next two days are regarded as days of rest, so this is her last day of Job Centre visits and interviews. I am excited because today is my day for reading the New Testament (or the 'Second Testament' as I call it).

Kirsty is cooking me a 'full English', which is very kind of her, last night's animosity seemingly forgotten.

MARCH 24 (b)

The telephone rang. Kirsty looked at her wrist clock. 'Jesus,' she said. 'This could be the clinic. It won't be a rejection by phone. They normally write out to you for that.' She hesitated by the telephone and then picked up the receiver. 'Hello? Yes, speaking… Oh, Mr Hulton-Little…' She turned to catch my attention and made herself go cross-eyed. 'Yes, yes, of course I would love to come in for a second interview. Eleven? Yes that would be fine. OK. See you at eleven then. Bye.' She put down the receiver.

I waited for her to tell me her news, but she just stared at the phone and bit her lip. Finally she said, 'Bollocks.'

I offered a smile. 'What's the matter?'

'It's looking like I've got the factory job.'

I knew what she meant. 'Piss poor wages?'

''Fraid so.'

MARCH 24 (c)

The Second Testament is absolutely fascinating. In many ways it sheds light on some of the less comprehensible things in the First Testament.

For example, in Daniel's book I had no idea as to the identity of the Son of Man who sits at God's right hand to judge the world. But in the Second Testament, the man Jesus constantly refers to himself as this Son of Man. It is also said that he is God's Son and The Word (God's spokesman?). He is born of a virgin girl called Mary, who has been overshadowed by the Father's holy spirit. I am understanding this to mean that the Word had his life force transferred to the womb of Mary so he could be born as a human being.

Jesus preached that the Kingdom of God in heaven would be extended to Earth. I am interpreting this to mean that all the ills which have come about since Adam's rebellion will be undone. Jesus also likens the final judgment to the days of Noah – all those who have rejected God will be destroyed.

All those people in ignorance, though. All those who cannot read or simply do not understand. All those people like Kirsty who are so disillusioned they cannot believe it. All those young children who will die when judgement comes. All those babies.

Is it right?

Like all the messengers of God before him, Jesus Christ was despised. The religious leaders hated him because he pointed up their hypocrisy, the political system saw him as a troublemaker, and the public first hailed him as their king and saviour, and then a week later demanded his execution.

I was completely and utterly choked when they killed him. I mean, the Firstborn, the Word of God, the Son in human form – murdered by the very people he had been sent to redeem. They whipped him with leather strands and sharp bones, made him drag a felled tree through the streets in humiliation, and then nailed him to it by his hands and feet. They mocked and jeered at him as he bled to death.

At that moment I wanted the Father to manifest himself in the skies and rain fire and sulphur upon this wretched,

143

sick world, with its pollution and factories and mass production, cigarettes, porn and television.

But on the third day after Jesus' death, the Father resurrected him back to life as a spirit son and he returned to the heavens to sit at the Father's right hand. His final admonition to his followers before departing was to preach the word of salvation throughout the Earth.

Destroying people, though? Is that right?

MARCH 24 (d)

Despite the noise and pollution, it is lovely to be outdoors. I have found a tiny park with grass, a pond and a few benches. Across the way I can see a homeless person taking a sleep, his hair all matted together, his skin rough and wrinkled, his clothes old and sticking to him. My heart aches for him and I feel an immense gratitude again toward Kirsty, my saviour. How would this man fare when the judgement comes? He probably doesn't even know it is coming. Would he be destroyed?

MARCH 24 (c)

Kirsty stood in the doorway, jaw dropped, more than a little aghast. I could not understand why. Glynis and Rich smiled and waved at her, but she did not respond. She just glared at me, as if struck with terror.

'Hello Kirsty, dear,' Glynis said. 'You didn't tell us you have a new lodger.'

'Wha – Wha –.' Kirsty could barely speak for some reason. 'What are you two doing in here?'

Ah, I understood it now. I got to my feet, took her coat from her, and offered to make her a brew. I also offered an

144

explanation. 'I invited them to visit. They have answered all my questions about the Bible.'

She looked at them and her voice was flat, nearly emotionless. 'Oh I bet you have.'

Rich began to chuckle. 'Yes, it was so strange, wasn't it, love?'

'Yes,' Glynis said with a smile. 'Normally people are shutting the door on us, or telling us they have a pan of milk on, or just running a bath, or asking us to leave because they have family coming *any minute now.*' They both laughed heartily as Glynis put deliberate emphasis on those last few words. 'But your friend here called on us and asked *us* to explain the Bible to *him.*' She smiled at me. 'You're a rarity, my dear, you really are.'

'He's also very gullible,' Kirsty said.

Rich gave a heavy frown. 'That's not been our experience. Baz made some very thought-provoking observations.'

My heart swelled when he said that.

But Kirsty was entirely dismissive. I felt a bit embarrassed for my guests. 'Yes, well, we've got a lot to do. I've got to put tea on yet.'

Rich stood up and Glynis did likewise. He led the conversation and led his wife to the door. 'Yes, quite right. Come on, love.' They turned before exiting, and smiled. 'We must do it again, Baz,' Glynis said. She looked Kirsty head-on. 'Maybe it would be better if we discussed it in *our* home next time.'

Kirsty smiled the most insincere smile I have ever seen in my whole life and shut the door – hard. Then she glared at me. As she approached I genuinely believed she might strike me. 'What the hell were they doing in here?'

'I invited them as my guests,' I said. 'You said they like to talk about the Bible.'

'I also said you must keep them at arm's length,' she retorted. 'Christ, if they think they can come in here, we'll never be rid of them.'

I gritted my teeth as she said Christ as one utters a curse. I had regarded it as an ignorant figure of speech before I read the Second Testament, but now I feel very differently. I could barely look at her, I felt so disgusted.

After everything Christ did for these wretched people. For Kirsty herself. That terrible death. A sacrifice to ransom her and all her kind from the effects of Adam's sin. And all they do is curse his name. They do not deserve to live. Technically, Kirsty should be destroyed. Only my love for her stops me wishing it true.

I followed her gaze to the coffee table. She picked up the *Light to My Path* magazine that Rich and Glynis had left me, casually flicked through it, and tore it in half. I was so aghast I could not speak. She dropped the two halves into the waste bin. Her voice was again flat, almost monotone. 'Don't ever bring that stuff in here again.'

'But they gave me that to explain how your people have inherited Adam's sinful condition,' I said, choked.

'Not that again,' she moaned. I watched her reach into her bag and pull out her cigarettes and lighter. Arsenic and cyanide. 'The world is in the state that it is because a man and woman ate an apple thousands of years ago? Bollocks.'

I was sheepish, turned instantly timid by her aggressive stance. 'It's not.'

'It is,' she insisted. 'Tell the starving millions in the third world that it's because Adam and Eve ate an apple. Tell those poor people in the war torn Middle East they are suffering because God is allowing a universal court case to play out to the end. He'll step in, make everything right, oh yes. But first he has to prove to all mankind that his way is best. And how does he do it? By leaving us to struggle and bumble from one disaster to the next. Nine eleven, the tsunami: he just watches, ever silent, to prove how useless we are.'

She strode over to the window and looked up at the grey clouds overhead. 'Well, OK, God!' she shouted. 'I say you've proved your point! We can't do it on our own! We're crap! Now come and save us, why don't you?!'

'Kirsty.' I choked. 'That's blasphemy.'

She sniggered, more to the heavens than to me.

'Blasphemy, eh? I can do better than that.' She raised an accusing finger, her unlit cigarette crushed in the palm of her hand. 'How's this for blasphemy, God? I don't believe you even fucking exist! You're a fraud! A fanciful idea, something to cling to while we all suffer! Well, I don't need you, God! And you can strike me down right now, for all I care. The life I've had. Picking up the pieces after what that bastard Uncle Tim made me do. Trying to keep it together when my dad died.' The shouting gave out, her voice becoming more of a tremble. And then she wept. 'I don't care anymore. I don't care.'

She tried to steady her shaking hands and put the crumpled cigarette in her mouth. She fumbled to get the lighter to ignite. I slowly got up, walked across, and held the flame for her. She drew long and hard, and the end of her little white stick glowed red hot. She inhaled slowly and deliberately, her streaming eyes closed tight.

I didn't know what to do.

'They're nice people,' Kirsty said quietly after a few seconds, smoke puffing its way from her lips and nose. 'They really believe all that Kingdom of God on Earth stuff, and they mean well.' She looked at me and gave a weak, defeated smile. 'But I don't want them in here. I only keep the Bible because my dad wanted me to.'

I put my arm around her and kissed her forehead. 'All right. If I talk to them again, it will be in their flat, not here.'

'And you won't discuss any more Bible stuff with me?' she asked. 'I really cannot be doing with it. I know you believe it, and I respect that. But I don't believe it – any of it – and I too deserve to be respected, right or wrong. Seeing is believing – that's what I've always said. So I'll believe when I see it, and not before.'

I pulled back and smiled at her. 'How about we make an agreement?'

'A deal?'

'Yes, a deal.'

'OK.'

She drew on her bent cigarette, the tracks of her dried tears lining her cheeks like raindrops on the window.

'You stop saying Jesus Christ as a curse word, and I will stop talking about the Bible. How about that?'

She considered and picked something from her teeth with her fingernail. 'OK,' she said. 'But I might find it hard at first. It's a bit of a habit. Like smoking, I started blasphemy very young.'

I got the impression that was supposed to be a joke, so I gave a gentle laugh.

As Kirsty slowly composed herself and headed for the kitchen to make a cup of tea, a thought struck me. 'How was your interview, by the way?'

'Oh,' she replied, stopping in her tracks. 'I got the job. I start Monday.'

MARCH 25

Had a long sleep this morning. Watched a bit of children's television. More pointless nonsense. Kirsty highlighted the fact that it is for children, but I just took the view that the children of my world would be insulted – which indeed they would.

We went for a walk in the park and fed the ducks. I asked her what she meant about that bastard Uncle Tim, but she was very reluctant to tell me. So we laughed about Stein's Baked Beans and broken biscuits and dodgy recordable DVDs.

Kirsty has suggested we go on a day trip to Glossop tomorrow so I can be in the countryside for a while. I must say I am very excited about it!

MARCH 26

Glossop was lovely. We've just got back and the pair of us are 'shattered.' That means tired. It was great travelling by train again too, this time with a friend to share the experience. I really soaked up the countryside, even though I could still hear the traffic on the road in the distance. That's what I miss the most about Home World, after my family, of course – the silence.

Kirsty is getting her things ready for her new job. I think she's a bit nervous about it. She'll be all right, I am sure.

MARCH 27

Well she went off this morning all serious and worried. She'll be fine, I know it. She understands the mindset of this society; she has an instinct for it.

As an exercise, I have put dates to all my diary entries right back to the day I arrived here. March 15. Wow, it's been twelve days. There's not much point in going back further, as in Home World we didn't measure time in such tiny fragments.

I'm off out now for a walk.

MARCH 27 (b)

'Jeez, what a day!' Kirsty exclaimed as she flopped on the settee.

Jeez is a substitute for Jesus.

It wasn't long before a cigarette was pinched between her fingers. I made her a drink and switched on the microwave. She frowned and I could contain my excitement no longer. 'I've made us dinner.'

'You have?'

'It was hard, what with all your processed foods and everything, but I did it.'

She smiled a warm endearing smile. 'What exactly did you do?'

'Meat and two veg.'

'Really?' She laughed. It was a tired but hearty laugh. 'You cooked dinner for me?'

'I did.'

'Well I don't know what to say.'

I put out the knives and forks and presented her with her meal, complete with gravy, of course. She looked very surprised. I don't know what she had been expecting.

'This is lovely, Baz,' she said, chewing on her sirloin steak. 'It really is.'

As I tucked into mine, I asked her what I had been desperate to ask since she had come back home. 'So, how was your new job then?'

Kirsty cleared her throat. 'Well,' she said. 'Where do I start? It was a typical factory. Walter and Lorraine upstairs prepare the mixture and release it to the production hall. Tin cans are formed in a machine. There's a girl on that, she's called Leanne. Then they go up a conveyor belt and into the filler. There's a girl on that too, she's called Bel, short for Belinda. Then there's a machine which puts the labels on.'

'And there's a girl on that,' I said, bored already.

150

She gave me a mock hard stare and continued. 'No, actually. He's a man in his twenties. Though I think he might be gay.'

'I'm amazed that anyone could be gay in an environment like that,' I scoffed. 'It sounds dreadful. Not like the Gay Village, which I assume is where he lives.'

Kirsty grinned wickedly. 'You don't know what I mean by "gay", do you? Now why doesn't that surprise me?'

'Happy,' I asserted.

'Nope,' she said, and chuckled. 'And I suspect you've never actually been to the Gay Village. Would I be right in saying you did not walk down Canal Street on a Saturday night when you were homeless?'

'Er, no,' I confessed. 'Though Jack and Kelly used to go.'

'I suggest you look up homosexuality in your encyclopaedia sometime,' she teased.

Homo Sexuality?

Then she stopped and collected her thoughts. 'And there's this ink jet thing that sprays the dates and codes and stuff on. The cans go into plywood boxes, the boxes go into the warehouse on another conveyor, and the lads pile them up on pallets for the forklift guys to pick up.' She exhaled loudly. 'And that's pretty much it. Tedious, but I'm earning at least.'

'And what part of the process were you doing?'

'The labeller. It's really tricky to keep the glue going. Not as easy as it looks.' She polished off the last of her meal. 'Ooh, that was terrific!'

I felt proud of my culinary efforts and served up the pudding.

Worn out, Kirsty curled up on her chair, lit herself a cigarette and watched the last of *Richard & Judy* on Channel Five.

MARCH 28

Went to see Rich and Glynis today. They told me more about their belief in the paradise Earth to come. I asked about the resurrection of the dead and they said the Earth, if the land was properly assigned, would be able to support not only everybody who is alive now, but everyone who has ever lived. An acre each, they said. I told them that if the water canopy was restored, there would be even more room than that.

We revelled in our conversation, they in their 'faith', me in my certain knowledge, which they termed as my 'strong faith.' They didn't seem to comprehend that I have *seen* the world they imagine to be future; that I have lived in it.

'It makes sense,' I said. 'When the accusations against the Father and against the creation have been fully resolved, the Earth and everyone who has ever lived will be restored!'

There was a brief silence at this point. I wasn't sure what I should make of it. Then Rich said, 'Of course, not everyone will, though.'

I expressed my confusion.

Glynis smiled. 'All those who died faithful, and all those who died in ignorance, who never really knew God – they are the ones who will be brought back.'

'But surely,' I began. 'Surely everyone will have their second chance?'

'Not everyone,' Rich interjected. 'There are those who knew God, knew his purpose, and still rejected him. Should they be given a second chance?'

I didn't reply. I was too stunned.

'Should Judas Iscariot be given a second chance, should those judged adversely and executed in the flood?'

Glynis cut across her husband. 'Should Adam and Eve?'

'Yes,' I said, shrugging.

They both smiled at me, as I might at my youngest daughter. 'You've got to remember that Adam and Eve weren't like us,' Rich said. 'We are born in corruption, we have genetically inherited imperfection. We battle fleshly selfish thinking and struggle with our emotions. Our motives are not always pure. In a perverse way, it is our natural state.'

'But Adam and Eve were not like that,' Glynis cut in again. 'They were perfect, uncorrupted. They had no such inner battle. When they chose independence from God, it was a deliberate act of rebellion, with full knowledge of the consequences, that they would bring the human race into a dying condition.'

I baulked at that last statement. 'I beg to differ,' I told them (another of Kirsty's expressions). 'There is no way they could have foreseen this world of yours, to know that their actions would lead to this narrow-minded, emotionally stunted, spiritually famished society. If they had known it, they wouldn't have done it.'

Rich tried to calm me. 'Well, we think like that because we believe that in the same situation we wouldn't have done it. But it was a question of their obedience, which was governed by their love.'

Glynis smiled. 'It was love that they lacked.'

'It wasn't,' I countered, exasperated.

The pair looked at me in silence.

'I know them,' I continued. 'They don't lack love, nor are they so self-orientated.'

Rich cleared his throat. 'You know them? You mean as a Bible student.'

'No,' I said. 'I know them. I have met them.'

'Met them?' There was a vague stammer in Glynis' voice as she exchanged looks and furrowed brows with her husband.

'When I visited the Euphrates.'

They were dumbstruck. Now it was my turn to speak with a reassuring tone. 'I think I should explain.'

More silence.

I told them that I grew up in a parallel world, a world where everything is perfect, where the global village is made up of lots of little villages; plenty of room, plenty of wholesome work. I come from a place that is in every sense of the word a paradise; the land, the climate, the food, the company.

Old age and death are experienced only by the animal kingdom, as part of the cycle and machinery of the Earth. By their calculation I am nine hundred and thirty-six years old. In a freak moment of curiosity I stepped over into this 'God forsaken' place (Kirsty again!) and now I am stuck here.

I haven't seen my wife and family for many days and it is only because of my flatmate that I am not utterly consumed by depression.

Well, they just stared at me, mouths agape.

Rich was the first. He cleared his throat, very obviously uncomfortable. 'Well, erm. That's very interesting.' He stood up, and Glynis quickly followed suit. 'But it's time we got started on dinner, isn't it, Glynis?'

'Oh yes, yes,' Glynis said, nodding almost frantically. She looked at her watch. 'Goodness, is that the time?'

I found myself being ushered towards the exit. 'But it's only three o'clock!'

'We're having guests, aren't we, Rich?'

'Oh yes. They'll be arriving soon, any time now, in fact. We really need to get ahead.'

Before I knew what was happening, I was standing in the hallway. They peeped through the door. I gave them a defeated smile. 'I thought you would understand. I am from that world. The world of your Yahweh.'

They cast their eyes to the carpet and quietly and gently clicked the door shut. Feeling pathetic and empty, I watched as their shadows moved away from the glass.

'Perhaps it's for the best,' Kirsty said when I told her. She was just relieved that my friendship with them had been brought to an abrupt end.

MARCH 29

I'm feeling riddled with guilt again. Even though I told Kirsty and she was more sympathetic than I ever could have conceived, I still feel bad.

It was boredom, you see. There are only so many books I can read and only so many entries in the encyclopaedia before tedium sets in. The television offers no relief. Most of what it serves up in the name of entertainment is childish at best.

So I went on the computer. I had looked up the subject of homosexuality, as Kirsty had suggested. I had guessed that it involved intercourse between members of the same sex like those in Sodom and Gomorrah, as implied by the words homo and sexual. The encyclopaedia said that the practice was outlawed throughout the world for most of the Christian era, but that in recent times, secular rulers have relaxed the law and legalised 'gay' sex.

I was completely overwhelmed by this knowledge. In my world, no such concept exists. Here it is perceived as just another lifestyle. And I knew that it would be represented on the Internet. I typed in 'homosexuality' at first, and found a number of web sites discussing the gay lifestyle and gay rights.

Again I was intensely absorbed. To my mind, the purpose of sexual intercourse is to procreate, to multiply the human race. But in this society, they engage in holy union not only to have children, but to enjoy the physical sensation of sex in its own right. I thought, and still think it an incredible concept.

They have manufactured a tight rubber bag, which goes over the male sex organ, thus preventing conception. As a result they can have union without pregnancy. This is how they are able to be so cavalier about it. And it enables them to have union with different partners.

Even now, I find it potent: To have sex for the sake of it. Naomi and I, in all the years we have been married, have never done that.

Their view of homosexuality seems to have come from a desire to have equal rights. If a man has no attraction at all to a woman, but is drawn to another man and loves him deeply, why should he not be allowed to demonstrate that love physically? And the same for women who are sexually attracted to other women rather than to men.

Almost every instinct within me dismissed the notion as unnatural and a perversion of what is morally right. The Father created sexual union as a means of multiplying the human race. It is a privilege. After all, he could have chosen to create each human being individually as he did Adam. But we have the ability to create our own offspring. Sexual relations between members of the same sex are fruitless and sterile.

But I say *almost* every instinct because I was still deeply curious, and I knew where I would be able to quench that curiosity.

Google: 'Gay porn'.

And sure enough, there it was. Men with men, naked, young, middle-aged, older. Ah, so *that's* what they do. How bizarre. How disgusting. How fascinating. How arousing.

How strange.

I recalled that some of these positions were also featured on the normal porn sites. Here the enjoyment of sex is paramount. It doesn't matter what it's *for*, it only matters how it *feels*.

In that moment I envied their freedom. Yes, I envied it so much.

I looked further. Women with women. Thoughts of being offended were a lot less present for some reason. It didn't bother me as much. Yet, I knew that if Naomi was to ever view these images, she most certainly would be sickened. But I wasn't sickened. Again I was aroused. I sensed the Father watching me, knowing my every thought and desire as they pulsed through me; every fantasy and every wish.

My heart thumped, my throat dried, and my head ached with the strain. But still I went on.

And on.

Until I heard Kirsty's key in the door.

'Look, I'm not bothered,' she said, laughing. 'Really I'm not. There are much worse things that you could be watching than that stuff. One of the most important things I learned at university is that we mustn't stifle our desires and fantasies. They are part of what makes us human. It's healthy. It's normal.'

I choked and stammered. 'But men with men and women with women.' I coughed nervously. 'And men and women with other men and women, and –.'

She cut in. 'Look, you've not been looking at men with kids, have you?'

I frowned. What on Earth did she mean? 'No,' I said, baffled.

She smiled, registering the truth in my face. 'If it really is becoming a problem for you.'

'It is,' I said hurriedly. 'I've got like you with your cigarettes. I can't keep away from it.'

She laughed again.

'But it's worse than that, because it's not just in my blood, it's in my mind,' I paused before adding the awful truth, 'and in my heart.'

Kirsty touched my cheek affectionately, her voice becoming motherly once more. 'If you're really troubled by it, I'll put the parental controls on so you can't access any porn at all. How's that?'

I felt instantly relieved. 'Oh, can you?'

'Yes.' Then a thought occurred to her. 'As long as you don't have any idea about computer programming. You don't, do you?'

'No.'

'Now why doesn't that surprise me?' She walked over to the machine and booted it up. Once running, she emptied the Google memory, the cookies and the history. Then she went into another part, moved some sliders to the left, clicked 'Save' and 'OK', and then shut down the computer. 'There,' she said. 'All done.'

My heart instantly relaxed, my muscles went numb. I was drowsy with relief. Weepy.

I cried.

MARCH 31

Every day seems like every other. What's the point? How do these people stay so motivated and positive?

I get up, wave Kirsty off, watch *This Morning* until I get weary of it. I watch the news. I do a bit of reading. I go for a walk. I come back. Get tea ready. I watch *Countdown* (it's so boring, I never get any of the puzzles wrong).

I watch the beginning of *Richard & Judy*.

This can be infuriating. It appears she is prepared to believe in almost anything – predicting the future by the movement of the stars, the dead living on in some kind of

158

spirit form, alien creatures from other planets visiting Earth and abducting people; he believes himself to be a great elder to the nation, full of knowledge and wisdom – embracing secularism and evolutionary theory, rejecting anything that cannot be measured scientifically, presenting his personal views as fact beyond doubt.

Both worship the system – its ideas, its philosophies, its fanciful dreams, its politics, its popular religions, its business empire, its entertainment, its celebrities: revelling in the emptiness of this life. I usually watch it with the sound off.

I spend the whole of the day waiting for Kirsty to come home.

I've just seen her through the window, right down in the car park area. She'll be walking through that door any minute now. She'll light up, have her cup of tea, and tell me about her day at the factory, and enjoy her meal.

I will love listening to it. To her.

MARCH 31 (b)

'And guess what?' she enthused. 'He said he'll give you an interview!'

I didn't know what to say. 'An interview?'

'Yes,' Kirsty said, bouncing up and down on her tiptoes for sheer joy. 'If he likes you, he'll give you a job. Isn't it fantastic?!'

It had all started earlier in the week when she realised that Mr Hulton-Little employed illegal immigrants. The law demands that he pay no less than an agreed minimum wage, but because these people have crept into Britain without permission due to being persecuted by their own Governments, and cannot declare their existence to the British system, Hulton-Little can pay them less than the

159

minimum wage in the full knowledge that they dare not complain.

I am not sure what to make of Kirsty placing me in this category.

'You can't live off me forever, you know, Baz.'

I stammered a little. 'I don't intend to. I just need some time.'

She frowned. 'Time? Time for what?'

'To work out how to get back.'

'Back where?'

I hesitated, but it had to be said. 'Well, back to my world, of course.'

'God,' she groaned. I didn't feel qualified to chastise her about the blasphemy. 'You're not still clinging to that, are you?'

She's in bed now. I cannot stop thinking about this job.

APRIL 7

Well, what a week. During the interview I felt a mixture of wonderment and nervousness. I thoroughly enjoyed exploring the factory, but I was also aware that I was being tested, assessed, as to my suitability as a worker, an employee.

Mr Hulton-Little led me upstairs to the mixing room. This, as implied by its name, is where the beans, the sauces, the flavourings, the colourings, and all the other chemicals are mixed inside a large metal urn. It is tested by Walter and Lorraine, and then released to the production area below.

Running parallel to the mixing room is the canteen. This is where all the workers go for a break. Fifteen minutes at ten o'clock, thirty minutes for lunch, and another fifteen minutes at three in the afternoon. Mr Hulton-Little pointed through the canteen window to a shelter positioned by one of the main exit doors. 'That's the smoke area,' he said. 'If you smoke, I'm afraid you will have to take your breaks in there. Are you a smoker, Mr Maher?'

Maher is the surname Kirsty said I must give. I am to call myself Barry Maher in the presence of these people, Baz for short.

'No,' I said. 'I am not a smoker.'

'Me neither,' Mr Hulton-Little replied. 'At least not now. I used to be a twenty-a-day man. Then I had my heart attack. Now I hate it. Filthy habit.'

I smiled. 'Full of lethal chemicals like formaldehyde, arsenic and cyanide. It is no wonder your heart was stressed.'

He nodded. 'Indeed.' Then he gestured round the canteen. 'There's a sink and a kettle, and brewing up gear. There's milk in the fridge. I supply that. We have a toaster too. The cleaner makes the toast at nine fifty-five. I've made that part of her job. She's an immigrant as well. Get Kirsty to introduce you.'

'I will,' I said with a smile.

Mr Hulton-Little waved a hand at another machine stationed in the corner opposite to the fridge. 'Oh, and as an alternative to the home-made drinks, or if you're in a hurry, there's the old Maxpax dispenser. Seventy-five pence will get you a brew from that.'

I laughed as I recognised the oblong box with its selections and small panel where the thin plastic cups appear. 'Getch yerself a cuppa caw-fee; machine down the hawl!'

'Quite,' Hulton-Little said, giving a slight cough.

We trotted down the stairs into the main production hall. It was exactly as Kirsty had described it. A huge machine formed cans from steel and dropped them onto the conveyor belt (itself made up of metal links, like a steel vertebrae). These travelled into a revolving structure and came out the other side full of baked beans.

161

Another device sealed the tops.

Then it was off to the labeller, the device which Kirsty had been learning, for the labels.

A final machine arranged the cans to be dropped into crates, which were then fed through a hole in the breezeblock (that is, a lightweight form of brick) wall to the warehouse.

'So what do you think?' Mr Hulton-Little asked, our tour now concluded.

What do I think? I think it is terrible that human beings should be cooped up inside a place like this for eight hours a day being not much more than extensions to the machinery. I think the fumes pumped into the atmosphere by this place will contribute to the already damaged ecosystem. I think the product itself is very poor quality. I think Mr Hulton-Little is a scoundrel because he is trying to become rich in monies off the backs of his staff, Kirsty included.

I now know this world to be entirely driven by the monetary arrangement. A few men and women at the top of the chain enjoy all that this perverse existence has to offer while most struggle to get by, and a few like Jack, Kelly and Shazia are pressed into all manner of debased activities just to eat, or at best, be induced to stupor so as not suffer unduly.

But most of all, Mr Hulton-Little is a scoundrel because he knows we are desperate. He fantasises about having holy union with Kirsty (she told me he watches her and the other young women from his office window) and he employs people like Waris the immigrant because he knows he can pay him less than the minimum wage decreed by the Government, since Waris is in Britain illegally. If I am offered a job, it will be on this basis.

I followed Kirsty's instructions to the letter. When I'd said I did not want to tell an untruth, she had a think about this and advised that I tell a half-truth. So I did. I said, 'I am deeply impressed by your organisational skills, Mr Hulton-

162

Little. You clearly understand how a business like this should be managed.'

He was pleased straight away. I could tell. He beamed at me. 'Why, thank you, Mr Maher.'

'Baz,' I offered. Kirsty said I should invite him to use my shortened name when I discerned he was at ease with me. 'Professional until he indicates otherwise,' she had said.

'So, do you think you would fit in here?'

I nodded vigorously and gave the impression that I was looking admiringly at his machines and conveyor belt. 'I do.'

He extended his hand, and I knew I should shake it. So I did. He grinned at me, keen with delight. 'I am pleased to tell you, Baz, you start tomorrow at eight o'clock.'

I thanked him.

Kirsty was 'thrilled to bits' by my news and said my obtaining a second-hand suit for the interview would have undoubtedly contributed to his decision. Personally, I believe my illegal status is what persuaded him most. She chose to celebrate by buying a bottle of wine. I had one glass, and, gradually, she had the rest.

The work itself is overwhelmingly dull. The production manager, a tall thin man called Aaron, dressed me in their customary white coat, paper hat and rubber wellington boots, and stationed me on the 'canner', the machine which presses out the cans.

I protested at the level of noise when the line was switched on. Deafening it was, the rattling of the line and the clanking of the cans, but nobody else seemed that bothered. Kirsty showed me how to put in the sponge earplugs, and I was grateful indeed for the noise reduction.

The machine pressed out the cans. If one fell over, I put it back up. If the machine jammed, I pressed a red button which turned it off so I could free the debris. As soon as the line stops, Aaron comes running down in a panic. Time is money, apparently.

And that is it. Eight hours a day, five days a week: the most mind-numbing task in the whole of my nine hundred and thirty-six years of life. But without it I have no money, no means of supporting myself, no hope of ever getting back to Elohah Village.

I keep reminding myself of these facts when the desire to simply walk out of the factory and never return overtakes me.

On my first day, I attempted to engage the workers in conversation. Not easy when the common practice is to mock the latest new employee. Kirsty had warned me this was likely to happen, but I had dismissed it as an exaggeration.

However, I soon realised the truth of the matter when I told Aaron he was likely to have been named in honour of Moses' brother in the Bible. He made a joke about it and everybody laughed. Kirsty smiled and looked at the floor, trying to hide her amusement. At that moment I was both foolish and disappointed.

At break time I met the other workers: Bel and Leanne are girls in their early twenties. I suspect they were hired for the same reason Kirsty was. They are slender, young, and attractive. Unlike Kirsty, they are grossly immature. Their conversation revolves around only a few subjects: clothes, current music trends, and their sexual partners.

Leanne is especially irritating since she has the habit of giving a little laugh at the end of nearly every sentence. 'Craig couldn't get up this morning. Ha, ha. He was too pissed last night. Ha, ha. I said, "It's your own bloody fault, getting pissed!" Ha, ha, ha, ha.'

The laughter isn't really laughter. By that I mean it isn't a response to something which has amused her. It's more a mannerism. She does it because she thinks everyone else is amused by her puerile stories.

She also has a habit of saying 'Christ' as her one reply to anything that vaguely surprises her, which sadly means she says it in response to almost every piece of information to which she is exposed. I cannot be certain she even knows who Christ is, or indeed that he is a person at all.

Bel might say something like, 'I bought that single at the weekend.'

To which Leanne would reply, 'Christ, did you? That new one by the Kaiser Chiefs?'

'Yeah. It's got a club mix on as a bonus track.'

'Has it?'

'Yeah. I think it's better than the radio one.'

'Christ.'

Thankfully both are smokers and once they have got their coffees they vacate the canteen to inhale arsenic and cyanide in the shelter outside. Unfortunately so does Kirsty, which means I am left with Lorraine, a middle-aged lady who talks almost exclusively to the homosexual man Ainsley.

I have to stop myself from staring at him because all the time he is speaking, I am thinking, 'You have sex with men like on the porn web sites'.

Walter, a greasy haired man in his mid-twenties, sits in a corner and reads a science fiction magazine without ever uttering a word.

We are also joined by the only warehouse workers who do not smoke. An older, oily looking man with a straggle of white hair, named Ralph, and a younger dark skinned man called Mo.

Ralph says 'Bleeding Jesus Christ' a lot, especially when matters of religion are discussed. No one is remotely affected by this. Personally I would like to nail Ralph to a tree and suspend it in the yard.

Mo practices a religion based on a sort of sequel to the Bible called the Qur'an. I would like to read it and make comparisons but I fear that Kirsty would finally lose patience with me and put me out on the streets.

Another man, middle-aged and yet handsome, wanders up from the front office every now and again. They call him Clint. He's always a cheery fellow and likes to listen to my ideas. Clint isn't his real name, though. They call him that because he bears a very, very slight resemblance to an ex-President of the United States named Bill Clinton (he has blue eyes, clean white teeth, and grey-white hair neatly arranged. He grins a lot too).

I have been far too tired in the evenings to write in my diary. Though the work is boring, it seems the boredom itself is fatiguing me. Like Kirsty, I watch a bit of telly, do a bit of reading, research things on the internet, but by the time nine o'clock has arrived, I am spent.

Today I was rather thrilled to receive my first piss poor wage. For all my criticism of the system, there is a curiously warm feeling about getting paid.

We celebrated by having a pub meal, and by drinking wine and eating chocolates in the evening.

APRIL 21

Most of this month has revolved around a celebration called Easter. The name is derived from Eastroe, which is Latin for Astarte, and Astarte is the pagan goddess of fertility. She symbolises worship of the sex act and rebirth, to coincide with the onset of spring. She, like all the other gods, is a creation of the human imagination. I told Kirsty this and she said my God is no less a human creation, which, to be perfectly frank, made me want to slap her as the parents of this world do their errant children.

The Bible (and Qur'an, so I'm told) forbids the mixing of false man-made doctrines with God's truth. So by turning the festival of Astarte into the celebration of Jesus Christ's resurrection in order to justify Christians participating is a direct violation of that scriptural principle.

But participate they do. I approached Mo to see how he felt about it, only to find that he had bought Easter eggs for all the women, and he's a Muslim! Not only does their holy book forbid the blending of truth and lies, but they do not believe that Jesus is the Son of God. So he's a hypocrite on both counts.

Kirsty warned that I should not say these things at work. I risked it with Mo because he entertains religious ideas, and I told Clint because he's nice. I didn't tell anyone else – until I was asked outright.

'What you doing about Easter, Baz?' Leanne quizzed one morning as she got herself a brew from the machine. I looked to Kirsty for guidance and her eyes widened slightly, indicating that I avoid the question.

'Oh, I'm having a quiet one,' I breezed, which seemed to do the trick. At first.

'Going anywhere or doing anything?' She took her drink from the machine.

I coughed. 'Er, no.'

'Christ. What, nothing?'

I shook my head, my throat dry again. 'Er, no.'

She stared at me, astonished. 'Christ.' Her astonishment gave way to puzzlement. 'Why?'

I shrugged. 'I don't believe in it.'

More puzzlement. 'You don't believe in it? Believe in what?'

More shrugging. 'Any of it.'

Leanne laughed. 'Christ, you don't have to *believe* it. You just have to enjoy yourself.'

At that moment Belinda walked in, slung her coat over a hook and made for the machine. 'What?' she said, grinning. 'What is it?'

'Baz isn't doing Easter because he doesn't believe in it,' Leanne declared. 'Ha, ha.'

Belinda snorted her disapproval. 'God, the only ones who really believe it are the kids. I mean, Jesus coming back from the dead and that.'

I offered a weak smile. 'Well it's not just that. It's the stuff about the fertility goddess.'

Kirsty tugged at my white coat anxiously. 'Come on Baz, we're gonna be late on the floor.'

Bel stepped between us. 'Hang on. What fertility goddess?'

'Astarte,' I said. I turned to Kirsty, frowning. 'Don't they know?'

'They don't know and they don't care,' Kirsty said, barely able to conceal her embarrassment. 'And neither do I. Come on, let's get downstairs.'

I followed her towards the stairs, still confused. Then I stopped and turned to Bel and Leanne. 'Have you never wondered what rabbits and eggs have to do with Jesus Christ? They are symbols of sexual fertility, not Jesus' resurrection.'

'Ha!' Leanne laughed. 'Res-erection!' At first I couldn't understand the remark. And then I realised. Resurrection rhymes with erection, penis erection that is. 'You're weird, Baz, you know that?' She put on her paper hat and urged me to follow in Kirsty's wake.

At lunch the discussion continued, my comments having found their way into the realm of the non-smokers. Mo was quite animated. 'It doesn't matter where it comes from,' he said. 'All that matters is that we are celebrating the arrival of spring. Goddesses, rabbits and eggs are just symbols. They don't matter.'

I found it hard keeping my emotions in check. 'They do matter,' I asserted. 'Astarte is an insult to the Father.'

The door flung open and Ralph entered, his sandwich box clenched firmly under his arm. 'Bleeding Jesus Christ!' he shouted. 'They had me run ragged in that warehouse.' He filled the kettle and hit the on switch.

A younger man, Gary, also marched in. 'Stick one in the pot for me, Ralph,' he said, and made for the table, newspaper already unfolding. Ralph did as instructed.

Lorraine exchanged glances with Ainsley and then grinned at me. 'The Father?'

Ainsley touched her arm, as if to say, 'Leave him,' but she was enjoying the controversy. Looking back I now see it served as a kind of puerile entertainment.

'God,' I said simply.

Ralph banged about behind me, clanking cups and clearing his throat loudly. 'Bleeding Jesus Christ!'

Gary lowered his newspaper and scowled at me. 'Look,' he snarled. He reminded me of a wild dog I had encountered in the park, teeth gritted, hard blue eyes bulging. 'We don't wanna know about your beliefs. We've come up 'ere for a break.' The paper returned to its position.

'Oh, I do,' Lorraine teased. 'What are your beliefs, Baz?'

I grimace now, thinking back. She wasn't interested at all. I answered her question as concisely as I could.

'Well,' I started. 'I believe the world wasn't originally meant to be like this. I believe God intended it to be a global paradise, a sort of worldwide Garden of Eden.'

The paper shot down again. 'What did I say?' Gary sneered. 'We don't wanna hear it?'

'Go on,' Lorraine coaxed. Ainsley frowned ever so slightly and looked at his boots.

'This world system came into existence when mankind declared independence from God,' I said.

'Bleeding Jesus!' Ralph shouted, hot tea wobbling over the rim of his cup and onto his fingers. He sat at the table and opened his sandwich box.

Ainsley looked up, genuinely intrigued. 'When did they do that?'

Before I could answer, Mo cut in, grinning all over his face. 'He means when Adam and Eve ate the apple.'

Lorraine was instantly amused. 'Do you, Baz?' she jeered. 'Do you believe that Adam and Eve were real?'

I was beginning to grasp what was going on, but I knew a denial would not be the correct path to take. I offered my answer humbly and with awkwardness. 'I do.'

'You think the whole human race was started by two lovers having a good shag in the Garden of Eden?'

Her tone implied aggression. She was difficult to read.

'Yes.'

'How can you believe that?' She laughed. 'The whole human race, whites, blacks, yellows, Europeans, Asians, the Red Indians, the tribes in the jungle dancing about stark naked – all from a single couple in the Middle East?'

I grinned back. 'It's much easier to believe than the human race descending from monkeys. Do you understand at all the kind of biological metamorphosis required for such a thing to take place? From a single celled organism to fish, plants, animals and man? I believe the human race descended from two physically perfect adults. You believe it descended from creatures that aren't human at all. Which is easier to believe?'

'And the world is the crap hole it is because they ate that apple?'

I swallowed, nervous, fearful of her anger. 'Yes.'

'Oh!' Lorraine shouted. 'So it's all because two people ate an apple thousands of years ago, is it? Kids being abused, people dying in earthquakes, my mum suffering with chronic arthritis, Clint's dad in the loony bin.'

I tried to maintain some composure. 'They were perfect. It was an act of outright rebellion. They were challenging the Father as God.'

'So he threw them out the Garden of Eden and now we're all in the shit.'

I shrugged. 'Looks like it.'

'Bollocks,' Lorraine sneered. 'I wasn't even born then. How can I be held accountable for what they did?'

'It is their legacy,' I stammered, but I knew it wasn't washing (to use Kirsty's expression). 'The Father is letting us rule ourselves to demonstrate how we much we need him.'

She glared out the window at the bright blue sky. 'So kids are molested by paedophiles, and my granddad dies of cancer, and those buggers in the Middle East are allowed to blow one another up and any poor sod who gets in the way, because God wants to show us we can't do it without him?'

'Yes.'

'Then he's nothing but a cruel ogre,' Lorraine said.

I offered a friendly hand and she recoiled. 'It won't go on indefinitely, though,' I said as softly as I could. 'Your Bible says he will step in the affairs of fallen man at his designated time, destroy the wicked, and return the Earth to the paradise it once was.'

Mo nodded, suddenly attracted. 'Judgement Day.'

Walter looked over the top of his sci-fi magazine momentarily. Then Clint walked in and the atmosphere immediately lightened up. 'What we talking about?'

'A load of bull,' Lorraine said.

Ainsley caught his eye. 'We're talking about when God transforms the world into a paradise. That's what Baz believes.'

'I'm afraid I don't believe in God,' Clint said, taking a chair and placing a paper bagged meat pie on the table. 'I don't mean to offend you Baz. Or you, Mo. Though I do believe in a paradise.'

Lorraine raised an eyebrow sceptically. 'You do?'

'Yes,' Clint replied. 'But it will be a paradise brought about by men, with everybody equal, a united brotherhood. No religion, no political nations, just people living in peace.'

'But that's –.' I nearly said that's where I come from, and cut myself short. 'That's what I believe in, but by God's intervention.'

'We don't need God to bring it about.'

I suppressed a snigger, but could not resist a smile. 'You really think human beings can turn this world into a paradise?' I'm afraid my tone betrayed my true feelings. 'Do you not watch the news on television? Are you not aware of your… our history?'

'Oh Jesus,' Ralph said, laughing. 'I was forgetting you're a commie, Clint.'

Clint grinned and tucked into his pie. 'I prefer Marxist.'

'Ooh,' Ainsley dreamed aloud. 'Imagine, a paradise with everyone living together in peace. Men and women, children, different colours and races, gays and lesbians, every creed and religion reconciled. It would be lovely.'

I shook my head, eager (too eager I now realise) to point out an oversight. 'Not homosexuals, Ainsley,' I said. 'There won't be homosexuals. It was never part of the Father's plan.'

They all glared at me, all but Mo. It was his turn to look at the floor. His religion teaches the same thing, but he wasn't going to say it. The silence was unbearable. And then Ainsley stood up and made for the brew machine. 'In that case,' he said finally. 'it wouldn't be paradise. Not for me.'

Aaron bustled in and went straight to the drinks machine. 'Who's got seventy-five pee for a brew?' He never had any money on him. He gave an over exaggerated frown. 'What?'

Gary spoke from behind his paper. 'You never told us you'd hired a Bible basher.'

'Eh?'

'Him!' he shouted, pointing at me. 'He's like the bloody God Squad knocking you out of bed on a Sunday morning.'

Everybody laughed. Although it was strained, I was grateful. Anything to shatter the tension.

On Easter Sunday, Kirsty insisted I join her in watching a children's film called *The Wizard of Oz*. She also insisted on singing all of the songs.

It tells of a young girl's search for a mystical wizard who has the power to send her back to her home, a dimension where everything is in shades of grey (apparently a means of showing off colour film around the time of its advent).

Kirsty thought I would identify with this aspect of the story, I having told her about my parallel world many times.

Joining the girl Dorothy on her journey is a man made of tin who has no heart, a brainless scarecrow, and a cowardly lion. Along the way, each finds the missing quality within themselves, so that by the time they find the wizard they do not need his special powers.

When they finally do get an audience with him, he at first appears as a frightening, booming disembodied face. Then, the little dog Toto pulls at a curtained booth, revealing the wizard to be nothing more than an eccentric elderly man, and the disembodied face an illusion.

'There you are,' Kirsty said, out of the blue. Her tone implied ridicule. 'There's your God. A clever party trick, all smoke and mirrors.'

I thought of the Father, his voice talking to me in the rainforest and in the temple. Could it be possible that he is an illusion, a creation of the elders? I could not stomach the idea at all. I mean, why would they do such a thing? To keep the community under their control?

Stop it. It's a twisted line of reasoning.

'I thought we had an agreement,' I said. 'No God from me, no blasphemy from you.'

She cocked her head and smiled. I love it when she does that. 'Agreed,' she said.

As a sort of precursor to Easter, there was Mother's Day (Astarte being the mother of all other gods, apparently). Again, no one cares about the origins. It's just a reason to shower one's mother with gifts and a means of boosting the economic system (lots of adverts on television to emotionally pressure the populace into parting with their wages).

173

Kirsty joined her brother Steve at their mother's. I offered to come along too, but she said it wasn't the right time.

I must admit I was encouraged to think about my mother too. I contemplated what she might be doing now. What does she make of my sudden disappearance? What are *any* of them making of it?

There is a scientist called Dr Jonathan Matthews. He writes for *New Scientist* magazine. I like his articles, so I'm thinking of sending him my idea on how a gateway could be opened using this world's technology and my knowledge of orgology. I am hoping he will be able to help me.

Section Six

MAY 31

Today is the anniversary of Belinda's birth. She is twenty-four years-old. It took some effort to prise the actual number from her, but Lorraine was unrelenting. Kirsty says Bel was reluctant to confess her age because it means next year marks her twenty-fifth anniversary and she is troubled by that knowledge because, 'it means she will be halfway through her twenties.'

The crew presented her with a card, a cake, and a bottle of wine. I thought she was going to burst into tears, she was so emotional. Then everybody applauded her. I do not understand this. Are they applauding her because she was born or because she has got a year older? And why applaud those things anyway? I mean, no one can take the credit for being born, can they? It's not like they planned it or anything.

Kirsty herself is twenty-nine and is even more bothered due to the fact that her next birthday will be 'the big three-oh.' That and the fact that she's 'ballsed up' her life. By that she means she was earning good money as a clinical psychologist, a vocation for which she had sacrificed a number of years in study, and in her first few months of practice had forfeited it by breaking the rules.

Leanne wanted to know my age. Kirsty had warned that this might be the case and had advised with the greatest severity that under no circumstances should I tell any of them that I am nine hundred and thirty-six years of age, even though it's true.

175

So I told Leanne and the others that I believe the anniversary of one's birth is not an essential observance. It places too much emphasis on self, which, when one considers the prime motivation for the troubles of the world is self-indulgence, is not a good thing.

'Christ, God Squad,' Leanne baulked. 'Don't you care about your life? Aren't you bothered at all?'

I said, 'Of course I care about my life.' Then I shrugged. 'I just don't want to celebrate the anniversary of my birth. Why should I?'

'Because it's a miracle any of us are here,' she said. 'I mean, when you think of the chances.' She looked to the others, but no one spoke. This happens often, whenever any of them show signs of considering more than the basic staples of life. Not one of them wishes to think about anything beyond work, pay day, Friday and Saturday nights, drinking alcohol, football (the men), pop music (the girls), family (the slightly older ones), and sex.

I acknowledged to myself in that instant that Leanne might not be as empty headed as she seems.

On spiritual matters, Bel will talk about the belief system of the Roman Catholic Church. This agency claims Jesus Christ as its founding member, yet the bulk of what is taught revolves around concepts dreamed up before the time of Jesus. Much of the doctrine is in direct conflict with his teachings and lifestyle as presented in scripture. The same goes for all the religions that have been spun off from this central organisation.

If Jesus were to return to the Earth in human form, he would condemn the hypocrisy of the Clergy as he did that of the Pharisees. And they would loathe him for it – and make sure he is silenced.

Bel claims to believe that when she dies, a spirit soul will survive the death of her body and live eternally alongside the resurrected Christ in the Father's dimension.

176

Yet, the way she speaks, the way she conducts herself, the things she focuses her life on, and the issues most important to her all belie that claim. She does not really believe she is destined for immortality with Christ, nor does she believe that her ancestors are already in such a state. She thinks she will live a brief span, physically deteriorate to the point that her body expires, and cease to exist.

They all do.

Leanne has no spiritual beliefs that I can discern.

Clint is an atheist (derived from Greek: Theo means God. Therefore a theist believes in and promotes the concept of God, and an atheist believes that God does not exist). He accepts and embraces the truth about his fleeting lifespan and seems unconcerned by it.

Walter fantasises about life evolving of its own accord without any intelligent guiding hand (as taught by Professor Dawkins in his book *The Selfish Gene*) but on other planets in outer space.

'If it happened here, it could happen on other worlds,' he says. I told him it didn't happen here, but that did not dissuade him. He loves to theorise about whether or not these beings have visited Earth, and if not, whether they will ever do so. I cannot be sure if he actually believes these things or just enjoys indulging in fanciful stories.

Lorraine just jokes about spirituality. Again I cannot discern what she actually thinks about the origin or purpose of life.

Ainsley is an atheist, but, unlike Clint, who has chosen by way of reason to be a Marxist, he was raised by 'humanist' parents and thus has grown up almost devoid of God. He understands the concept, of course, but does not see it in the natural world.

Gary is like Kirsty, in that he not only disbelieves religious texts like the Bible and Qur'an, but is embittered by the suffering he has experienced in his own life and that which he has witnessed via the media. He hates the whole

177

notion of God and would like to see it eradicated from the human psyche.

And Ralph? 'Bleeding Jesus Christ!' says it all.

Waris is a Buddhist. He says he does not believe in a Creator God and isn't religious in the true sense of the word; yet he chants prayers, lights candles and directs his meditations towards a statue of Buddha.

Like Bel, he thinks all humans have a spirit soul which survives the death of the body. Unlike Bel, he doesn't expect to go to another dimension. He says we have all existed previously in lives that we cannot remember, and each time we die, our soul migrates and is reborn as another person, an animal, or even a plant. Who or what we come back as is determined by how we live our current life. I asked him who decides if it isn't God, and he said, 'Fate,' which doesn't really answer the question.

I asked him what purpose being reborn time and time again would serve, and he said it was to attain 'Nirvana', a state of non-existence with no thoughts, no memories, and no emotions.

That's death, isn't it?

So we go through an almost endless cycle of rebirth in different forms just to finish up completely dead?

I also asked how we are supposed to strive for this condition if we have no memory of our previous lives. How can we be sure we are not repeating the same errors? Then he started talking about race memory and how key memories are retained by the soul. I think he was just making it up by this point and I grew weary of the discussion.

The person who intrigues me most is Mo. He is very open about his faith in the Qur'an. He heralds the book as the Word of God and says it complements the Bible, even though a good portion of it is in direct contradiction (I bought a copy in spite of Kirsty's protests!).

Adam is the father of the human race, but Jesus is a prophet rather than the Son of God. The whole volume was written by the prophet Muhammad over an estimated twenty years, following a series of revelations from God via the angel Gabriel. Amazingly it has a built-in clause which says that if a later verse contradicts an earlier one the reader must accept the later one.

There are no miracles or special signs in the Qur'an. Yet it is traditionally believed that Muhammad did perform some. While mountains and lakes burning with fire and strange nightmarish creatures are employed in the Bible as metaphors, in the traditional legends of Islam, Muhammad literally engages trees and mountains in conversation.

The Qur'an agrees with much of the early Bible record and Abraham is considered to be of extreme importance. However, while in the Bible the genetic line producing Christ descends from Abraham's son Isaac (whose own son is Israel), in the Qur'an the true worshippers of the Father descend from Ishmael, the son Abraham had with his servant girl Hagar.

Faithful Muslims will be blessed with eternal life in Heaven, while the wicked and godless will burn, their flesh melting off, restoring back, and melting off again, over and over, for all eternity in an underground place of blazing torment.

There is great animosity between the Jews and the Muslims. Both claim to be the people of God. Many a war has been fought over these claims, millions have died as a result, and yet both peoples are descended from the same ancestor, Abraham. They are, in effect, brothers and sisters.

Both factions have a hatred for orthodox Christianity, it having butchered their peoples in times past. The Roman Catholic Church invaded many lands and murdered those who refused to embrace their form of religion. To keep people in ignorance they kept the scriptures in the dead language of Latin, and if anyone dared to translate them, those individuals were burned to death. And all this in the name of Jesus Christ!

I see similarities between corrupted Christianity and Islam: heavy emphasis on ritual and the scrupulous observance of days, seasons, months and years.

Mo claims to hold all of this dear, following the rituals with strict adherence, and yet flouts the basic principles of spirituality. I've heard him blaspheme on many occasions, whispering 'God' under his breath when angered, 'Oh my God' when surprised, and 'Jesus!' when shocked. He joins in all of the godless banter in the canteen. But, interestingly, he never uses Muhammad's name as a curse word.

I'm not saying that all Muslims have double standards, just as not all Jews and Christians have double standards. But there are a hell of a lot who do, and Mo is one of them.

Hell 1. Derived from the Greek word Hades. Denotes the grave to which all animals and humans go.

Hell 2. Derived from the Greek word Gehenna. Denotes a burning rubbish tip near Jerusalem in the first century.

Mo, like Bel, draws a certain comfort from his belief system, but he too is open to persuasion. He is utterly fascinated by my truths, I can tell.

It's as if none of them really know what to believe.

And so I find that I cannot blame any of them for giving so much emphasis to the onset of spring and the anniversaries of their births. They are, all of them, very aware that they have been born to die. Their whole approach to life is governed by the fundamental truth that they shall certainly die. The knowledge haunts them every day. It's in their art and literature. They are obsessed with it. They are prisoners of their own condition.

It is very sad.

I made a mistake today, and I think it might have been a serious one. It was at lunch time as the smokers collected up their sandwiches, and in retrospect I see that I was being set up as the butt of a joke – again. They were all giggling and sniggering, and then Lorraine called over to me. 'Hey, God Squad!'

'What?'

'What did Jesus say when he was dragging his cross through the crowds?'

The tone implied a riddle rather than a genuine question. 'I don't know,' I said, bored stiff by her primitiveness. 'What did Jesus say when he was dragging his cross through the crowds?'

Lorraine kept as composed as she could. 'He said, "Fuckin' 'ell. If I knew the carnival was going to be like this, I would have stayed at home!"'

The reaction of her audience was immediate. They roared with laughter. Leanne held her tummy; Bel shook her head in a weak attempt not to laugh, while Clint and Gary exchanged glances and pointed at me. Ralph wiped tears from his eyes, his face red and full. Even Kirsty had to turn her back, her shoulders bobbing uncontrollably.

My reaction was also immediate.

Rage boiled in the pit of my stomach, rose into my chest and filled my head. My nostrils flared and my eyes bulged. I was consumed and driven with a fury I had never before known.

'Is there *any* reason why *any* of you should be permitted to *live*?!'

In that moment I was engulfed by a hatred for them all. And, in their shocked silence, I saw that the feeling was mutual. Kirsty was deeply disturbed by my outburst and later told me I should not have said it.

I am wishing I hadn't.

JUNE 30

Just come back from a week in Grasmere. It really is the most lovely place. I took Kirsty to see Margaret, who was delighted to find that I have 'landed on my feet.'

I also took her up the path leading to Easedale Tarn and to the spot where I first stepped foot on this world's soil.

'Just think', I enthused. 'Right here on a different dimensional plane is Elohah Village. My wife, and all my generations of children are all here.'

And then I broke down crying. Kirsty ignored me and continued on to Easedale Tarn, and I had no choice but to follow.

We also visited Windermere and Ambleside and went on a boat. In the evenings we walked hand in hand around Grasmere village, with its trails and the fields. It really was lovely.

Kirsty was different again, in her approach to the guesthouse owners and the shop keepers, the bus drivers and the people in the streets, smiling and being polite. And she never used a single curse word – well, apart from oft times when alone with me. But even then it was much milder. I felt the need to broach the subject.

'I don't change personality,' she countered, trying hard not to be offended.

'You do,' I pressed. 'When it is just me and you together you talk one way, when you're at work you talk more like our workmates, and now you're in Grasmere you smile and say hello to people on the road.'

'When in Rome you do as the Romans do,' Kirsty said, as if it explained everything.

'What?'

'It's a skill,' she said. 'Granted it's one you don't have.' I could not tell if it was supposed to be humorous or if she meant it literally.

'A skill?' I said. 'How can being a traitor to your own self be a skill?'

'I'm not a traitor to myself.'

'You are,' I asserted. 'At work you laugh at comments that you don't really think are funny. Is it because you want their approval?'

She didn't like that, I could tell. She took a deep breath and grasped my arm. 'Look Baz, they're called social skills: the art of interacting and integrating.'

'The art of being false,' I countered. 'The art of cowardice and lies. You people are so afraid of what your peers think. And you know what the lunacy of it is? You all worry the same thing about one another. And that's how your unspoken but mutually agreed social rules have come about. You are all so paranoid and insecure.'

I shook myself free of her hand and headed to the fields. She just stood there watching as I marched off.

I deeply regret doing this. She has been more of a sister to me than my own sisters back home. And I love her for it.

Thankfully, the remainder of the week was spent enjoying walks and boats and meals and shopping. And lots of laughter.

I don't want to go back to work.

JULY 31

Life at the factory continues, as tawdry as ever. I hate it. Kirsty says I would be much better off in an office job because in an office there is a certain professionalism required, a standard. More pretend etiquette, but I would welcome it right now.

Everything was fine until Kirsty contracted what she calls a summer cold, which is a malfunction in the glands controlling the production of mucus. On Thursday her eyes and nose were streaming so much she phoned work and told them she was not going in. And so, for the first time, I went to work alone.

Morning break came, and there was the usual confrontation. The smokers took their cigarettes and coffees to the shelter, and then Lorraine began her torment. 'I bet Kirsty is glad to be rid of you at last,' she said, nice and loud.

Gary lowered his paper. 'I bet she is.' His paper returned to its position.

I said nothing.

'Do you know she's not been on the razzle once since he shacked up with her?'

Ainsley was genuinely surprised. 'What, never?'

'Never.'

'I'm not sure I could live with that,' he said, thinking aloud. 'I like a glass of wine.' He grinned at me. 'Or three.'

I attempted to smile in return, but it was half-hearted, which, in retrospect is a shame because Ainsley is the only person in the place who truly does not have any issues with me. He disagrees with what he calls my 'world view', but he does not hate me for it.

Lorraine continued. 'She's not been with a fella for months, she never goes on the town; she has no life.' She glared at me. 'Don't you feel guilty, God Squad? You've ruined her life since she rescued you from the gutter.'

Clint arrived and re-boiled the kettle. Lorraine called over to him. 'Clint, I was just saying God Squad was rescued from the gutter by our Kirsty.'

He didn't want to get involved, keeping his back to us. 'Did she? That's very generous of her.'

'Yeah.' She wrinkled her nose and I saw hatred in her eyes. I don't think I have ever felt so despised by another human being. 'You're fucking killing her, God Squad. You need to get out of there and let her live her life. She's thirty next year. You should let her get down the clubs and go

184

with as many blokes as she can. Let her enjoy herself, for God's sake.'

At that point I got up from my seat, threw my coffee and cup in the sink, and made for the exit, Lorraine's raucous laughter echoing behind me. Someone else followed. I heard their chair scrape on the floor and I made haste down the stairs to the yard outside.

My pursuer turned out to be Mo. 'Baz, it's me!' he called. 'Ignore her, she's a bitch.'

Female dog.

I kicked a lone crate in anger. It skidded across the tarmac ground and fell on its side. 'I can't take much more of this fucking godforsaken bloody place!!'

Mo remained standing at a distance. 'Baz, man,' he said, more than a little startled. 'This isn't like you. You don't swear.'

The truth of his words hit me like a slap in the face and I wept. Mo took a couple of steps forward. 'You're not like anyone else I have ever met.'

I half laughed, half cried. 'You really have no idea how true that is.'

'And there you go again, those cryptic statements. You talk as if you're from one of Walter's alien planets.' He stood opposite me and I wiped my eyes with my sleeve. He offered a hanky and I blew my nose. 'And when you said "this godforsaken place" just then. You didn't mean the factory, did you? You meant the whole world.'

I croaked a response. 'It is God-forsaken.' I looked up at the deep blue of the sky. 'Father, why have you forsaken me?'

'There you go again,' Mo said with a gasp. 'Who are you? What do you see yourself as? Some kinda messiah or prophet?'

I looked at him. He was very puzzled, that much was clear. 'I see everything in this world as it really is,' I told him. 'You have tried every form of Government there is, from communism to capitalism to monarchy to dictatorship. And none of them have truly worked.'

Mo took exception to that. 'Hey, hang on, Baz, man. I'd rather live in this country under this Government than some others I could mention. I wanna be free.'

Free? I tried not to laugh. 'You are a slave.'

No answer to that one.

'You are a slave to the system and a slave to yourself. You all are. Your Governments fail because you are all greedy and selfish.'

I sensed a feeling in him. Exasperation. He was exasperated. 'What, everyone?'

'Everyone,' I said. 'None of them can be trusted.'

'Oh, Baz, man. You can't go living your life like that.'

'Why not?'

'It's so depressing.'

I countered, 'And it's so true.'

'Don't you have faith in *anything?*'

In that moment I realised what he was implying was right. It took a second or two to hit me, but Mo had pinpointed something in me, a fact I had not ever considered. But it was true. From the moment I severed contact with the Father. 'No,' I said simply. 'I don't have faith in anything. Not here, not in this world.'

'So they're all corrupt, all the politicians, everyone?'

'Yes,' I said. I could see anger in his eyes. This is nothing particular to him. They are all the same: liars believing their own lies. So used to hearing excrement, they spout it out themselves and don't even notice.

I told him, 'I'm sure young men and women are sincere when they first enter politics, but once they're in, and certainly once they're in power, they realise that none of it is as simple as ever they thought. The issues cannot be settled quickly and simply, the answers are not going to be easy. And that's when they sell out. They get a taste for the power, for the importance that they feel, for the limousines and free lunches, for the favours and the sex. They sell out to the corruption within themselves. Then all they want is to maintain that power.'

Mo stared at me, mouth agape. 'God,' he breathed. 'You really have thought this through.'

'I have.'

'So what's the answer?'

Oh, that was easy enough, but not at all popular. 'You must do things the Father's way. It is the only way that works.'

'The Father?' Mo repeated. 'You mean God, right?'

'Yes. Where I come from, everything is in harmony with the Father's design, and as a result it is perfect.'

More exasperation. 'But we've *had* rule by religion. It doesn't work.'

'Ah, well, that's because your religious leaders are corrupt too. They're not interested in the Father.'

He laughed out loud, but it wasn't a wholesome hearty laugh, or an incredulous laugh. It was a knowing, troubled laugh. 'How can you say that?'

I smiled into his expectant eyes. 'They're not. And deep down you know they're not. All of you do, deep down. It's why you secretly hate them. Through the ages religious leaders have lorded their authority over the ordinary people. Again, they might well have been sincere in their youth, but many of them, and certainly all who hold political office, are in it for the power first and foremost.'

Mo was shaking with emotion. 'But, but,' he breathed. 'But if you believe in God, you must see some value in spirituality.'

'Oh, I do.' He was completely baffled now. I smiled as softly as I could. 'But you all think you've got the one true path. The Jews because they were chosen by the Father to represent him, the Muslims because God revealed the truth to Muhammad, the Catholics because they were the first orthodox Christian organisation. The Latter Day Saints are expecting Christ's kingdom to be built in their Salt Lake City, the Born Again Christians claim to be already saved, and the atheists believe we make our own path and then die and are forgotten, as though we had never lived in the first place.'

'But isn't that the beauty of diversity, the freedom to choose?'

I countered the question with another question. 'How can being in confusion be beautiful? It is pitiful. You all are pitiful. Inside I weep for you.'

He was about to offer an angry retort, but I was on a roll now. 'When you're not killing one another with your bare hands, you are dropping bombs on one another, and when you're not doing that you are driving animals to extinction, and destroying rainforests, pumping filth into the atmosphere and poisoning the seas. I don't know why the Father hasn't just stamped you all out and given up.'

'He obviously sees something in us you don't,' Mo said. Then he shook his head. 'What am I doing? I'm acting as if you're not one of us. You always say "you" when you mean "we".'

'Oh, I know what I mean,' I told him. 'You asked where I come from. I'm from the world where Adam and Eve did not eat the fruit. They passed the test of loyalty. The corrupted spirit son, the one you call Satan, was destroyed, and the human family was granted to eat from the Tree of Life, in symbol of being given unending life. I have lived for nine hundred and thirty-six years in a global paradise where all my ancestors still walk the Earth, where no one dies, and where all progress and advancement is guided by the Father: a perfect world.'

Mo frowned. 'You mean in another life? Like Waris and his reincarnation?'

'No, I mean literally, like a couple of months ago.' I baulked at my own stupidity. 'If I had listened to the Father, I would never have got stuck here.'

'What?' Mo was finding it all too much, but I could not help myself in my frustration. 'You mean you have spoken to God, like, direct?'

'Yes.'

'Like Abraham did?'

I nodded, staring at the sky. 'Like Abraham did.'

The bell rang and the smokers moved out from their shelter toward the main door. Mo scurried off. With some hesitancy I walked back to the factory.

Everything was fine. Until the filler broke down. Mr Hulton-Little told Aaron that he would have to find jobs for us to do while the fitters worked on the line. The girls were given cleaning equipment, the warehouse lads brushed the warehouse floor, and Aaron and I climbed onto the tank which fed the filler. We pulled off the top panel and peered inside.

'Mm,' Aaron mused. 'It's still half full. If we can't get the line going soon, we might have to release the tank and wash it out. Perhaps send everyone home early. Best check with the boss. Wait here.'

I waited.

And then it happened.

A group of workers congregated at the base of the steel steps. Gary, Lorraine, Walter, Ralph, Mo, Bel, Leanne, Waris, and a couple of teenagers from the warehouse. They all looked angry, their eyes full of hatred. Gary shouted up. 'Think you're better than us, don't you, God Squad?'

I choked. 'No.'

'Yeah you do!' It was Lorraine. 'You think you're perfect. Mo told Clint and Clint let it slip. You're perfect and we are the doomed sinners.'

Mo? I thought I could trust him.

Leanne started her fake laughter. 'Christ, I'm a sinner and proud of it! Ha, ha.' Everybody jeered their approval. 'You ask that Paki I went with on Saturday night!'

I said nothing.

189

'From another world, eh, God Squad?' It was Gary again. 'A perfect world?'

'Another dimension.' I could not resist it.

Leanne's eyes bulged and she addressed the others in astonishment. 'Christ, he really does believe it!'

Mo snarled, 'I told you he does. Thinks he's the second coming or summat.'

Gary put a foot on the bottom rung. 'He thinks he's better than us.'

I AM better than you.

Suddenly Gary was making his way up, and the others were following. I backtracked as far as I could along the gangway. 'Let's get him!' I heard Gary say. 'Fucking religious nutter.'

Cheers were followed by the clanging of metal, and before I could think of a possible escape route, they were bearing down upon me. 'Take his legs,' Gary commanded and the two warehouse lads did so. Gary himself grabbed my left arm while Mo took my right.

Before I knew what was happening I found myself suspended in the air, the dizzying drop below me. I panicked and wriggled and fought. 'Help! Help! Aaron! Mr Hulton-Little!!!' The ensemble roared with laughter.

Lorraine shouted. 'A one, ar, two, ar.' They swung me to and fro in time to her voice. 'Three!' And on three dropped me into the tank.

I thudded to the bottom, instantly immersed in baked beans. I coughed and spluttered for air, only to be met with the sickening stench of tomato sauce and more raucous laughter.

'Bleeding Jesus!' I heard Ralph jeer. 'He's had that coming a long time.' Suddenly the mood was broken and I could hear rushing and feet clanging on metal. Then silence.

My eyes adjusted to the darkness of the tank. I could feel the bean mixture sliding down my neck and back as I attempted to stand. I reached up to the light, the roof of the factory all bright and appealing, but as soon as I attempted to climb up, my feet gave way and I fell back on my bottom. This was greeted by more laughter.

A few beans dropped from my matted hair. It was awful.

More clanging of metal. Two pairs of footsteps. A face appeared in the opening. 'Oh, Baz.' It was Ainsley. 'Can you stand?'

'Yes,' I said.

'OK.' He turned to another person. 'Sure you'll be able to keep me steady?'

'I am sure, son.' It was Clint.

And so I stood up, slowly and precisely, as Ainsley lowered himself gradually through the opening. He grabbed my arms and then called out to Clint. 'Right, pull!'

Ainsley hauled me up, yelping as his stomach scraped across the sharp ridge of the metal frame. He staggered backwards into Clint's arms. I grabbed the edges of the opening and dragged myself up and out.

'I'm sorry they did this to you,' Ainsley said as I lowered myself onto the gangway carefully. I felt nothing but relief and gratitude.

Kirsty insisted that I go into work as normal today, but I refused. I could not face the humiliation. Then Mr Hulton-Little phoned and said Clint had told him what had happened and that he had disciplined those involved. I felt better at knowing that.

Of course, he only phoned because we have got behind with production and he needs a complete workforce to get back on target. That said, I went in and everyone was very nice to me. Ainsley and Clint are my closest friends now.

JULY 31 (b)

Kirsty had the latest issue of *New Scientist* magazine waiting for me when I got home this evening, which is lovely of her.

I was greatly angered when I found Dr Jonathan Matthews' article on the possibility of harnessing the life force of plants and trees 'and maybe even animals and people' as a means of 'utilising a new kind of energy'.

'He's stolen my proposal!' I seethed.

Kirsty was in-between blowing her nose and lighting a cigarette. 'What is it?'

'I wrote to Dr Jonathan Matthews and gave him a few pointers about how one can harness natural energies including the life force of living things and meld it with your own technology,' I explained. 'I was hoping he might be able to help me generate a porthole to get me back home.'

As was her custom, Kirsty ignored my references to Elohah Village and drew hard on her cigarette. 'And?'

'And he's written the piece up as his own.' I was livid. 'He stole my idea and published it as his own. The bastard!'

Kirsty sat up, choking and laughing at the same time. 'Baz! You're setting me a bad example!' She grinned mischievously. 'You naughty man.'

I grinned back, but inside I was furious.

I still am.

AUGUST 5

Kirsty's mother has found out about me. A mutual friend spotted us walking in the park and now her mother has invited us for dinner. The day for this will be a Sunday.

Kirsty is not happy about this, but she has agreed.

Personally, I'm rather looking forward to meeting her mother.

AUGUST 28

'Now, what did I tell you?' Kirsty asked as we approached the door of the house.

I recalled the instruction. 'I mustn't let her get inside my head. I mustn't tell her anything that could be used as ammunition against me, and more to the point, you.'

'Did I really put it like that?'

'Yes.'

'Word for word?'

'Yes.'

She exhaled noisily. 'I have a feeling this is not going to be good. She'll read you like a book. It's obvious what you are.'

'It is?'

'Yes,' she said. 'You're a child.'

The house is a semi-detached. It looks much better than Kirsty's flat. Kirsty's mother is called Mary Ingham, and Mary has two floors with a number of rooms all to herself. The house is nicely decorated, the furniture is of a much higher quality, and there are many plants, large and small.

Plants! I was in my element as soon as I walked through the door.

Kirsty called her mother and Mary scurried into view, eager to get a look at me. 'So this is Barry, is it?'

'I am Barry,' I told her. 'Barry Maher, Baz for short.'

Mary cocked her head as a dog does when differentiating sounds. 'An interesting accent you have, dear.' She studied me from the top of my head to the boots on my feet. 'My, my, what a handsome specimen. You really have done very well for yourself, Kirsty, dear. Your father would approve.'

193

Kirsty twirled on her heels. 'Don't start!'

'Don't start what?'

'Don't start using Dad on me.'

Mary gave a subtle laugh and shook her head. 'I don't know, Barry,' she said, walking into the living room. 'She's so touchy. I don't know how you put up with it.'

'I find your daughter delightful,' I told her. 'She is a great credit to you.'

Mary gestured that I sit. I did. 'Such a well spoken young man. Kirsty has never brought anybody like you home before.'

'I am indebted to her for doing so.'

'Really?'

Kirsty changed the subject. I trusted her judgement. 'Baz is into plants, Mum,' she said. 'Big time.'

Mary looked at me keenly. 'Are you really, Baz?'

'I am.'

'I love them. I go to the garden centre every week and pick up a new one.'

I surveyed the room. There were plants of varying sizes all over, nicely arranged to enhance their surroundings, but plenty of them nonetheless; plants in baskets, plants on the shelves and mantelpiece, large plants in buckets in the corners of the room.

It might just be enough, I thought.

There was a knock at the door. Mary got up. 'That will be our Steve.'

Kirsty seemed alarmed. 'You invited Steve?'

'Of course,' Mary smiled. 'We can't have a family meal without your brother, can we?'

Kirsty scowled as her mother went to the door. 'I bet Jennifer and the baby aren't with him, though, eh Mum!'

She was right. Steve had come alone. We sat around the big table in the dining room. The food was good. I complimented Mary on her cooking. After a while Steve began asking questions about my country of origin.

'I'm from Finland,' I lied.

'Finland?' Steve said. 'I went there with some lads from uni. Which part are you from?'

'The city,' I said.

Kirsty tried to cut in again, but Mary spoke across her. 'And what brings you to England?'

'Work,' I said.

'Work?'

'Yes.'

'And where do you work?'

'At Stein's. Kirsty got me the job.'

Mary smiled. 'Ah, that's nice.' She smiled at Kirsty. 'Can I take your plate, love?'

Steve brought over the sweet, a very tasty trifle. I wasted no time in getting stuck in. It was delicious.

Another question, this time directed at Kirsty. 'How did you two meet?'

Kirsty glared at her mother in silence. I kept looking at the Yucca plant in the corner and the potted plants in the kitchen.

To break the silence I said, 'When I arrived I had nowhere to live. I was starving on the streets. It was Kirsty who came to my aid.'

My heroine rested her forehead in the palm of her hand. Embarrassed perhaps?

Steve looked at her, his face almost a picture of contempt. 'God, I bet I know where this is going.'

Kirsty refused to catch his eye and just stared at the table. 'Don't start, Steve.'

'Another waif and stray, sis?'

She turned, violent with fury. 'No, actually. I was being mugged, set upon by a gang of layabouts. They were after my bag and cards. And Baz chased them off.'

'This is true,' I confirmed. 'And Kirsty took me home.'

'I knew it,' Steve sneered.

195

Mary gave more of a snigger, a snort, and a mocking smile. The eyes were like those of Lorraine before her discipline. They dazzled with a morbid enjoyment. 'Well,' she said. 'Well you bloody fool.'

'Mum.' Kirsty was shaking now, her voice a tremor, her blue eyes glassy with tears. 'Mum, leave it.'

'You took in a loser off the streets, it cost you your career, and now you've done it again.'

'Mother.'

'You're like your father,' Mary continued. 'He was a fool too.'

Kirsty threw back her chair, made for her bag, took her cigarettes and lighter, and slid a single white stick from the packet. The action was swift and precise after years of practice. 'I need a cigarette.'

'You'd better get out back then,' Mary pointed an accusing finger. 'Don't light up in here.'

'Don't worry, I won't.'

Mary turned to her son. 'Go and see her.' He did as instructed. Then Mary looked at me. 'You really have no idea, do you? No wonder she has you around.'

I nodded my agreement. 'She has lost the ability to trust. I do not blame her.'

'You don't?'

'No.'

'Why?'

'Because so many people have abused her. The system, individuals within it.'

She snorted again, dismissing my observation. I looked her right in the eye. 'I think it all started with her Uncle Tim, though, don't you?'

The snorting stopped. 'What has she told you?'

'Enough.'

'Tim's my brother.'

I nodded once. 'I know.'

196

I too could use words and tones and silences to great effect. It's an art, one of this world's absurd 'skills', but handy when learned.

It had the desired effect as well. Mary headed for the backyard. 'Kirsty!'

A great deal of shouting and crying ensued. This was my chance. I pulled down the blind in the kitchen, gathered as many plants together as I could, rolled in the four larger plants from the living room, and the Yucca from the corner. Then I shook them from their pots, exposing their roots.

In all my time in this corrupted world, I had not forgotten how to combine the plants together to form a mini circuit. All I needed now was some raw power and a connection with the human mind. I used the flex from the kettle, the power from the toaster, the food blender and the microwave, and a helmet made from the roots of a pot plant.

And then I turned on my menagerie.

Sparks flew, the room hummed with electricity, my head shuddered and vibrated, but I was not for giving in. I could feel my brain reacting and interacting, the life force of the natural elements around me pulsating. The veins in the leaves became more pronounced, the green colour began to fade. 'Come on!' I screamed. *'Come on!'*

And there they were. Tiny pinpricks of blue and green, floating like fairy dust right before my eyes. I wanted to reach out, but I dared not. My head was frying but I could not switch off.

A voice, shrieked. 'Christ almighty! What the hell are you playing at?' Mary stared in horror. The plants burst into flames. My hair curled up, but I could not switch off. I didn't want to. I could smell the fragrances of home. Kirsty was frozen, beautified by her awe.

Steve lunged at the plug of the kettle and yanked it free. Then he scrambled to the blender, the toaster and the microwave, and suddenly all was silent. The plants wilted, and so did I.

'It works,' I whispered. 'It *will* work. I can get back.'

Mary stared at me, for the first time speechless.

Steve's face was more of a scowl. 'You mad bastard. What were you trying to do?' He turned to Kirsty. 'What's wrong with you, sis? What is it with these creeps?'

Kirsty ignored them both. Her voice was level and calm. She took my hand. 'Baz. What were those things floating about, those little lights?'

'Natural light,' I explained. 'Real in this room'.

'Tiny lights,' Kirsty said, trying to comprehend. 'The top ones blue, the ones underneath green. And could I hear a bird squawking? Like a parrot or something?'

I smiled. 'The blue is the sky, the green is grass. And yes, that was a parrot.' I looked into her soft eyes. 'Here, but not here. In this room on this world in this time, but not.'

Kirsty's eyes widened and she stared at the space where the pinpricks of alternate reality had hung suspended. Her voice was a whisper. 'Your world.'

'Yes.' I nodded. 'My world.'

It goes without saying that we were ordered to leave Mary's house. Kirsty feared that her mother might involve the police, but she didn't. And I knew she wouldn't, because I knew she had seen the spectacle for herself, as had Steve. They were frightened of me, and that fear kept them at bay along with their threats. So long as we remained estranged from them, we would be safe.

'I want to help you, Baz,' Kirsty said as we walked home. 'I want to help you get back to where you come from.'

'I'll need more than your help,' I told her. 'But I appreciate the offer. It is nice to know that you believe me at last.'

'Well, seeing is believing,' she said. 'That has always been my yardstick.'

'I wish the Father would open a portal for me.'

Kirsty stopped dead. 'Look, Baz. I believe you're from this other dimension. But can we keep our agreement about God for now?'

'You do not want me to talk of him, even though you are persuaded?' I did not understand.

'I believe you are from this other dimension, this alien community you talk about. But conversations with God? Well –' She broke off, shaking her head. 'Any number of things could explain your hearing a disembodied voice.'

I smiled. '*The Wizard of Oz*?'

'In a way, yes.' She looked apologetic, and I felt moved to put my arm around her shoulder.

'All right,' I said. 'The agreement stands. No blasphemies from you, and no God from me.'

We continued to walk, thrilled to be in one another's company.

AUGUST 28 (b)

Kirsty is fascinated by my diary. 'Is that really ancient Hebrew?' she's just asked. Her interest in the *Tonight* programme cannot be maintained. She's watching me now and has no idea at all what I am writing.

I have just told her it is earlier than ancient Hebrew, a purer form.

'Read it to me,' she begs and I just laugh. But she is unrelenting. 'Why not translate it into English so everyone can read it? No, go on. Why not? You could have it published.'

'Published? For the world at large?'

'Why not?'

I am considering titles for the work. 'How about *The World of Lies*?'

'My world, I presume?'

'Of course.'

'Mm, too direct. It's unattractive.'

'Ha! Like your world!' I am reconsidering. 'All right, what about *The Treacherous Planet*?'

'No, it's still too negative.' She's thinking. 'I think it should reflect you.'

'*A Lamb Among Wolves*.'

She's clicked her fingers. Her smile is instantly beautiful. '*Parallel Man*!'

'Parallel Man?'

'Yes! *The Diary of a Parallel Man*. How's that?'

Mm, I like it. 'I like it.'

Maybe I will translate it for her, just before I leave.

SEPTEMBER 11

What a day. The minds of all and sundry have been preoccupied with something called Nine Eleven. I now realise that they are referring to the ninth month and the eleventh day. At eleven o'clock the factory ground to a halt. Everybody stopped moving and speaking. Most stared ahead in a trance with dour expressions on their faces remembering those who had died.

The newspapers were full of it, and so was the canteen. I remained quiet, knowing instinctively that my views would provoke hostility. And then I was asked outright, by Ainsley, of all people.

'It is diabolical,' I said, keeping my comments as generic as possible. 'To kill another human being because he does not hold the same world view. Your lives...' I rephrased this bit. 'Our lives are so fleeting to begin with, to deliberately bring a life to an end prematurely. It's... well, it's hard to grasp.'

They all looked at me, puzzled. Somehow I don't think I had answered the question in the way they were expecting. Maybe in their minds I did not answer it at all.

Only now, this evening at home, do I fully comprehend the horror of what they were memorialising. There have been references to the event on the television news, with relatives of those killed offering tearful reminiscences. Kirsty and I have just finished watching a documentary about the tragedy.

A group of individuals had embraced a view of the Qur'an not held by the wider Muslim community, namely that God wishes all non-Muslims dead, and in particular those in the 'Decadent West'. They regarded the Governments and populace of more affluent countries to be corrupted. They also believed themselves to be devoted to the cause of the One True God, Allah, and determined to carry out his will. In their minds his will involved the overthrow of the United States of America as a world power.

To achieve their ends they boarded a number of aeroplanes destined for key areas in America. These were the twin towers of the World Trade Center (a symbol of America's commerce), the Pentagon (a five sided building used by the governing body) and the White House (the building in which the President lives and which symbolises the heart of America's Government).

The plan of the believers was to take over control of the aeroplanes and pilot them into the buildings, causing them to collapse, and in the case of the Pentagon and White House, kill key members of the Government and hopefully the President himself.

This would, of course, result in the deaths of the believers too, but this did not concern them since they were convinced God would bless their disembodied spirit souls with eternal life in a heavenly paradise.

The documentary contained some disturbing images. The live action recordings of the great passenger planes crashing into the twin towers were wholly sickening. Kirsty mumbled 'God' a few times under her breath. I vomited.

Sound recordings of people on the planes phoning their relatives to tell them they were about to die were also played. The shaky weeping voices, and most disturbing of all, the voices of children, embedded themselves in my mind. I still hear them now.

The authorities tried to evacuate the towers, but many people were trapped. More deeply overwhelming images had been captured on camera. I watched as individuals, faced with the certainty of being crushed by the rooms in which they were trapped as they caved in, chose to jump from the windows to their deaths. One of the towers collapsed in its entirety, killing everyone inside, followed a while later by the other.

Survivors of the tragedy were seen on their hands and knees thanking God for their lives.

The plane heading for the Pentagon crashed into one of the five walls. The other one, headed for the White House, crashed before it reached its target. It is felt that passengers confronted the terrorists and sabotaged the mission.

This sort of behaviour can be traced right back to the first murder on human record. Since that time, people have fought over possessions, land, political views and religious belief. On nearly every occasion, if religion has not been the direct cause, it has been effectively used by politicians to stoke up hatred for the perceived enemy.

The Father would not approve of any of this, even less so any war conducted in his name. The religionists are more reprehensible than anyone else in this regard.

The people of this world have employed all manner of device at their disposal, from bows and arrows, horses, metal armour, to explosives projected from guns and cannons, to aeroplanes dropping bombs, computer driven missiles; and scientific breakthroughs in splitting hydrogen atoms have led to the murder of thousands in an instant.

Interestingly, only the United States of America have ever employed the latter in warfare.

Hypocrites.

SEPTEMBER 30

Christmas is coming. It's a sort of festival. People at work are very excited about it, Bel and Leanne in particular. Lorraine moans about all the shopping she's going to have to do and says she's only just paid off her debts from last year. Gary is only doing it for the kids. Clint has no opinion one way or another.

The word Christmas is derived from 'Christ's Mass', a Roman Catholic term. Strictly speaking, Christ's Mass would be the time when Jesus died, but I couldn't be bothered telling them this. For, according to Kirsty, Christmas is a celebration of, not the death, but the birth of Jesus Christ.

Why do they celebrate the birth of someone they either a) don't believe existed, b) believe existed but wasn't the Son of God, c) believe was the Son of God but don't adhere to his teachings?

It is said that Jesus was born on December 25, that he was visited by three wise men who bestowed gifts upon him, and in celebration today, parents wrap up gifts in colourful paper and give them to their children. The date is a national holiday (derived from 'holy day'), families get together for a meal, and then in the evenings many indulge heavily in food and alcoholic drinks.

However, according to my encyclopaedias, Christmas has nothing to do with Jesus at all. It originates with an ancient Roman celebration in honour of their imagined sun god. The festival was held in late December, involved the exchanging of gifts and indulgence at wild parties. The

203

parties often descended into orgies where individuals and groups of individuals would have sex with one another, rather like those on the porn web sites.

The Bible doesn't give the date of Jesus' birth, but it does condemn the fusing of false man-made beliefs with its truth – assuming that the Bible itself is not man-made, of course.

It seems that, as with Easter earlier in the year, some three hundred years after Jesus, the orthodox churches blended the winter festival with the account of Christ's birth in an attempt to popularise Christianity. Later other ingredients were added, such as a mysterious benefactor who visits the homes of children with sacks of presents on Christmas Eve, and a fir tree decorated with lights (again, fir trees are not commonplace in Bethlehem).

While I remained silent on this subject at work, I did ask Kirsty today. She says she doesn't care what its origins are.

And, it seems, neither do my workmates, whether they be Christian, Muslim, Marxist, or atheist. All are eagerly looking forward to it.

I *do* care. A lot.

OCTOBER 31

I keep crying, silently. I've learned to do that. People do not empathise with my emotional outbursts, largely because they have become so desensitised to the terrors and unnaturalness of their world. But what a mixed-up day it has been.

Just before leaving for work, Kirsty was able to pick up the post. It came early that morning (October 26) for some reason. And lo and behold one of the letters was a report from a 'private investigator.'

'I spent a good dollop of our combined savings hiring him,' Kirsty said.

I was confused. 'Combined savings?'

'Yes,' she said. 'I've been putting a few quid aside for us, for a rainy day.'

What would we do with the money on a rainy day?

She opened the big envelope and slid out a letter, a couple of photographs of a building with long windows, and a map. She was thrilled. 'Ha, ha! He did it! I knew he would.'

More confusion. 'What is it?'

Kirsty grinned with delight, bouncing on her tiptoes. 'The home address of Dr Jonathan Matthews!' She took my hands. 'The one person who could help you get back home!'

And suddenly all was clear. *She was right.*

I thought of nothing else as we took the bus to work. With Matthews' understanding of this world's technology and an elementary grasp of orgology combined with my expertise, I could open up a gateway large enough to jump through at the very least.

Conversation during morning break was almost exclusively dominated by talk of Christmas. I am getting heartily sick of that particular subject, not to mention the crowds in town on a Saturday. What a big fat fallacy. Anyway, I continued to obsess about how I would get back home, as they continued to obsess about their empty festival – until Gary said something. He said it more to himself than to any of us, from behind his paper.

'Huh,' he grunted, 'I've got no sympathy.'

Distracted, Lorraine turned. 'What's that?'

The paper lowered enough for us to be able to see Gary's eyes. 'Some hooker has died of a drug overdose. Heroin, I think. And they slap it on the front page like it's important.'

Lorraine clicked her tongue. 'Heroin, eh? Serves her right, fucking druggie.' She swivelled round to address her audience. 'Not to mention all the sick bastards who betrayed their good ladies by going with her.'

Clint cleared his throat and took a swig of tea.

Pleased that he had elicited a reaction, Gary decided to read out the headline. 'Prostitute Dies Of Overdose: A popular Salford girl loved by the community where she was raised died last night from a heroin overdose.' The paper lowered. '"Loved by the community" being the operative phrase there,' he said wickedly. Paper went up.

I stirred my tea, half dreaming about the rainforest back home.

Gary continued to read. 'Shazia Patel, aged twenty, had grown up in the Swinton area and had proved popular with her schoolmates and neighbours. "It's such a shame," said Mrs Roach of Kildare Street. "She was a lovely girl, but she got in with the wrong crowd. Drove her family to distraction." Miss Patel became dependent on the drug heroin, which she procured from local dealers, and financed her habit by prostitution. She was found unconscious on Manchester's Deansgate and rushed to hospital. She was pronounced dead on arrival. Police have not ruled out suicide.'

Lorraine shook her head in denial. 'Bollocks. And how did the reporter get that quote?'

'Probably a client of hers,' Gary offered.

'She had got pregnant and had an abortion,' I whispered.

Ainsley looked worried. 'Hey, are you all right, Baz?' he said, touching my hand. The others instinctively followed his movements, anticipating my reaction. I did not react. 'Baz? You all right? You look as white as a sheet.'

I stared at them, dumbstruck. 'She had an abortion. It had really upset her, I could tell. She pretended that she didn't care, that she was as hard as nails, but she wasn't really. She was in mourning.'

206

Ainsley squeezed my hand with a gentleness I'd known only from women. 'You knew her?'

'Briefly.'

Gary's paper went back up. 'Oh aye?'

Lorraine turned and snarled. 'Leave him!'

'I can't believe it,' I kept saying, as if saying it more than once would somehow help me grasp the enormity of the fact. It didn't. Someone, a real person, a person whom I had known, with thoughts and a voice and memories and feelings and views and a beautiful body, a real breathing person, had died. I burst into tears.

Ainsley squeezed my hand tighter. 'It's OK.'

'She's gone,' I cried. 'She's gone. Shazia, gone. How can she be? So alive and real, and now non-existent, an empty shell. An empty shell like a spent battery.'

The whole canteen radiated embarrassment and awkwardness. Bel put her hand on top of Ainsley's and then looked at me. 'She had a crap life,' she said softly. 'But just think, she's gone to a better place. God will forgive her sins and she'll be in heaven with him.'

I wiped my tears with the sleeve of my white coat and looked through raw eyes at Clint, who looked at the table. He did not believe in such things, and at that moment neither did I. Shazia was dead, in every sense of the word.

When Kirsty returned from the smoke shelter, she took in the drama. 'What's up?'

Gary gave a typical retort as he folded his paper. 'Baz's hooker friend has topped herself.'

'Shaz?' Kirsty said, her face pained by the sight of mine. I nodded. She touched my shoulder. Her hybrid odour of perfume and cigarettes hit me. 'Oh Baz, I *am* sorry.'

I keep dabbing my eyes with a tissue. Tonight is not helping. Tonight is Halloween, a celebration devoted to sorcerers, the art of magic, and the disembodied souls of the evil dead. Kirsty says it's a laugh and has sculpted a hideous face into a hollow pumpkin. A lit candle finishes off the effect. She keeps chastising me whenever I turn on the lights, but I find the pumpkin unnerving even though it's just a vegetable.

Children in the hallway are tormenting Rich and Glynis because they think Halloween is an insult to Yahweh and won't give the children any money. I went out and gave them some of mine and asked them to leave. I think Rich and Glynis were thankful, though still a little wary of me.

NOVEMBER 11

'You should be grateful,' Ralph barked when I said people are too preoccupied with war. 'Those men died so that we could live and be free.'

'No,' I countered. 'They died because they were terrified of saying no to the Government. For example, that poor man who was shot by his own army because he wouldn't go back to the front line.'

'He was a coward!' Ralph sneered. 'He wouldn't defend his country.'

Insulting.

'He refused to take part in the murder of other human beings,' I said, calm but firm.

Ralph's teeth were gritted now. 'Jesus,' he said. 'So you think we should have just let the Nazis walk right in and take our land and rape our women, do you?'

I remained as composed as I could. 'No.'

He pointed a finger in my face. 'If everyone thought like you, we would have lost the war.'

I ignored his finger and looked him right in the eye. 'If everyone was like me, there wouldn't be any war.'

Clint smiled his approval. 'I like it.'

'It's not realistic!' Ralph shouted. 'In war it is "kill or be killed". The Nazis would have won.'

208

I shook my head. 'No they wouldn't. Not if everyone was like me.'

'How can you say that?'

I smiled. 'Because if everyone was like me, everyone in the world, there wouldn't be any war at all. It's only because we have these ridiculous borders drawn up that people fight over them. In my philosophy there are no such borders.'

He put his face very close to mine. 'We don't live in your philosophy; we live in the real world. Your paradise Earth, and,' he indicated Clint without looking at him, 'and his brotherhood of man do not exist. Greed and jealousy exist. War exists.'

'But if everyone was like me, it wouldn't.'

He gave up.

Today is Armistice Day. At eleven o'clock we had two minutes' silence in honour of the men who died in the war. I wonder what the people in Germany do at eleven o'clock.

How utterly futile and narrow-minded.

NOVEMBER 30

Kirsty took me to Shazia's funeral. We dressed up in black clothes and attended the crematorium in Salford. I could not help but stare at the image of the crucified Jesus at the front. There were flowers too, and cards with the question 'Why?' written on them.

Why, indeed.

The Patel family took up the front row, the mother barely able to compose herself. We sat a little further back.

An assortment of middle-aged men sat right at the back, briefly nodding to one another, but not ever making eye contact. All were red-faced and sullen.

A piece of haunting music was playing, the main vocal almost dragging tears from me, it was so sad (something called 'Madam Butterfly', I later learned, a favourite of Shazia's).

A serious white haired man stood at the front and indicated that we all stand. And then the box containing Shazia's lifeless body was carried in by four black clad men. I trembled as they passed me by; the idea of her dead flesh being so close was difficult to cope with. I kept thinking *she was so alive.*

'I've never been to anything like it,' Kirsty said when we came out. She had been expecting a Muslim funeral at a mosque, but it seems the family were so ashamed of Shazia's hooker job, they didn't want to be observed by any of their religious elders or friends. The service was conducted by the white haired man, who kept his remarks as generic as possible, making no direct references to either the Qur'an or the Bible.

His opening remark made me angry. He said, 'Many of you will be wondering why this has happened, why God could allow one of his children to stumble so far.' He shook his head. 'I will be honest, I don't know why. God in his wisdom moves in ways that we cannot understand.'

I wanted to shout at him. I wanted to say, 'Why don't you know? What are you doing up there if you don't know?'

He avoided any mention of drug abuse or prostitution and focussed exclusively on Shazia's childhood. The newspaper reporter was right. She was well loved. I told her mother that I loved her too as a sister of the human race. She nodded her acknowledgement, but could not speak because of her grief.

The box was placed on a platform, which Kirsty later told me led to a furnace. Shazia's lifeless body would be destroyed by fire until there was nothing left but ashes. When the curtains started to close for this process to begin, the girl's mother threw herself on top of the box, sobbing and shouting about her 'baby girl' and crying out to God. Her family had to drag her off it. The depth of pain in her

210

voice disturbed me greatly. At that moment I despised the Father for his silence and inactivity. Later I obsessed about how he would know my thoughts toward him.

I spent the rest of the day thinking about the funeral, as well as the people who died in the war and those I had seen jumping from the twin towers, and the voices of the frightened children on the mobile phones.

What a bloody awful world.

A few days later we had another stupid celebration. This time it involved building a big fire, upon which went an effigy of Guy Fawkes, who hundreds of years ago was thwarted in his attempt to demolish the Houses of Parliament.

'Remember, remember, the fifth of November, gunpowder, treason and plot' goes the rhyme. Kirsty took me to an organised event held in the park that evening where they lit the big fire and sent colourful explosives up in the air. They were very pretty – and loud. We also had potato hash, treacle toffee, and toffee apples.

All this because of what some man did hundreds of years ago. Talk about bearing a grudge.

For the most part I hated it and couldn't wait to get back to the flat, and for the most part Kirsty ignored me and said it was fun.

DECEMBER 23

We are on the train and heading for Milton Keynes, which is near Buckingham where Dr Jonathan Matthews lives. To pass the time, I bought a big A4 pad and sketched a drawing of Naomi, she being on my mind more and more these days as I anticipate our reunion.

Kirsty was astonished. 'Bloody hell, you're brilliant! Where did you learn to draw like that?' She held up her

211

hand before I could reply. 'No, don't tell me. It's because you're perfect.'

I laughed. 'Well, it is!'

As I gave the picture some finishing touches, Kirsty stared at it in wonder. 'Is that really Naomi your wife?'

'It is.'

'She's beautiful.'

'Isn't she just? Not a blemish or a wrinkle, a perfect complexion, lovely bouncy brown hair, the most enchanting smile. The day she fetched up water from that waterhole… It was as though I was bound by one of your Halloween spells.'

'Does she really drive a horse and cart like that?'

'Oh yes,' I cooed, recalling the real thing. 'She adores that cart.'

'You really do love her, don't you?'

'Of course,' I said, still dreaming. 'She is my wife.'

Kirsty is watching me write this diary. She is wishing I would translate it into English, I can tell.

DECEMBER 23 (b)

Dr Matthews was quite shaken when we first told him who we are. That and the fact that we had got into his house on false pretences (Kirsty told him she was his biggest fan!). When he knew what we were really there for he poured himself an alcoholic drink. 'Oh Lord.'

'Are you going to deny you stole Baz's idea?' Kirsty pressed.

Matthews downed the drink in one. 'No,' he said. 'It was so revolutionary, and his letter suggested a man without a university education, I couldn't help myself.' He shrugged and offered a weak smile. 'I am sorry.'

212

Kirsty seemed uncertain how to take the apology. She looked at me. 'So what now?'

The answer was obvious to me. 'I want to combine our knowledge and experience and open a porthole.'

Matthews stared at me intensely, poured another drink, downed it, and stared at me again. Finally he said, 'Do you think we could?'

'Yes.'

He poured himself another drink. 'Oh Lord.'

'I have a story to tell you,' I told him.

Kirsty gestured. 'You might want to sit down for this, Dr Matthews.'

'Yes,' Matthews said. 'I think I might.' He made a telephone call to his wife. 'Susan, I'm working in my study. I want no disturbances. OK. I will be done by supper. Bye.'

And so I told him. Kirsty remained silent throughout. Finally Matthews responded by whispering, 'Fascinating.'

After revelling in his reaction, Kirsty leaned forward. 'So do you think it could be done?'

He widened his eyes. 'We'd need a much stronger power supply,' he said. 'Something much more powerful than a toaster and a microwave.' We all laughed at that. 'If I were to book the lab, get some small trees brought in, of your choosing naturally, and young Miss Ingham and I were connected to the circuit –.'

'It could be done?'

He nodded vaguely. 'Yes.' Then he pulled a face. 'Oh, but my lab is in London, you said you came through at Grasmere.'

I chuckled at this. 'Listen, I don't care where I go through. I would gladly walk it all the way back to Elohah Village if you could get me through to that dimension. Just get me through!'

'OK.' He nodded. 'I'll get you through.'

Dr Matthews has put us up in an expensive hotel. Kirsty is very impressed with it. The experiment won't be

213

conducted until New Year's Eve, which unfortunately means we will have to suffer Christmas with his family.

Section Seven

DECEMBER 25

Dr Matthews' family is delightful. His wife Susan is a very polite, very well mannered lady. She is skilled in the art of conversation and what Kirsty calls social etiquette. Much of what she had to say revolved around us. She asked us where we were from, if we worked and what that work entailed. She demonstrated more interest and wonderment about the production of baked beans than either me or Kirsty ever has.

Was she really interested or did it just come with practice? A seasoned chatterer, perhaps?

Love for her children is more than apparent, and respect for her husband and his achievements in the world of science borders on worship.

Their children are well balanced polite children, nothing like the ones in Manchester, but similar to the ones I have seen in films like *The Lion, the Witch and the Wardrobe* (Kirsty had insisted I watch that too. It was nice, I suppose, and bore some resemblance to my own experience).

Mitzi and Roza are six and ten, while Jeremy is fifteen. Roza in particular was very talkative both before the meal was served and during. Susan chastised her for her inquisitiveness once or twice, but I was not offended by the child's questions. In fact I found them fascinating. Roza is not dissimilar to Daisy in that respect. I am so looking forward to seeing her again, after all this time.

Jeremy was more talkative once the meal was over. Dr Matthews had told him we are investigating the theory of

215

parallel dimensions and I was astonished when the boy shared his own ideas. In a way he reminded me of myself when I was his age.

'We cannot rule out the possibility simply because we cannot see it,' he said. 'There are life forms on this planet which are not aware of our existence, partly because of their limited perception and partly because of their size. They perceive the three dimensions differently.'

'That's right,' I said, eager to reward his inquisitiveness. 'We cannot put limits on what God has designed.'

His response shocked me. 'I do not believe in a supreme being personally, but I do believe that the elemental forces of the universe are eternal, without beginning or end. They existed before the dimension of time.'

'Well I don't believe that time is a dimension at all,' I countered. 'Not in the way most people here... not in the way most people do. Time is merely the measurement of events as they occur. Hours and days and years were agreed by men as they interpreted the seasons and the movement of the Earth in its orbit round the sun. Time is not an entity. It is an illusion.'

'Fascinating,' Jeremy said. 'You don't believe in the dimension of time, but you do accept the possibility of extra dimensional planes of existence.'

I had not thought of it like that. I also hadn't thought of what he proposed next.

'I wonder how many different spatial dimensions there are.'

Jonathan, Susan and Kirsty watched the exchange patiently, Roza played with her new toys, Mitzi lost herself in a world of her own. I was mesmerised by the boy's imagination. 'What do you mean?'

'Well,' Jeremy said. 'How many alternative universes are there? Is there one where life evolved differently to the way it did here? Is there one where the planet is completely dead? Is there one with duplicates of ourselves?'

I thought of something and put it to him. 'Hypothetically, if God existed, how would he preside over all these universes?'

Jeremy considered, his brow furrowing, his eyes burning. 'Interesting – The supreme being, an intelligent living First Cause, a vast mind with full comprehension of every universal possibility, seeing and knowing them all simultaneously.' He broke off. Then he added, 'Or what if each universe has its own God, or variations on the same God persona? Is there a dimension where God exists and one where he does not?'

It was all too much for me.

As for the Christmas paraphernalia, well what can I say? Lots of bright coloured lights, cheerful but erroneous songs about the birth of Christ; equally cheerful songs about fir trees, snow, Santa Claus and reindeer. The main meal consisted of turkey, vegetables and gravy, and the sweet was a sponge cake filled with currants. For some reason Susan chose to set it on fire before she apportioned out our slices.

It was all very tasty and enjoyable.

And empty. Like everything else they do for 'fun' in this world; nice, but no substance, no real purpose beyond simple relaxation and a distraction to stop them dwelling on the shortness of their lives.

I read that in the First World War (imagine that, a *global* war!), the soldiers in the trenches stopped fighting on Christmas Day and played football, only to return to killing one another the following day.

This is pointed out in documentaries and on the local news and is romanticised. But it tells me with all certainty that if another conflict flared up, all of that romanticism would be forgotten and the Government would be using the media, the religions, and the populace's already stupendous national pride to whip up a fever and condition them to fight and kill.

That's all Christmas is to me: not a day of peace, not Christ's Mass, but another reminder of how primitive, self-centred and narrow-minded this culture really is.

On December 31 there is going to be another show of immodesty. They call it New Year. Again the dating has been adopted from an ancient Roman festival in honour of a false human god. This time Janus, who has two faces, one looking into the past and one looking to the future. It will be another pointless passing of time, dressed up to be a period of reflection where one is supposed to consider one's progress over the last twelve months. In reality, of course, it is just another 'reason' for them to overeat and get drunk.

I have nothing but contempt for their approach to life, and yet, because of the staggering briefness of their lives, I find I cannot condemn them wholly for it.

The one big plus for me is I can get to work in the laboratory, with the help of Kirsty and Jonathan, and finally, *finally*, go home.

I think about nothing else.

DECEMBER 31

Well, the world is gearing up for its New Year celebrations, and I have been spending the day translating this diary into English. Some of the wording has been a problem because I needed to convey my confusion upon arriving in this world and the fact that I could not read English. I also had the problem of finding names in the English language that are close to the names back home. Still, I think I've done a reasonable job.

Amazingly, the name Mahershalalhashbaz is in the Old Testament. It's the closest pronunciation to my real name.

I have made Kirsty promise that she will not read the diary until after the experiment.

DECEMBER 31 (b)

Dr Jonathan Matthews was late arriving at the laboratory. 'I'm in the doghouse with Susan,' he said. 'She hadn't realised I would be slipping away from the party so soon.'

'I appreciate you doing this,' I told him.

'Not at all,' he said, smiling. 'I'm glad to get away from the sycophants and politicians, and I've told you, Baz, you can call me Jonathan.'

This is true. He said it on Christmas Day.

The laboratory was larger than I had anticipated. We had to go through a number of doors with special electronic coding, and Jonathan kept having to explain to various individuals who Kirsty and I were. At one point he was fearful we might be detained for questioning, but we weren't, he having authority in his voice and the respect of many powerful people.

The main room itself was a large area with green walls. A bank of instruments and switches dominated one wall, while a glass window partition separated us from the variety of plants and trees that Jonathan had assembled, all interconnected as I had described in my original letter with two leaf connection points suspended above a couple of stool chairs. A thick electric cable ran and split to a tangle of smaller cables, each linking with the largest of the plants.

'I know in principle that this will work,' Jonathan said.

Kirsty was unsure. 'How?'

'Because I tried it on a much smaller scale after receiving Baz's letter. I succeeded in creating tiny particles, and what sounded like the noise of a stream.'

I smiled. 'Actually, that wasn't just the sound of a stream. It would have been a stream literally.'

219

Jonathan nodded. 'I realise that now.' He gestured to the small jungle amassed on the other side of the partition. 'Hence all of that.'

Kirsty suddenly spun on her heels and took my hands. 'So this is it, Baz.'

'Hey,' I said, squeezing her hands tight. 'Don't cry.'

We embraced.

This is it. I am going home.

DECEMBER 31 (c)

Jonathan flicked a series of switches. The room began to pulse with power. 'When I throw the final lever, we will have fifteen seconds to event time. That's fifteen seconds for Kirsty and I to attach ourselves to the circuit, and fifteen seconds for you to ready yourself. I am hoping that the bubble will form in the centre space, but I cannot guarantee it. So be ready for it merging at any point in the room.'

I nodded. 'I will.'

'I also cannot guarantee that the bubble will remain intact for any length of time, so once it has stabilised, you will have to jump through it.'

'I know.' I released Kirsty and headed for the partition. I felt driven to stop and turn. Kirsty bumped into me, Jonathan's hand was poised on the final lever. 'If anything goes wrong, though,' I said, 'you must disconnect the power. Your safety is paramount.'

The hum of power had been steadily rising, and I knew what Jonathan was thinking. 'Don't worry,' he called. 'I won't put our lives at risk. Now get into position before the power shorts. You have one shot at this. Get it wrong and you're stuck here forever.'

I needed no further incentive. I climbed through the branches, exposed roots and cables into the central clearing, knowing that Jonathan had now thrown that final switch.

The room throbbed with energy. Kirsty sat on her stool and very hesitantly attached the leaf helmet to her head. She looked so frightened, poor thing, yet she was doing it. She was doing it for me, and I loved her for it. Jonathan, on the other hand, was very cold and methodical about it, perhaps deliberately, so as not to let emotion get the better of him.

The hum of the room began to vibrate the very air. Suddenly my companions gripped their seats. The leaves on the trees and bushes flexed and coiled like monsters coming to life, their veins bulging and yellowing.

Above the racket I heard Kirsty moan, 'God, it hurts,' and Jonathan respond, 'Just stick with it. It shouldn't be long now.'

And sure enough, large football sized globules of reality formed from the air and floated about the room. I counted a dozen of them. Two collided and I feared that they would burst. But instead of bursting they merged to become one bigger bubble.

'It's working!' I shouted.

Three more bounced together. Kirsty forgot her pain and pointed excitedly. 'Look! I can see stars and the moon!'

She was right. A night sky was forming, and below it a ragged mountainous scene. Odd houses dotted about were only distinguishable by their candlelit windows. And then the fragrances of winter hit me, not the diluted winter of this world, but the full, unpolluted winter of home.

'I can hear the river again!' Jonathan shouted.

The final bubble merged with the whole, and the globe of wobbling reality bounced against the branches and leaves. I stared at it in wonderment, my heart beating tempestuously.

I turned to Kirsty, who was now holding her head in the palm of her hand. At that moment I wanted to rip off the

221

helmet and nurse her, but I knew I could not. I waved at Jonathan, who glared back at me, teeth gritted. 'The plants are starting to give out!' he shouted. 'If you're going, go now!'

'I'm going!' I shouted back.

I leapt in the air, as high as I could.

'Baz, I love you!' It was Kirsty. The last words I would ever hear from this world.

Except they weren't.

As I hit the bubble of alternate reality, it popped. I crashed down, yelping as I hit a couple of sharp up-pointing roots. Leaves curled and browned, and suddenly the plants were on fire. The three of us coughed and wheezed as the blaze rapidly spread. Instinctively I dragged Jonathan and Kirsty from their helmets, and as if responding to my actions, the water sprays in the ceiling were triggered.

Jonathan shut down the power and we scrambled from the room. They were traumatised; I was beside myself with frustration. I paced about, unable to speak.

Only then did I break down crying.

I'm crying now.

DECEMBER 31 (b)

Kirsty keeps blaming herself because she distracted me right at the crucial moment. I've told her not to, but she isn't yielding. It was my own procrastination, really. I should have jumped into the bubble the moment it was big enough.

It was my own fault.

God, I'm depressed.

We sat in Jonathan's car for a while, not speaking. Kirsty suggested going back to our hotel to pack.

I suggested going to back to Jonathan's, to the party.

They didn't have to be asked twice.

JANUARY 1

I have drunk four glasses of wine now, and the din of the music is still irritating me. Kirsty insisted that I get up to dance, but what she calls dancing isn't dancing.

Then someone put on the television, and an image of the Big Ben clock in London appeared. The crowd of people outside the clock counted down the seconds to midnight, as did everyone at the party. 'Five! Four! Three! Two! One! Happy New Year!'

The cheering and clapping overwhelmed me. I couldn't wait to leave the room. Not an easy thing when everyone is shaking your hand and wishing you 'All the best.'

I stood in the corridor pinching the bridge of my nose. Footsteps approached. God, who is it now? 'All the best, Baz.' It was Jonathan, with two glasses of wine, one for him and one for me, his voice low and calm.

'How can you say that?'

'Look,' he said. 'We'll try again. It's not over yet. We'll find a way.'

'We won't,' I said. 'We had one chance. I had one chance.' I stifled the onset of tears. 'And I blew it.' I took the glass from his hand and knocked it back.

'Baz.'

I turned. It was Kirsty holding my translated diary open in her hands. Oh no, she's been crying. I really don't need this now. 'What is it, Kirsty?'

She wiped her left eye with her sleeve, not letting go of the book. 'Do you really think I'm more of a sister to you than your own?'

I exhaled noisily. 'I wouldn't have written it if I hadn't thought it.' I took another swig of wine.

'No one has ever said that about me,' she said. But I could not respond. I was too angry about the singing coming from the other room. 'What the hell is that?'

Jonathan laughed. 'It's called 'Auld Lang Syne'. They're singing in the new year.'

These people are something else, they really are. What's the difference between this year, last year, the year before that, or the year in three year's time? Nothing. Years are just measurements of time, collections of twelve month periods, nothing more, nothing less. They are celebrating nothing.

I finished my wine and let out a loud burp. I'm stuck here. Stuck amongst primitives and empty heads.

Bollocks to it.

JANUARY 2

Kirsty and I are on the train. It's been a long journey, and it's nearly dark. The carriage is full of cretins.

Mentally deficient.

Cretins with cans of beer, talking loudly. I don't appreciate this, especially as I'm suffering from the remnants of what Kirsty calls a hangover. Not a pleasant experience. I really don't understand how people at work can say things like, 'I had a great night on Saturday. I got completely rat-arsed. I was so pissed, I can't remember anything, and I had a banging head on Sunday morning.'

Imbeciles.

Kirsty is reading bits of my translated diary as I continue to write this one. She's looking at me right now with a measure of horror on her face.

'What is it?' I've just asked.

'You made your daughter cry when you attached her to the apparatus.'

Oh, don't remind me. 'I know, I know. I feel terrible about it, all right.'

'So you should.'

'Look, if I ever do get back there, I'll make it up to her big time.'

She's satisfied with that.

Now she's sniggering to herself.

'What? What is it?'

She's pointing at the book as though I know. 'You thought that old chap with the dog was a monster.'

Old chap? 'Which old chap?'

'The one when you first arrived on the path that leads to Easedale Tarn. You talk about his skin looking like that of a shrivelled piece of fruit!'

'Well I didn't know about old age then, did I?'

She's laughing. Bloody hell, am I going to have to put up with this all the way home?

A middle-aged man and a boy have just got on. His grandson, perhaps? The cretins are still being cretins, all the same. They keep saying the F word. The boy is looking at Granddad and Granddad is telling him to ignore it. The boy is obviously distressed, and the man is apprehensive, fearful. I am going to do something about it.

I have just stood up and shouted, 'Look! There's a young boy on here. We don't want to hear your filth. OK?!'

I'm back now. When one of them challenged me I advanced upon him, took his can and threw it out the window. The others backed off and I grabbed the main culprit. 'Do you have any doubts at all that I couldn't throw you off as well?'

He didn't answer.

'The problem with this world,' I told him, 'is it's full of brainless imbeciles who don't give a shit about anybody but themselves.' I paused before I added, 'And I have a problem with that.'

I let him go and he scurried off to the far end to join his fellow idiots. The granddad gave a brief nod of approval and then looked out of the window as I returned to my seat.

Kirsty is looking at me again.

'What?'

'Do you really think I'm very pretty when I smile?'

Oh God, why did I agree to translate it? 'Yes,' I have just told her. 'I do think you are pretty when you smile.'

I really don't need this at the moment.

JANUARY 2 (b)

It's late, and we've just got in. Kirsty is running a bath. I've just made us some sandwiches for supper. I've also just made up my bed on the couch.

I cannot bear the idea of spending the rest of my days in this flat and working in that factory, as lovely as my host is. It was always only meant to be a temporary measure.

I think I am what Kirsty sometimes terms "clinically depressed."

I can now understand why some individuals in this world choose suicide as a way out.

Suicide: Self murder.

JANUARY 2 (c)

Kirsty has cracked open the wine. We've decided to get ratted. She's lit herself a cigarette and is now reading more of my diary. She keeps going back and forth reading different bits. She says she can't put it down. She really is so lovely, sat coiled up on her chair in her pyjamas and dressing gown.

'You cheeky bugger!' Kirsty exclaimed, not quite looking up from the diary.

I feigned shock. 'What?'

'You tried a cigarette while I was in the bath!'

'Well, I had to see what the appeal was in something so lethal.'

She laughed and took a drag. 'Get lost, you!' Then more reading. 'God, I remember that. Your clothes stank.'

I sipped my wine and began to draw her on one of my fresh blank pages. Her silhouette was simple enough, the shape of her face, the short spikes of her dyed blonde hair, the blueness of her eyes – an innocent child in many ways.

I think I'll have my bath now before I hit the bottle for proper.

JANUARY 2 (b)

When I came out of the bathroom I was met with Kirsty's eyes, all tearful and glassy. I groaned inwardly. Not my diary *again*.

But it wasn't the diary she was holding. It was the sketch I had done. She looked down at it and then gazed at me, and then repeated the action before standing up.

'What's the matter?' I said, not entirely sure what had provoked the tears. 'Does the picture offend you?'

She scrunched her nose, her bottom lip quivering with emotion. 'Do you... Do you really see me like this?'

'Like what?'

'Like this.'

I didn't know what to say. 'Is it not a true likeness?'

'No.'

'I'm sorry, I just thought that –.'

She cut me off, looking down at the picture in her hands. 'No, you misunderstand me. It's not that I don't like it.'

'Well, what then?'

She looked right at me, holding back the tears. 'This isn't really what I look like, Baz, and you know it. I have never looked as good as this. The girl in this sketch is an idealised version of me, but she's not me as I am. She's beautiful.'

I approached her, aware of the need to maintain control, and placed my hands on her shoulders. My smile seemed to reassure her. 'You *are* beautiful,' I said softly. 'You are beautiful in appearance, and you are a beautiful person. I drew what I saw. I drew you.'

She finally broke down, and I was not ready for what followed. She launched herself into my arms, wrapping her own tight around my back. I nursed her as a father does an emotional daughter. 'Hey, it's all right.' She raised her forehead and I kissed it tenderly. I kissed it again, and then a third time.

I could not help myself. As I leaned down a fourth time, she lifted her head more subtly, and pulled me forward. And my lips met hers. She kissed me.

I was stunned, but I did not let go. She cast her eyes to the floor. 'I'm sorry. I shouldn't have done that.'

'It's all right,' I said, still not letting go. We remained locked together.

'Baz,' she said, her eyes still grounded.

'I know,' I replied, my throat drying. And I did know.

'I think I'm in love with you.'

I placed my forefinger at the base of her chin and gently lifted her head. 'I know,' I said softly and kissed her tenderly on her lips. She responded to it as though it was the most natural thing. The feeling was deep for both of us. It reached simultaneously into our souls. Her fingers made avenues in my hair. I touched her face with the tips of mine, my left arm pulling her closer, tighter.

It was like we were possessed. Eventually she prised herself free. 'I think we had better stop,' she said. 'You will regret it in the morning if we go all the way.'

I was overawed by my own feelings. I could not think. 'All the way?'

'You know,' she nodded, with a hint of apprehension. 'If we… If we make love.'

I took her hand. 'I want to make love.'

She didn't wait for me to repeat it. Kirsty kicked open the door to her bedroom.

And we made love.

And we loved it.

She is in the bathroom now, washing herself. I am dazzled, but ready for more. I think she will be bringing the wine and her cigarettes.

I have never been pleasured like this ever before.

JANUARY 3 (5 am)

Kirsty is fast asleep. I am sat in the living room.

I am racked with a dreadful awful treacherous guilt. I feel terrible. Oh Naomi, I'm sorry. I'm sorry, Naomi. How will you ever forgive me? How can I ever face you now?

Father, please help her forgive me.

Father, please forgive *me*.

I keep crying.

JANUARY 16

The weather in winter is appalling. It's not helping my mood. Neither is my work at the factory. It is so monotonous, as is the conversation.

Kirsty tries to cheer me up, but it's no use.

I doubt I will ever be truly happy again.

JANUARY 28

The most astonishing thing happened this afternoon. I was making dinner for us both when the phone rang.

'Oh, hi Jonathan,' Kirsty said into the receiver. 'How are you? Ahuh. And how's Susan and the children? Oh right. Really? I bet you're dead proud of him. Yeah. Baz? Yes, he's here. Mm. Well, depressed, really. Mm. Oh, OK then.' She called to me. 'Baz! Jonathan wants to talk to you.'

Not more condolences, I thought. I can do without them. They only serve as reminders. I handed the cooking over to Kirsty and took the call.

'Hello.'

'So how have you been keeping, Baz? I must say it's lovely to hear your voice again.'

I thanked him.

'How have you been keeping?'

I sighed loudly. 'Well, I've let myself go a bit. Took a couple of days off work. Can't stand the place, really. I've got no motivation. And I just keep sleeping, you know. When I'm asleep I'm not thinking, not aware. There's no ache in my head, you know.'

Jonathan was perplexed by my remark. 'You get an ache?'

'Yes,' I said. 'It's around my forehead and on the bridge of my nose: a dull ache.'

'Sounds like depression, my friend,' he said. 'A colleague of mine got it pretty bad when he was made unemployed for a while. He had been discredited for his unorthodox approach.'

'Kirsty will identify with that,' I told him. 'With me it's the knowledge that I'm going to be stuck here forever. You forget that I am physically perfect. I will outlive both you and Kirsty, and your children, and their children. I'll be like Connor MacLeod in that bloody *Highlander* film.'

'And that's what is depressing you?'

'Yes,' I said. 'Well, that and the guilt.'

'The guilt?'

'Never mind.'

He paused briefly and when he spoke again there was a beguiling cheerfulness to his tone. 'I think I have the solution, Baz. To the main cause of your depression anyway.'

I don't believe it, but I'll play along. 'You do?'

'Yes.' He was getting quite excited now. 'You know about that holiday complex called Eden World, don't you?'

I remembered it. Some domed place near the Lake District.

'Well, I've been called in to help out with the tropical side of things, and I have access to the place for a whole month.'

'Right.'

'Well I was thinking, this place is an artificial tropical paradise. It has lots of trees and plants, many varieties, and plenty of room.'

I knew what he was suggesting, but I wasn't sure I could face another emotional episode only to fail again. 'OK,' I said.

'You don't sound very excited.'

'Well,' I told him. 'It's a case of once bitten, twice shy.'

'But I think we could make it work this time. The place will be practically empty, we will have a proper sizable power source to hand, and the scope of the place will equal that of the forest you conducted your original experiment in at the very least. I see no reason why it should fail this time.'

And at that moment neither could I.

'So what about it?'

I took a deep breath and then exhaled with pleasure. 'Yes!'

Kirsty appeared at the kitchen door.

'Yes! Yes! Yes!' I said. 'Let's do it!'

Kirsty mimed, 'What is it?' but I could not answer. I indicated the phone.

Jonathan proposed a date. It was perfect.

'March the fifteenth? Perfect.'

'It will give me enough time to get things set up and run a few tests,' he said. 'And it's near Grasmere, which means you'll come through quite near your home village.'

I thanked him profusely and put down the receiver.

Kirsty danced in on her tiptoes, excited in my behalf. 'What is it? What is it? Tell me.'

I smiled and touched her cheek. 'Kirsty, my love.'

She looked at me expectantly.

'It seems I really am going home!'

We embraced momentarily.

'I'm so happy for you,' she said.

FEBRUARY 14

Today is Valentine's Day. The origin of this one is a mixed bag, partly to do with one of the Roman Catholic saints, partly to do with a mythological baby angel who fires heart tipped arrows at individuals, causing them to fall in love.

I looked it up. Tradition has it that the admirer secretly bestows gifts on the one he loves along with a card signed 'Guess Who?' However, it appears that the commercial system has very typically sunk its teeth into the proceedings and now everyone is expected to buy gifts for their wives, husbands, boyfriends and girlfriends. Even Ainsley is making special plans for his partner Wayne.

I surprised Kirsty today by having a huge bouquet of flowers delivered to the factory. She was overwhelmed and glassy eyed. The girls were more than a little jealous. Clint thought it was very romantic. And Lorraine? Well, Lorraine asked the question most were probably privately wondering.

'I don't get it,' she said. 'Are you two shagging now, then, or what?'

I looked at Kirsty, Kirsty looked at me. Our eyebrows raised at exactly the same time. And then much to the bemusement of everyone present, we laughed.

MARCH 15 – ACCORDING TO DR JONATHAN MATTHEWS

It was the most extraordinary day.

I agreed that I would pen this account, but I am not sure where I should begin. I suppose everything which precedes this is self-explanatory, so logic dictates that I bring events full circle.

Logic also dictates that I set the scene.

Getting access to Eden World was not at all difficult, nor was the transportation of my equipment and the modification of the main power room. The skeleton staff assigned to assist me did so without question, despite finding my requests somewhat puzzling.

I arranged the main circuit of trees exactly to the diagram that Baz had emailed across. The wider circuit was linked together by primary roots, a process which left the general design and floor plan relatively unchanged. I was confident that my staff would be able to restore it before the administrators returned for the launch of the spring season. We would be packed up and gone and they would be none the wiser.

Baz and Kirsty arrived at their rented apartment on March 14 and I issued them with uniforms and electronic passes. Once inside the complex, though, Baz insisted on changing into his original handmade garments. Kirsty had prepared them especially, so he could go back exactly as he came. A nice touch, I thought.

On the day itself, Baz and Kirsty were subdued, changed considerably since the last time we had all met on that fateful Christmas week. I busied myself at the console, Baz double-checked all the connections, and Kirsty just stood, hands in pockets, watching him. It was as though she was soaking up every last image of him. She had fallen in love with him, that much was clear, and I recall being somewhat saddened at the realisation, for she would know that he would be alive and living right here in this area on this Earth, but not here, not in any sense that could matter.

Once the machinery was ready, Baz wasted no time issuing orders. There was a coldness about him, a determination. He was not going to allow sentiment and love to get in his way.

I threw the final switch and Kirsty and I took our positions.

And then it started, exactly as before: a build up of power, but not as intense this time because of the spacious area. There was a sense of something in the air, but the trees and plant life showed no signs of giving out, they were entirely resilient. The mental pressure for Kirsty and I was the same, though. I bore it with gritted teeth; Kirsty endured it with her head in the palm of her hand.

Pinpricks of blue and green pressed themselves into existence, thousands of them. I'm sure I heard the sound of a horse and cart passing on a gravel road and the distant laughter of children. The dots hit one another rapidly, forming great wobbling blobs of landscape, an image not unlike an alpine spectacle, only with smaller mountains. It was certainly more Eden-like than the fake paradise we were residing in.

Baz hissed a triumphant 'Yes!' as the three shimmering, vibrating images bounced together and formed one giant bubble of alternate reality. I was astonished by what I saw: a

234

lovely pastoral landscape, a sky bluer than any shade of blue I had ever seen.

Kirsty, still holding her head, chanced a look, and was immediately awestruck. 'Oh – my – God,' she said, her voice just audible above the hum of power. 'It's real. It really is ... real.'

Baz stood before the enormous spectacle, briefly acknowledged us both, and took no chances. He ran at the image, picked up some speed, and launched himself up in the air.

Suddenly there was a flash of light. It was blinding in its intensity. Kirsty and I had to shield our eyes. When we recovered we were hit with an all pervading sense of melancholia.

Baz was lying face down on the floor. He had failed again.

Yet the bubble was still intact, the paradise image stable and very present. I exchanged glances with Kirsty as Baz dragged himself from the floor, dazed.

'What happened? I ran at it hard enough. Why didn't I go through?'

'Oh – my – God,' I heard Kirsty say again. I followed her gaze.

The most astonishing spectacle had merged with the main picture, something that looked in shape and size like a sword. It was no ordinary sword, though, but rather one seeming to be comprised of flame. It spun and rotated with brilliance, and then I perceived two other shapes merging behind it, tall and white, with energy like lightning, and yet vaguely human shaped. It was an illusion, it had to be.

'They look like angels,' Kirsty whispered, and before I knew it she had slipped from the leaf helmet to her knees.

'Kirsty!' I shouted above the din. 'Get back in place, you'll break the circuit! You don't know that they are angels! It could be a trick!' But as I looked about me, I saw that the circuit had not in fact been broken. It defied logic.

235

Baz, now fully recovered, stepped forward and addressed the phenomena. 'What is this?'

A voice: human, yet not human, masculine, yet feminine, in the image, in the complex, in my head. Some form of advanced telepathy, no doubt.

'Mahershalalhashbaz,' the voice said. 'It has been decreed that you shall not enter here.'

Baz had a look of obstinacy about him. 'By whom?'

'By the Father,' the voice said.

He shrugged. 'How do I know you are telling the truth?'

There was a pause before the voice replied. 'I do not understand your question.'

I sensed the power in the complex winding down, the whole system stopping, but not burning out, just stopping of its own accord. Yet the bubble remained afloat. All that could be heard was the gentle wafting of the fiery blade and the muffled country noises coming from behind the two apparitions.

Then another voice occurred. It was similar to the first voice, but wider and deeper. A parental voice, authority mixed with a tender love. Baz recognised it straight away, I could tell. His face expression was one of anticipation and relief.

'Father,' he said, looking into the bubble and up to its bluer than blue sky.

Kirsty collapsed into a trembling heap. 'Oh no,' she whispered. 'It's real, it's all real. Forgive me, Lord. Please, please, please forgive me. I know I have sinned many times, I know I have blasphemed against you, I know I have taken your name in vain, I know I have denied that you even exist. And that was wicked of me, Lord. I know it was. I am nothing, Lord. I am an ant.'

I tapped her on the bottom with the tip of my shoe. 'Kirsty, you're rambling. Get up.'

She ignored me. 'I have had a life of woe,' she said. Woe? Not usually a Kirsty word. 'And I'm not making excuses, but, but –.' She rocked back and forth, her voice disappearing as she spoke. 'I am sorry, Lord. Please forgive me.'

I tapped her on the bottom again. 'It's not listening to you, Kirsty. It seems only to be acknowledging Baz.'

She turned her head very slightly, not rising. 'Don't you fear God at all?'

I considered. 'God?' I'd ruled out the notion of organised religion in my teens and dismissed the concept of an all knowing, all loving heavenly father figure by the time I was thirty. 'This?'

I took in the image before me. The gelling of the two dimensions can be explained scientifically, I decided. It can be measured. The sword and the figures behind it are an intricate illusion, as is the disembodied voice. It's a clever advance of our own telecommunications, or perhaps a mental projection, a form of telepathy.

'Mahershalalhashbaz,' the new voice said. 'How is it that you are here?'

Baz cleared his throat. A little nervous, I thought.

'Did you pursue that course which I had forbidden?'

Baz frowned. 'You know that I did,' he said. 'You can read hearts and minds.'

A good answer, I thought. Challenge it. Though I doubt he was actually challenging the phenomena at this point. That would have been counterproductive.

The voice sounded at once angry and disappointed. 'What is this you have done?'

Baz began to stammer a little. 'I was curious. I knew I could open the gateway, so I tried again. I mean, what's the point of you giving us an inquisitive mind and resources if you will not allow us to use them?'

'You have acted contrary to my will,' the voice said. 'You have taken an independent course.'

'I was curious,' Baz repeated, sounding rather pathetic now.

Kirsty slowly and deliberately got to her feet, slowly and deliberately because she was overcome by fear. Yet she did it. Her voice was coarse and dry, but she managed to speak. I was fascinated by the exchange. 'Forgive him, Father,' she offered. 'Please forgive him.'

The phenomena spoke only to Baz. 'You were not like this people,' it said. 'They are descended from corruption. They battle with themselves internally. The law of the principled mind wars with volatile, unbridled emotions.'

I nearly snorted at this remark.

The voice continued: 'And some disregard the war and indulge their fallen flesh.' Baz turned to face us with, I must say, a measure of contempt. He listened as the character assassination continued. 'You had no such hereditary imperfection in you. This makes your sin all the more grave. You, although perfect, chose to disregard my standard, my law. You chose disobedience and independence. And so, independent you must now be.'

Realising before either Kirsty or I what that actually meant, Baz twirled on his heels to face the voice. 'No!' He was suddenly in a blind panic. 'I am not like these people, I cannot live among them. I do not belong here. I belong at home with my wife and children, my family. I belong with *you*.' His breathing was faltering, he coughed. 'Father, please.'

'I am not your father,' the voice said, now more authoritative than parental. 'You are estranged from me.'

'No!' Baz stuttered. 'What about Naomi, what about my wife?'

'You will stay with your new wife here.'

Baz took on a look of incredulity. He stabbed a finger in the direction of his saviour. It was an aggressive stab, an accusing stab. He didn't even look round to face the girl, and she was reduced.

'What, *her*?' he spat. 'She's not my wife. She's a simpleton like everyone else in this –.' He carefully avoided the phrase 'godforsaken', along with his next words. 'I know I sinned against you, against my own flesh, and against Naomi, my dear Naomi, when I took this girl into holy union. But she seduced me. You don't know what these people are like.' He corrected himself. 'Well, of course, you *do* know what they are like. So, why did you allow me to get mixed up with her?'

The voice came back, dismissing everything Baz had said. 'I have permitted Naomi to engage in brother-in-law marriage.'

Baz clutched at his chest, wounded by the announcement. 'You have given her to one of my brothers? Which one?'

'You will stay here with your new wife,' the voice repeated. 'And your son.'

Silence.

Baz looked into the other world, his face a distortion of anguish. And then Kirsty found the strength to stand up fully. She staggered, light-headed. 'It's me.' She laughed. It was the kind of laugh a person laughs when in shock, but a happy laugh nonetheless. 'It's me, Baz,' she said. 'I'm pregnant. I am carrying your son.'

Baz covered his face with the palms of his hands. 'No,' he mumbled. 'No, no, no.' Then he looked into the bubble again. 'Father, I have sinned. I know that. But I am repentant. Does that not count for anything? I know I have been corrupted as I have lived among these people, but I can be purified. Please.'

'You sinned before you entered that world,' replied the voice Baz called "Father". 'You sinned the moment you disregarded my will.'

I could not help but wonder what this Father phenomenon actually was; an illusion, a carefully concealed secret known only to a few elders in the community? What must it be like to live under the authority of such a thing?

Was it one man supplying the voice, several men, perhaps a character part passed on down the generations?

Kirsty later insisted that the Father couldn't have possibly known certain facts about Baz's life since arriving in our dimension if he had been an illusion or the product of a controlled society. But I beg to differ.

A society that can advance genetics to such a finely tuned degree and control human development to the point that individuals can live indefinitely, perpetually regenerating themselves, can easily develop a theology and create a God figure and maintain the illusion.

Those posing as the God would have the means to detect Baz's attempted return, and it wouldn't take a stroke of genius to guess that a man and woman who have lived in one another's pockets for a whole year may at some point in that duration succumb to their sexual desires, especially when in a weakened emotional state.

Mahershalalhashbaz, because you disregarded my will and chose a course of independence, the Father continued, his tone implying the passing of a judicial sentence, 'cursed is your flesh. In the sweat of your face you will work in the system to which you have become accustomed. You will eat the product of that world until you return to the ground from which your forefather Adam was taken.'

Baz choked on the words, his eyes bulging in disbelief. 'You are condemning me to die with these people?'

'Out of the dust you were made,' the voice said. 'And to dust you will return.'

Ashes to ashes, eh? Fascinating.

The image started to break apart. Baz launched himself forward, screaming, 'Father! Father! Please!'

Relentless sobbing ensued as he fell to his knees and the fragmented bubbles burst, one by one.

I could not help but whisper, 'Incredible.'

Kirsty acknowledged me for a second and then touched her tummy with the palm of her hand. 'I am going to have a baby.' She smiled. 'Baz, I am having your baby!'

But Baz did not answer – the frantic sobbing having given way to a pained whimpering. He just rocked back and forth on his haunches, devastated. Kirsty and I mourned his loss in profound silence. He swayed to and fro for a good ten minutes, and then suddenly got up and fled from the building.

He wept bitterly.

MARCH 15 AND THE AFTERMATH – ACCORDING TO KIRSTY INGHAM

I always said seeing is believing.

Jonathan reckons any number of explanations are possible, but I know in my heart that everything Baz has told me since the moment we first met is all true. And that haunting supernatural voice will stay with me forever. I know what I saw and I know what I believe.

All that stuff in the Bible about miracles and supernatural power makes a lot more sense to me now, and I can take a lot of it at face value, though the narrative is still crazy at times and I think I can see whopping contradictions.

There are certain things I cannot get the hang of. I still don't buy the thing about us suffering. I didn't rebel in the Garden of Eden; I didn't challenge the Father's sovereignty. I wasn't born then – and neither were any of the billions of people who have lived since Adam and Eve.

Rich and Glynis say that that's why we need the sacrifice of Jesus. He mediates with the Father on our behalf. I'm not sure I buy that either. Waris at work reckons we are permitted to suffer so that we can learn humility and to be better people. Seems a very cruel way to teach us. I'm not sure about the Qur'an either. I'm not sure about organised religion. In fact, I'm not sure about any of it. All I know is what I saw.

I'd ask Baz, but he has become distinctly uncooperative. He says he agrees with Jonathan and that he has been indoctrinated with a lie. I tried to point out that his language was altered from some kind of ancient Hebrew to English upon arriving in our dimension and that although he has lived for nine hundred and thirty-six years, he is now set to die as one of us – so his Father God must exist.

But he's having none of it. He says the change in his language matrix could have been induced telepathically by his elders and that his aging will be brought on by living in our poisonous atmosphere.

An interesting turnaround, I must say. And that's not all. He's read, underlined, and wrote in the margins of Dawkins' *The Selfish Gene* and Darwin's *On the Origin of Species*. He's gone from laughing at evolution to insisting the human race has descended from apes and that God is a creation of Man.

He somehow managed to persuade our Steve that he's not bonkers and goes round to his place to listen to doomy Gary Numan songs and Marilyn Manson. Poor Jennifer, is all I can say.

At work, they love him. He goes to all the nights out and swears like a trooper. He's very fond of saying 'Christ on a bike' at the moment. He and Gary are now fast friends. They go down the pub together and sometimes he comes back with spaced out eyes and smelling of weed. He thinks I don't know what he's been up to, but he forgets I've done it all.

I was disappointed when he took up smoking cigarettes regularly. I mean, after all the lectures he's given me about arsenic and cyanide, and especially as I'm now trying to give up. I have a baby on the way. I'm trying to stay off the ciggies, partly for the baby and partly because knowing the

Father exists has given me a conscience about it (I light up and then find myself looking up at the sky in a fit of guilt). I bought the inhaler and nicotine patches, and they seem to be doing the trick, but all the while Baz is standing in the kitchen by the window bloody puffing away.

At first he was coming back drunk nearly every night. I had to lay the law down about that, and he threw a wobbler. I told him I understand he is depressed and he has my sympathies, but he cannot come in shouting the odds and keeping me up half the night.

I've also discovered that he's learned how to overcome the parental controls on the computer. He's up till two and three in the morning, drooling over it. I've told him that if he starts searching for the illegal stuff, he'll be out on his arse. I won't care if he finishes up back on the streets, and he knows it too.

You are probably wondering right now why I even put up with him at all. That wouldn't surprise me because I'd be thinking the same if I were you and you were me.

Well, OK, it's because I'm having his child. But that's not all. Before he received his really bad news, he was the loveliest, kindest, most warm-hearted man I have ever met. And deep down, under all the hang-ups and shit, he still is.

At nine hundred and thirty-six years of age, Mahershalalhashbaz is having to face the truth about the world in which he lives and the truth about himself. Basically, the world is a bit crap, it's unjust and cruel, it's run by liars and rats, a lot of the people are treacherous, half of the populace is living in luxury while the other half starves, the rainforests are being uprooted and the environment is being destroyed.

And in the middle of all this, he's realising that he's not got long to live, not really. He will make it another twenty years if he looks after himself and if he's lucky. Provided that cancer and heart disease don't get him, he might make it another twenty or thirty years after that, and if he's still around after *that* he will be slow and weak and aged.

There are a number of ingenious ways to die. The Father must have known that we would develop cancers and heart disease and leukaemia, that we might well go blind or have to suffer the indignity of limb amputations or have a plastic bag on our side, or go senile and not recognise even our nearest and dearest.

I believe in God now. I shudder at the thought of him. But I cannot conceive a single good reason why any of the above should be permitted. If we have to die, well, OK. But in such a horrible manner? Why?

If he were a politician or a member of the medical profession, I'd say he's a cruel and vindictive bastard for allowing us to go like that and I'd vote him out of office or demand that he be sacked. And yet I talk to him at least once every day, usually while I'm in the park or doing the washing. He never replies, of course, but I talk to him anyway. Don't ask me to explain it. I can't.

And so Baz is having to deal with what the rest of us start to realise in our teens, and in spite of being centuries old, he is reacting the way we all do. He denies it, he resists it, he gives two fingers to it, he says fuck it, he indulges his pleasures – but in time he will do what the rest of us do: he will accept it.

I know in my heart that he will come to his senses, he will recover. And when he does, he will be the best husband a woman could dream of and a brilliant dad. And I will love him for it.

Is this desire
Or a disease
If I surrender
Will you come for me

Will you come for me

Is this your mercy
Or sacrifice
No absolution
If you come for me

If you come for me

So will I suffer
Humility
Divine forgiveness
When you come for me

When you come for me

"Desire" by Gary Numan
from his album *Sacrifice*.

About the Author

Mahershalalhashbaz was born nine hundred and thirty-six years ago. He moved to Elohah Village in the Northern Hemisphere where he met his wife Naomi. He has eleven children, twenty-six grandchildren, twenty-nine great grandchildren, thirty-seven great, great grandchildren, forty-two great, great, great grandchildren, fifty-seven great, great, great, great grandchildren, and eighty-four great, great, great, great, great grandchildren. He now lives in Salford.

The author and publisher extend their thanks to the following people.

Theresa Cutts
Stephen Gordon
Will Hadcroft
Matthew Mutch
Ruth Wheeler
Colin Emery
Marie Hill
Ruth Gordon
Julie Euston

If you enjoyed 'Diary of a Parallel Man', you'll love this, from www.hundredpublishing.com

**Deus Ex Humanus
By C.P Leigh**

*...A Dan Brown-style conspiracy story
wrapped in a sci-fi spacesuit...*

We are all searching for something. Alan Hold is searching for a news story to revive his flagging journalism career. But has he found it in the mysterious Chris Connell, who claims to have taken a perilous journey to the farthest reaches of space in search of the Creator.

An ancient and manipulative organisation that secretly control religion, politics and commerce are desperate to prevent the truth emerging. Unravelling who they are tells us much about control, manipulation and our own personal searches for meaning.

Whatever happens, Chris and Alan's view of the world will be changed forever... and so will yours.

Paddytum
By Tricia Heighway

At one thirty-three in the afternoon, on the second Wednesday
in May, something happened which was to change Robert
Handle's life forever. At the time, he did not realise it would be a
change for the better. Rob is man who has reached his forties
without achieving anything at all. To his mother's dismay, he
has dug himself into a rut so deep it will take more than a shovel
to dig him out. It will take someone...or something, very special.
Paddytum is the funny, poignant and heart-warming story of
one man and his bear.

"A gentle, funny life-affirming novel"
- Paul Magrs, author

Also from www.hirstpublishing.com

Life Begins at 40
By Mark Charlesworth and Chris Newton

Two thirty-something Doctor Who fanatics sharing a flat in
Blackpool, out of pocket, out of luck and clinging to the hope
that Life Begins at 40...

Jeff is a barman, constantly forestalling marriage to his neurotic
new-age girlfriend, preferring the company of Pete, an
agoraphobic misfit with some serious baggage. United by their
social detachment and love of Doctor Who, their world view is
tainted by too much cult TV, and the walls between reality and
fantasy begin to blur, with hilariously disastrous consequences.

With middle-age fast approaching, can they really spend the rest
of their lives hiding behind the sofa? 'Life Begins at 40' deals
with the big questions. Should we get married? Are children a
good idea? And, in the future, will we all be walking around
with one eye and no arms from too much teleporting?

Also from www.hirstpublishing.com

A Dinner of Bird Bones
By Robert Hammond

"A Dinner of Bird Bones" is the story of Lloyd
Inchley; of heartbreak, new best friends, a girl called
Atom, and how the terrible power of sudden new
geometry links a mystery now and in the past - and
how it is all witnessed by a presence that has silently
observed the unspooling events for decades... "A
Dinner of Bird Bones" is a story about love.

Also from www.hirstpublishing.com

Vanitas
By Matthew Waterhouse

When you wish upon a star...?

Your dreams come true...? They did, at any rate, for Florinda Quenby, though not in the way she had planned. When she flew out to Hollywood to become a movie star, she could not imagine the terrible struggles ahead of her, from riches back to rags, or that fame and wealth would finally come from an entirely different quarter, her fantastical soup factory in Harlem modelled on the Taj Mahal... Once she was famous, she became one of New York's grandest hostesses and one of America's most beloved celebrities. Her parties for the Christmas season in her huge, gold-lined apartment overlooking Central park were an unmissable part of Manhattan's social calendar. Those parties grew wilder and wilder every year, until finally she decided to throw one last party, designed to top all the others... This is a tale of ambition and wealth and fame and vanity. This is Florinda's incredible story.

Also from www.hirstpublishing.com

Look Who's Talking
By Colin Baker

To many, Colin Baker is the sixth Doctor Who; to some, he is the villainous Paul Merroney in the classic BBC drama The Brothers. But to the residents of South Buckinghamshire he is a weekly voice of sanity in a world that seems intent on confounding him. Marking the 15th anniversary of his regular feature in the Bucks Free Press, this compilation includes over 100 of his most entertaining columns, from 1995 to 2009, complete with new linking material. With fierce intelligence and a wicked sense of humour, Colin tackles everything from the absurdities of political correctness to the joys of being an actor, slipping in vivid childhood memories, international adventures and current affairs in a relentless rollercoaster of reflections, gripes and anecdotes. Pulling no punches, taking no prisoners and sparing no detail, the ups and downs of Colin life are shared with panache, honesty and clarity, and they are every bit as entertaining and surreal as his trips in that famous police box... for a world that is bewildering, surprising and wondrous, one need look no further than modern Britain, and Colin Baker is here to help you make sense of it all, and to give you a good laugh along the way.

Also from www.hirstpublishing.com

Amusements, Carousels and Candy Floss on Sticks
By Brad Jones

Meet Bernard Stint. A marriage guidance counseller from Hendon, North London. A rather meek and mild man whose idea of a fun day is sitting at the local transport depot collecting bus numbers. Wife, Angela. Son, Sam. Bernard's life is turned upside down one day, when arriving home from work, Angela announces she is leaving him in favour of a muscle-bound fitness instructor. Realising he can't counsel himself when his own marriage breaks up and losing his job shortly afterwards for drunkenly assaulting Angela's new man, Bernard decides a new life beckons. Somewhere new. Somewhere miles away. Closing his eyes and putting a pin in a map of the UK, he moves to the sleepy north-east town of Lympstone-on-Sea. There he meets Melody, newly arrived from Southern Ireland, a music hall style singer who plays to an nearly empty pier theatre most nights. Can Bernard build his new life and revitalise Melody's flagging stage act? Will success and fortune prevail? Will Bernard and Melody fall for each other in this land of amusements, carousels and candy floss on sticks

Also from www.hirstpublishing.com

Tales in Dark Languages
By Cynthia Garland

Geoffrey Midori is a magician and raconteur - a purveyor of ancient tales, lost arts, and dark secrets - and he is having trouble sleeping. His nights are plagued by vivid dreams, bouts of sleepwalking, and a strange sensation that he is not alone in the dark. He takes a break from his travels with a caravan of performers to visit friends, only to find that their daughter is having troubles of her own. She has come of age, and is exhibiting certain specific traits from a vilified race that was exterminated centuries ago - traits that elicit fear and suspicion from those around her. When the authorities come to investigate, Geoffrey takes her on the run. Aided by his companions in the caravan - a soothsayer, dream interpreter, medicine showman, astrologer, and strong man - he must use his fragmented knowledge of ancient mythologies to unlock the secrets of the dead races - all the while battling his own demons and keeping one step ahead of the agents who are pursuing them.

Also from www.hirstpublishing.com

Lemon
By Barnaby Eaton-Jones

Spencer was an insignificant Data Input Operator and this
suited him fine. However, when he is mistaken for someone
actually significant, due to a mix-up by the Post Office, then his
life becomes complicated. By complicated we're talking murder,
sex, violence, car chases, beautiful women, and an annoyed fat
cat (both of the feline* and big business variety). Spence didn't
like complicated things and he was as far removed from being
James Bond as Shakespeare was from being a hack plagiarist.

A week in Spence's life usually consisted of nothing more than
dull, repetitive, time-wasting tedium. But, not this week. This
week was going to be different and Spence wasn't going to like
it one little bit.

*Just to add some extra zest to this 'Lemon', you can read all about
Spence's love-hate relationship with his feline nemesis in 'Eric's Tale'
at the end of the book.*